NOTHING IS LOST

Cloé Mehdi

NOTHING IS LOST

*Translated from the French
by Howard Curtis*

Europa
editions

Europa Editions
27 Union Square West, Suite 302
New York, NY 10003
www.europaeditions.com
info@europaeditions.com

Copyright © Editions Jigal, 2016
Published by arrangement with Agence littéraire Astier-Pécher
All Rights Reserved
First publication 2023 by Europa Editions

Translation by Howard Curtis
Original title: *Rien ne se perd*
Translation copyright 2023 by Europa Editions

Library of Congress Cataloging in Publication Data is available
ISBN 978-1-60945-822-5

Mehdi, Cloé
Nothing Is Lost

Art direction by Emanuele Ragnisco
instagram.com/emanueleragnisco

Cover image by Emanuele Ragnisco
Original photo by Lino Lombardi/Pixabay

Prepress by Grafica Punto Print – Rome

Printed in Canada

NOTHING IS LOST

Prologue

That's it, you've found him. There he is.

He's walking with his hands stuck deep in his pockets and his eyes down, as if he instinctively feels the threat. He isn't safe here, and he knows it. He should never have set foot in this town again. He isn't at home. It's a matter of territory. A matter of revenge and memory.

The two of you are walking behind him, side by side, staring at the back of his neck. On your lips, a question you can't bring yourselves to utter. What do we do now? You don't know. You haven't thought about it.

You've found him, that's all.

He walks to the main door that leads out onto the street and leaves the hospital enclosure. You wait a few seconds and join a group of visitors so that you can get behind him, hoods pulled down over your heads so that they can't identify you later in the footage from the security camera over the entrance to the grounds.

There he is, at the other end of the path. You walk faster to keep up with him. What now? He's bound to notice that you're tailing him. You aren't professionals, you aren't cops. He knows your faces. And you wonder once again if he wakes up in the night thinking about you, about him and what he did to him, the thing that nobody has ever made right.

Face facts: you aren't dispensers of justice. Give up. You don't have any weapons, any protection, you have nothing, you are nothing, that's why things are the way they are.

I beg you. Give up. The fire is out, and that's it. People have forgotten. Nobody will help you. Nobody will forgive you.

It's already been fifteen years. It's too late. You should have done something at the time. But you were too young. Too angry. The people who could have done something preferred to play by the rules. How can you blame them?

You know it won't bring him back. So what are you looking to do? Balance the scales?

Turn back. If you refuse to play the game they'll make you pay a hundred times over. They're allowed to cheat but you aren't, and nobody ever said it was fair.

He gets on the bus. So do you.

Night closes over you.

1

A few months earlier

I saw it yesterday afternoon when we parked near the hospital. Graffiti sprayed in red on the wall of a factory that already had thousands of other images. It showed the face of a teenager, and the words *JUSTICE FOR SAÏD*.

Obviously, it struck me as weird. I knew that graffiti well. It had been all over the walls in my neighborhood when I was little, but time has done its work, they've demolished the high-rises, and the memories along with them.

By the next day they'd repainted the wall white. The other graffiti didn't matter, but they couldn't let that one resurface.

I almost told Zé when we passed it. Our eyes met and I saw the shadows in his. I preferred to keep silent.

We were going to see Gabrielle and he didn't care about anything else, especially not the face of a boy who died fifteen years ago.

* * *

The hospital bed.

Gabrielle, pale-faced, a needle in the hollow of her elbow, bandages around her wrists. Her breathing slow and deep. Shutters half closed to keep out the gloom of an October Wednesday. Outside, it's cold. Inside, the hospital is well heated.

Gabrielle, her eyes wide open. She's been staring up at the ceiling for days now.

Zé sitting at the foot of the bed, a book in his hand. Lamartine's *Méditations poétiques*. They don't talk. They don't look at each other. No expression on their faces, nothing but a great emptiness. Hence the bandages, the drip, the hospital.

A nurse comes in. Forty-something. Lines around her eyes. A small scar at the base of her neck. She doesn't take any notice of Zé, she's used to his studious presence. She goes straight to the bed. She greets Gabrielle with a somewhat insincere, slightly curt "hello." She's tired, it's obvious. Neither of them look at her. She removes the needle, dabs at the tiny orifice in the crook of the elbow with a sterile compress, and sticks a Band-Aid over it. She gets ready to leave the room without uttering another word. It isn't that she's doing her job badly. The hushed atmosphere of this place is contagious.

But then she sees me and gives a start.

"What . . ."

This reaction tears Zé from his reading. He turns to her, then to me, as if he'd forgotten my presence.

"Who is this child?" she asks, recovering.

"He's nothing," the visitor replies (*thank you very much*). "Just my ward."

"Your ward?"

She looks at us in turn, trying to figure out if it's a joke, given the difference in our ages.

"This department is out of bounds to anyone under the age of fifteen, monsieur."

"Fine, are you going to pay for a babysitter? Because I can't. Be a good girl and piss off, this is a family reunion."

She looks him up and down. I feel her anger rising. Lots of little bits of anger accumulated in all these years spent trying to find a fragile balance between ethics, humanity, and the bitterness and stress of the job. Every humiliation probably reminds her of all the others. Zé has already turned away from her and plunged back into the *Méditations*. Zé's a real bastard when he wants to be. He isn't even reading. He knows Lamartine by heart.

Gradually, the tension in the nurse's shoulders relaxes. She'll crack some other day. It won't be long now, I think. Maybe she'll just insult a patient. Or else increase a patient's daily amount of potassium chloride. A few grams, just enough to kill him and then argue that it was a mistake in the dosage. Or maybe one morning she'll walk into the hospital with a shotgun. Zé says I have an overactive imagination.

"There's no need to use that tone, monsieur. I realize you're on edge, but you shouldn't take it out on the staff."

She leaves without waiting for an answer that wouldn't have come anyway. I'm not even sure Zé heard her. If he did, he doesn't give a damn. He doesn't give a damn about anything, pretty much, except for a few hand-picked poets. And—of course—Gabrielle.

Her wrists are bandaged. You can't see the stitches, which have had Betadine applied to them, or the width of the cuts before they were sewed up. The hospital is clean, hygienic, and so are the bandages. Not like the back seat of the car where Zé and I found her, her eyes as empty as those of a fish out of water.

She's looking up at the ceiling. That's all she's been doing since it happened.

I observe the two of them—they aren't paying any attention to me—before plunging back into my own reading. It's an English textbook for school. I pretend to read but I'm listening. You never get bored in a hospital. There are the comings and goings of the nurses, who are always running. There are the patients, in less of a hurry, going to get some air, smoke, or stand by the coffee machine. A factory with its machines, its workers, its foremen, its own laws.

Gabrielle has been here for a week. She's taking a long time to recover. Zé says she's resting.

In her room, day after day, the silence expands.

* * *

Zé came to fetch me from the schoolyard. My friends moved aside when they saw the tall, stooped figure of this weird guy wearing a big raincoat—he looked like a pedophile—and the teachers stepped forward, but I said, "He's my guardian." And nobody believed me. He'd come ready for this, and brandished the paper from the family judge like a divine defense.

He said to me:

"I need you to keep an eye on her."

What I understood was:

"I need you to keep an eye on me."

That's why I've been skipping school for the last two days. It's not as if I'm missing much.

* * *

At night, after the trays have been collected, the nurse's aide forces Zé to leave the premises. He resists for form's sake, but it's a diversion. I already slipped under the bed as soon as there was a knock at the door. The footsteps of the nurse's aide move away, and now I'm alone with Gabrielle. It's better than being alone with Zé.

I lie full-length under the bed. I'm tired. I'm not supposed to sleep, but there's no point overdoing it. I'm only a kid and I need my sleep, and anyway, it's really not my business.

I doze off despite the staff talking too loudly in the corridors. Gabrielle's voice pulls me out of my lethargy.

"Mattia?"

That's me. Mattia, not Matt. Not for my friends, not for anybody.

"Shhh," I say. "I'm not supposed to be here."

She laughs softly. "Was it Zé who told you to hide?"

"Zé's a bastard."

"Not all the time."

I drag myself up onto my elbows and emerge from my shelter. Gabrielle has twisted around in her bed. She's looking at the wall. I guess she's bored with the ceiling. Her braids rest on the pillow on either side of her face. They hide part of her bright eyes. I don't know if it's the fever, the tears, or the moonlight that makes them shine like that.

The silence, feeling uneasy, retreats to the bathroom. I sense it huddled there, ready to leap out at the first sign of weakness like an animal tracking its prey. I get to my feet. I try to meet her eyes but find only a lurking half-light that keeps me from seeing into them.

She smiles into the emptiness. The silence is already taking a tentative step outside its hiding place. I try to shoo it away (pathetically).

"How are you?"

"Fine."

The silence springs out, crushing us with its formless mass. My shoulders yield under its weight. I slide back under the bed but don't get to sleep before dawn.

I think about Saïd. He died before I was born. I wonder who took the trouble to demand justice even now, even though justice gave its answer a long time ago.

But I hear Gabrielle breathing gently and I try to concentrate on the present.

* * *

The next morning, following Zé's instructions, I wait for the change of shift in order to leave the room. It's a time when the team doesn't want to be disturbed. The treatment room is closed and I'm too short to be seen through the window. I'm able to walk quite calmly along the corridor. I pass one or two patients who look at me curiously, surprised to see a young boy alone in a psychiatric ward, but people are too monopolized by their own ailments to ask questions. There's nowhere better than a hospital to pass unnoticed.

I get a hot chocolate from the drinks machine and go to the cafeteria to wait for Zé. He finishes work at the same time as the nurses start their shift. He's a night watchman in a supermarket. He says it's boring as hell but necessary.

He arrives at seven-thirty on the dot. He looks around the room, and his eyes don't linger when he sees me. He sits down opposite me.

"How is she?"

He has a thermos of coffee with him. Distractedly, he offers me some. I shake my head.

"I don't know. She hardly spoke."

"What did she say?"

"I'm hungry."

The skinflint gave me only enough money for a drink. Sometimes he forgets I need to eat. He buys me two croissants and a raisin Danish, which is unusually generous for him and leads me to think he's aware he made me spend a pretty rough night.

"What did she say?" he repeats once I've stopped eating.

"Nothing. She just asked if it was you who told me to hide here. I said you were a bastard. She said: not all the time."

He smiles. That must be the nicest compliment he's ever had in his life. He brushes the croissant crumbs from the collar of my jacket. I knew I was dirty but I was waiting to see if he would notice. He's taken much more interest in me since realizing how useful I can be to him. Gabrielle should try to kill herself more often.

"I'm going to see her," he says. "Are you going back to school?"

"Nah."

I feel like going back to the apartment, but he doesn't offer to drive me there. He still needs my presence to decorate the silence. That irritates me. I say nothing. I follow him to the third floor. There she is, translucent, asleep. She'd blend into the sheets if they didn't have a narrow brown border. And he looks at her with a tenderness he's never shown me.

I turn away, stifling the bitterness that climbs up through my oesophagus.

My English textbook does nothing to cheer me up. Any more than Lamartine can help Zé forget, even for a minute, that the only person in the world he loves cut her wrists last week. He's lost weight. He hasn't been eating since she left.

Love should be banned.

* * *

And so should school.

After a week, Zé suddenly snaps out of it and remembers he's my legal guardian. He forces me to go back to school as abruptly as he took me out of it.

Sitting on the passenger's side, I look at the back seat in the rearview mirror. I remember the blood it was soaked with. I spent half of one night cleaning it while Zé, in a state of shock, stared at the wall in front of him—like Gabrielle in the hospital. There's no trace left of the suicide attempt. At least in the car.

We don't talk. The silence again, on the ride to school. I have no desire to go back there.

"I don't want to go."

Silence.

I touch Zé's shoulder. "I don't want to go!"

"Don't be a baby."

"Everyone's going to ask me why I skipped school."

"Make something up."

"Can't I just tell the truth?"

"If you like, but your friends are going to end up thinking you're jinxed."

Silence again. It's a monster, the silence! A beast with a forked tail, with no tongue, no teeth, no palate, but with lips so it can laugh at us.

Stunned by his own words, Zé realizes what he's just said. So do I.

"Son of a bitch," I murmur.

He parks in front of the school. His fingers shake around his cigarette.

"I'm sorry. You can stay with me today if you l—"

"I'd rather go to school," I say, slamming the car door.

And he knows how much I hate school.

* * *

The whole class is in love with the teacher, except for me. She's beautiful, apparently. She's twenty-eight, her arms covered in Brazilian bracelets (not bandages), short hair, freckles, her name is Madame Sivrieux. At the beginning of the year she liked me. She called me her "little prodigy." Not because I had good grades but because, one, I kept quiet, which gave her the mysterious impression that I was listening to her lessons, and two, I understood quickly and helped the others to understand, just so people would find me likeable and leave me alone.

Then came the first assessment, and Madame Sivrieux realized I wasn't the little genius she'd thought I was. She quickly dropped me and concentrated on the others, the ones who were genuinely intelligent, the studious ones. All the better. I didn't like being thought of as top of the class. My place has always been near the windows.

In double file in the covered playground. It's raining. I realize I left my bag behind at the exact moment everyone else notices. Fingers point at me. Madame Sivrieux approaches, more anxious than stern.

"Where were you, Mattia? A whole week without hearing from you. We were worried."

No parent's note to excuse my absence, of course. But how could I blame Zé? I shrug as a sign of contrition.

"I was in the hospital."

"Were you sick?"

"Not me. My guardian's girlfriend."

I see in her eyes that such a distant relationship doesn't justify such a long absence. All right. I didn't want to mention it but she asked for it.

"She slashed her wrists. My guardian needed me."

Her smile freezes. I slip back into the line without waiting for her reaction. Let Zé figure out how to explain it. It's not exactly my fault if everyone in my home is a loser.

* * *

Four-thirty. Zé is supposed to pick me up, but he never arrives on time. I don't blame him: for once, he has a good excuse. He must have spent his day at Gabrielle's bedside, sharing in the nothing.

I hang about on the corner of the street, going over my math lesson just to have free time this evening to watch cartoons. With this hospital business, I've missed a week's television.

That's when I see them.

Two men, one about forty, the other a bit older, sneakers with solidly knotted laces on their feet, one of them wearing a suede blouson, the other a khaki jacket, standing in the doorway of the post office on the other side of the street. They're talking and looking at me out of the corners of their eyes.

I'm not scared. Pedophiles don't usually work in pairs, and kidnappers are only interested in rich kids (and those whose absence would be noticed, which probably isn't the case with me, given that Zé seems to have forgotten I even exist, the old bastard).

I'm bored and it's nearly time for my favourite series. I look at my watch. I'm about to walk home when the guy in the suede blouson makes up his mind and crosses the street. He walks up to me, a smile on his face.

"Hi," he says.

"Hi."

"Is your name Mattia Lorozzi?"

"Why?"

He laughs for no reason and holds out his hand, but I don't take it. He puts it back in his pocket after a few seconds. He doesn't let go of his smile. "I'm a friend of Zé's. You live with him, don't you?"

I don't reply.

"I haven't seen him in years, I'm trying to get in touch. I was hoping he'd come and pick you up from school. I wanted to give him a surprise."

"How do you know he's my guardian?"

"I followed the story."

The other guy pretends to be interested in the flow of traffic, but he's watching us fairly discreetly. I think they're lying. Having friends isn't in Zé's nature.

"And who's the guy over there? Your bodyguard?"

This time he stops smiling. I prefer that. He leans down until he's the same height as me. I look at him defiantly.

"You're oddly sure of yourself for a six-year-old kid."

"I'm eleven."

"I'm just trying to get back in touch with an old childhood friend. Why are you so suspicious, have you been told not to talk to strangers?"

"Precisely," I say and start walking.

But he catches up and walks alongside me.

"You know your guardian is a murderer?"

I stop. So does he. I smile. He doesn't. I turn to face him. His friend hasn't followed us. He's still there by the post office, his hands in his pockets, looking elsewhere as if he's sensed how suspicious I am of him.

"Yes," I reply.

"You live with him but you're afraid of people on the street?"

"I'm not afraid. You're pissing me off, that's all."

I do an about-turn and walk off in the direction of the hospital. This time he doesn't try to catch up with me. I see his reflection in a store window. He hasn't moved. Standing in the middle of the road, he watches grim-faced as I walk away, and he doesn't turn until I'm outside his field of vision.

In other words: a cop or a gangster.

* * *

Zé isn't in the hospital. A nurse tells me he's just left. He's finally remembered I exist. He doesn't have a cell phone so I wait for him patiently, sitting in a corner near the window. Gabrielle doesn't respond to my attempts at conversation.

Zé keeps me waiting until about six. He rushes into the room and his eyes are full of relief when they come to rest on me.

"You came here on your own?"

"I had to! You were late."

"I'm always late."

"There are some guys looking for you."

I hesitated a bit, not sure I wanted to talk about this in front of Gabrielle, but I'm the child, not her; and just because she's refusing to speak doesn't mean she has to be kept out of our conversations.

"Who?" he asks, quite calmly, taking off his blouson.

"Cops or gangsters. They were waiting for me outside the school. They asked me if I live with you."

He shakes his head, indicating Gabrielle, who hasn't reacted.

"Please, one problem at a time."

I laugh to myself. If that could be a rule of the universe I'd still be living with my real family.

2

When I was five, I wondered why life was so unfair, so unjust.

When I was seven, I told myself that if it had been fair and just it would have lost all meaning, because we wouldn't be driven by the hope of improvement.

When I was eight, I searched desperately for a way to right wrongs—but I didn't find one because most injustices are irreversible, that's why they're so unbearable.

At the age of nine, I decided to stop asking myself questions.

* * *

It's a strange story, Zé and Gabrielle. A love story according to him. Her, I don't know. She never talks about it. She doesn't feel the need to give things a name. She looks. She learns. She's never been a big talker. Zé, a little more. He talks to say nothing, to talk bullshit, or to recite Baudelaire—which comes to the same thing. It averages out.

I like observing them. It distracts me. It stops me thinking about more unpleasant things. It's better to concentrate on nice things, even if they're distributed with a parsimony that verges on avarice.

I've been with them for four years. At least as far as Zé is concerned. With Gabrielle, it must be two years. I seldom see one without the other. My shrink says it's called intense bonding. She also says it may be unhealthy. That's for sure. But it's too late. The harm has been done, you can't turn the clock back. They met and they fell in love just like in the songs. Now it's impossible to separate them.

I tried and it didn't work.

Don't blame me. I'm possessive. I wanted Zé for myself. Like a big brother, I mean. Or like a father, or a friend. Does it really matter? After all the shit that happened in my family, I hoped when I ended up with him that the wrongs would right themselves. How stupid I was. It was a time when I still believed in a kind of balance, even in a kind of justice. But I digress.

Zé and Gabrielle. And one big problem, otherwise there wouldn't be a story. They're madly in love and they're both unhappy.

I don't know which of them is trying to save the other, and how long they hope to survive together, or even if they really want to.

My shrink says I should take a little less interest in other people and a little more in myself.

* * *

The day after I started school again, at the end of the afternoon, Dr. Kadouri (his name is written on his white coat) sees us in his office. He indicates me with his chin.

"I'd rather we had this conversation without your son being here."

"He's not my son," Zé says, as if that settled the matter.

The doctor gives a slight, disapproving pout but doesn't insist. He's young. Thirty tops. Barely out of his training, but Zé wouldn't trust him even if he taught at Oxford. He has an ink stain on his left pocket. A little notebook. A stethoscope around his neck, just so we don't confuse him with some plebeian paramedic.

Day ten since Gabrielle's brush with death. An anonymous office in the hospital, a few doors down from her room. The doctor, Zé, and me (I'm always invisible, except when they talk about really serious things. I don't know how I manage to make them forget me to that extent. It would be perfect if it was intentional. A real ghost. I sometimes wonder if I'm alive).

Outside, it's raining cats and dogs. Gabrielle can't be cured but she's healing in her way: slowly.

A word pulls me out of my thoughts.

"Charcot?" Zé says in a faint voice.

I know it. It's the psychiatric hospital just outside town. Zé gives me a tense look. I'm pleased that he remembers me and my story before he takes me with him. He knows it, too. He spent time there during his "crazy youth." It's where he met my father before he hanged himself in that very hospital, they shared the same room.

Yes. When it comes to losers, we have quite a record in my family. It's not even me who says it, it's my shrink (she didn't say "losers," but it's what I understood).

"You do understand," the doctor resumes, unaware of our silent exchange. "Your partner attempted suicide."

"No kidding."

"Her life is no longer in danger, but she isn't communicating. Not even with you, it seems. I'm afraid she might try again if we let her leave without aftercare."

"I'm here. I'll take care of her."

"Will that be enough? You were also there before she . . . I mean, that didn't stop her from acting on her impulse."

Silence. From the doctor. From Zé. From me, too. I look out the window. Three cranes rise above the buildings. A flock of birds is perched on the metal arms. They all fly up at the same time. A billion feathers invade the sky, and it's beautiful, but I'm the only one who notices.

"She goes through phases," Zé says in desperation. "You must know that. It happens to everybody. One day you're laughing. The next day you want to die."

"This isn't the first time she's tried to take her own life."

"If we locked up all the people who wanted to die—"

"It's not a question of locking them up, but of restoring their taste for life."

"She's already been in that hospital. It didn't help her much. What will you do if you can't convince her that it's worth it?"

The doctor falls silent, thus betraying the extent of his powerlessness (his own, that of his whole profession, and ours, too).

"She won't go," Zé says.

"I'm sorry, but you won't be able to stop it."

He isn't being brutal about it. It's just that he knows people. Zé exudes intransigence. No point trying to mediate.

"What does that mean?" Zé almost yells. "That you can put her in that hospital without consent? On what basis?"

"The cuts on her wrists, monsieur. She was ten minutes away from dying of a hemorrhage. Are you prepared to take that risk?"

"No psychiatric hospital. It's out of the question."

"It's for her own good."

"You don't know her. She hasn't said a word to you. I live with her. I love her," he adds stupidly, as if it was necessary. "She won't go to Charcot. It's a fucking death trap."

The doctor decides to postpone the transfer in order to "give you a few days to think about it." As far as thinking about it goes, Zé acts the very next day. He wasn't born yesterday. He knows the doctor doesn't give a damn what he thinks. So, during the afternoon change of shift, while the nurses and the nurses' aides shut themselves in the treatment room and I, dragged reluctantly into being an accomplice, keep an eye on the corridor, he speaks to Gabrielle.

I stand in the doorway, listening with one ear, the other focused on the sounds outside. I listen but I don't hear anything.

He's whispering. She turns her brown eyes to him, her features furrowed in concentration. Zé's nose is buried in her hair.

She doesn't utter a word. But in the end she agrees. She leans on Zé's shoulder, trying to manage with her bandages. I approach to offer my arm but he stops me.

"Tell us if the coast is clear."

Yes, boss. I obey. The medical staff is still changing over, but unlike me, Zé and Gabrielle are too big not to be seen. So I improvise. I walk confidently down the corridor and knock at the door. I insist until I hear a highly irritated "Yes?" I go in. The two nurses and the three nurses' aides are waiting, determined to see which patient would dare disturb them in the middle of their break.

They melt completely.

"Hello, Mattia."

They know me by now. In a way, I've become the ward's pet. There are advantages in being just a child, even an invisible one.

I put on my most hangdog look.

"When is my mom going to leave?"

I mean Gabrielle. She's not my mother and I've never called her that before, but it always works. And my tears overflow while the nurses, distressed, search in themselves for a compassion they've long forgotten. They press around me to console me, which means they aren't paying any attention to what's going on in the corridor. Out of the corner of my eye, I see two intertwined figures edge past the window.

I remember the day of the funeral very well.

It was January 2, a Thursday, I was five years old. Mom turned to me and said:

"Never get attached to anybody because everybody will end up abandoning you."

She was right. It might not have been the kind of thing you should say to a child, but the reason I love my mother is that she isn't one of those adults who keeps talking bullshit to you on the pretext that you're too young to understand.

She turned toward the grave. She was holding my hand and I was holding hers. She was squeezing me a bit too hard. Her nails were digging into my fingers, making tiny scratches.

"You see, you lower your guard for a second, you give your trust, you fall in love, and that's what happens."

She pointed to the gravestone. A simple marble slab with a name and two dates, the crescent moon of Islam above them. Dad hadn't been a believer for years but all his family was, my grandparents, uncles, aunts, and cousins, and Mom thought he would have liked that to be taken into account. He didn't leave any instructions before his death.

My brother and my sister were standing a bit farther back, with the rest of the cortege. I looked at his grave, frowning, it was very beautiful for January, birds were singing everywhere in the cemetery.

"You fall in love, and look what happens."

She spat out these words. Worse than an insult. I imagined the spittle hitting the stone, hitting the name, that name staring at us there, mocking us. Dad must be laughing in his grave. I don't know. I didn't know him. Nobody did.

"Not even me," Mom murmured.

She held me so tight, my fingers hurt. I didn't say anything. I started to be silent one fine January day, when the words started to drop away, when I realized how powerless language is to deal with the depth and complexity of things. We think we're intelligent, with our gift of words, but in the end we never know what to say when the worst things happen.

She never blamed him. She blamed herself for loving him too much, too strongly, someone who didn't love himself and no longer loved other people, in any case not enough to want to stick around.

"Never get attached to anyone," she repeated. "Or else,

bear in mind that you'll always be alone, however many people are around you."

My brother came up to us.

"Don't tell him things like that."

"Why, do you think I'm wrong?"

My sister, her fists clenched down by her thighs, lips full of scratches from biting them too much, joined us near the grave. For the first time in my life, I had the feeling of what a "united family" might be.

"It's not fair," she said.

Nobody replied.

"Not fair," she repeated. "They may not have hanged him but they were the ones who killed him all the same."

My mother let go of my hand.

"Be quiet. Not in front of the child."

And that silence . . . that silence.

* * *

A group of girls from my class can't stop looking at me in the canteen. Puzzled, I pretend nothing is happening. I'm not especially the kind of boy who interests girls. Usually they don't pay any attention to me.

To my right, Julien nudges me with his elbow.

"Hey, you're popular today."

Actually, I think they're making fun of me, though I don't say anything. Ever since I started in elementary school, I've learned to conceal my complete lack of interest in myself. But others notice it easily and always end up by using it against me.

After lunch, I wander in the schoolyard waiting for the start of the afternoon classes. The girls are still following me with their eyes, but it's not the kind of look you give someone who intrigues you or someone you like: they're talking among themselves in low voices, they look solemn.

The bell finally rings. I join the line for my class. Much to my surprise, one of the girls, Camille, the oldest, breaks away from the others and comes up to me. She's dancing from foot to foot. I seriously start to think I've made a hit, and I wonder how you're supposed to react in this unheard-of situation, but she speaks first:

"The other day someone came to see us during recess and asked us questions about you."

I immediately remember the two suspicious guys outside the post office. What with Gabrielle's escape, they'd gone completely out of my head. I hadn't seen them since, and Zé hadn't said anything about them again.

"Who were they?"

"Some old guys. Same age as our parents. It was last week, while you were away. They asked us if we were in your class. At first we didn't understand who they were talking about, they called you Mattia Younès."

Younès. That was my father's surname. I have my mother's. A choice made by my parents so that my sister and I wouldn't have trouble getting work later on.

"Anyway, there aren't that many Mattias," Camille continued.

"What did they want to know?"

"How long you'd been away and if you were coming back. We said we didn't know."

"Is that all? Didn't they say who they were and why they were looking for me?"

"No. Strange, isn't it? It was a bit like in the movies, when the cops make inquiries."

She gives a strange laugh as we climb the stairs leading to the classrooms.

"Did you do something?"

"Of course not."

"That's what I thought. You're so quiet, I can't see you doing anything that would make the cops look for you."

Just to be sure, I ask her what they looked like. She mentions the suede blouson and the huge size of the other guy, the one in the khaki jacket, who was a real bull. There's no doubt they're the same people. That's fine, at least there aren't fifty of them after me—after Zé.

I thank her as we sit down behind our respective desks.

It's almost the first time since the start of the semester that one of the girls in my class has said anything to me.

* * *

Night.

The supermarket. All decked out for Halloween. Grinning masks everywhere. Movie monsters, pumpkins, witches. The aisles are deserted. I love walking down them alone. I love these nights when Zé takes me with him to his work, although I don't tell him and I pretend to go reluctantly. I love being alone with him.

He's left Gabrielle in the apartment. With all the goodwill in the world, he can't force her to come with him to the store.

He's patrolling the aisles. Somewhere in the middle of the store, a radio is sitting on the floor and playing a tune I can't identify.

He recites:

"Vous n'avez réclamé la gloire ni les larmes
Ni l'orgue ni la prière aux agonisants
Vous vous étiez servi simplement de vos armes
La mort n'éblouit pas les yeux des Partisans."[1]

---

[1] You did not ask for fame or tears/Organs or prayers for the dying/You simply took up arms/Death does not dazzle the partisans.

Aragon, *L'Affiche rouge*. Thank to Zé, I'm unbeatable when it comes to classic French poetry. He even curses in alexandrines.

And he's a night watchman. A job to pay the rent. Like all jobs, he says.

"Vous aviez vos portraits sur les murs de nos villes
Noirs de barbe et de nuit hirsutes menaçants
L'affiche qui semblait une tache de sang
Parce qu'à prononcer vos noms sont difficiles
Y cherchait un effet de peur sur les passants
Mais à l'heure du couvre-feu des doigts errants
Avaient écrit sous vos photos 'Morts pour la France'
Et les mornes matins en étaient différents"[2]

I'm going over my English lessons. They're the worst of all, because I've never heard an uglier language than English. Go figure why the only language in the world that's really nasty has replaced all the others. There must be a life lesson in that, but I'd prefer not to put it into words.

Zé has arranged a little corner for me near the comic books, in case I want to clear my head instead of doing my homework. Sometimes he tells me to work hard at school, but that's as far as his parenting goes. He's not the kind to check my diary in the evening.

We've brought the tent we never use. It's good for sleeping in without being caught on camera.

---

[2] You had your pictures on the walls of our towns/Black of beard and at night hairy and menacing/The poster that seemed like a bloodstain/Because your names are difficult to pronounce/It was meant to scare the passersby/But when the curfew came, wandering fingers/Wrote on your pictures "They died for France."/And the grim mornings were quite transformed.

His voice comes closer as he recites. He kneels to see inside my cocoon.

"It's midnight, Mattia."

"So?"

"Go to sleep."

"I'm studying."

He laughs.

"You, studying? I know you. You're still messing around. Let your little brain rest a bit. Sleep. Children need their sleep."

He talks as if he's just seen a documentary on the subject. I could point out to him that he wasn't so concerned about my getting enough sleep when he asked me to spend my nights in the hospital, hidden under Gabrielle's bed. But I say nothing.

"Zé . . ."

"What?"

"A girl in my school mentioned these two weird guys who were asking me questions about you. She said they came when I wasn't there, they wanted to know if I was coming back to school."

I watch his face, ready to detect a lie, but he remains totally impassive. The only sign of anxiety is a vein throbbing nervously at his temple.

"They're not after you. Don't worry, who'd want to cause problems for a child?"

I don't know. One thing I'm sure of is that problems find you regardless of your age.

"Sleep," he says again. "It must be a mistake. They'll realize sooner or later."

"Goodnight," I mutter.

"Sleep well."

His voice is full of warmth. I'd sell my soul to have him always speak to me like that.

* * *

My real father started losing it well before I was born.

Apparently, it was his job that made him flip out (my shrink calls it "decompensating"). He was a special needs teacher at the community center in our neighborhood, Les Verrières. There he is, leaving school at twenty, pleased with his diploma, and applying for a job that nobody else wants. He's oh-so-optimistic, stupidly convinced of his ability to get things changed. He meets his young charges, there's enthusiasm in the air—on his side, at least—he spends twelve hours a day on the job, goes out again at midnight whenever a kid who's being held for questioning by the police calls him, doesn't sleep for a week when one of them is sent to prison. Basically, he's passionate about it.

My father discovers the vicious circle. School, bad grades, car theft or the equivalent, prison, release from prison, no job no money, endless problems, more car theft or the equivalent, more prison, with increasingly heavy sentences as the years go on.

And the faces turning haggard, the lines appearing at the age of eighteen, nineteen, twenty, the anger, the exhaustion.

And then, one day, the police kill someone.

His name was Saïd. He was fifteen years old, and he died near the community center. Just an identity check that got out of hand, as happens all too often. His friends appearing on the scene. The first bottle thrown, followed by many others. Night after night lit by police floodlights, the flashes of cameras, burning barricades. My father calling for calm, as teachers tend to do, although nobody listens to them. Why should they? They move on parallel lines that never meet. Ever. He didn't understand that, and neither did his colleagues.

He meant well, my father. Convinced like everyone else that

he was working for the greater good. That's the most pitiful part of it.

A massive number of arrests. One, two, three, thirty sentences for assaults on police officers, and a commensurate number of years in prison.

The local people demand justice. They believe in the Republic. They form a collective around Saïd's family. They look to democracy, human rights, the whole kit and caboodle. They demand that the person responsible for the killing face trial.

The riots stop by themselves: a spasm can only be temporary, however legitimate. Internal Affairs investigates. The cop is suspended. A few months pass. The cop is reinstated. My father takes sick leave. He's had enough. He can't bear the fire in these kids' eyes, reminding him how totally powerless he is. He awaits the verdict of the courts.

It comes three years later: acquittal. The cop leaves the courtroom carried in triumph by his colleagues. It's a common enough story. But everyone has forgotten it. Until the next time, the next fire, the next inquiry, the next dismissal, a snake three quarters devoured from eating its own tail.

And confinement in Charcot as far as my father is concerned. He never came out again.

I was six months old.

They say the ground was already fertile. That this business was just a catalyst, the spark lighting a powder keg that had always existed, just like a riot. They say no psychosis appears as if by magic in adulthood. I don't know. I never knew my father without what they called his mental illness.

All I know is that it gnawed away at him for five years until he hanged himself in his hospital room. That the fifteen-year-old is still dead, and that his killer is still plying his noble trade.

A fat lot of good it does me.

* * *

I was at the window, counting the clouds and waiting for the rain, when Mom came and rested her chin on my shoulder, I felt water running down my neck and realized she was crying, I prepared to endure the worst but the worst couldn't get in, I'd already built an indestructible barrier between me and it, between me and other people, between me and the world.

My defenses worked all too well.

3

I would throw stones in the pond and count the number of times they bounced. I was a realist. I set the bar high.

Five, Dad would get better.

Six, he would be back home in time for my birthday.

Eight, he would never be sick again.

Later, I changed it to: Five, he isn't really dead.

I never managed to get past three. Maybe, deep down, I didn't want him to come back. Maybe it was my fault he didn't.

My fault he hanged himself.

* * *

She's as diaphanous as ever, her long braided hair hitting against the back of her neck as she walks.

He's duller, hanging onto her arm, hanging onto her life.

It's three weeks since her suicide attempt and Gabrielle's still alive. She's taken care over her appearance today. She's had a shower for the first time since she left the hospital. Even Zé is scented. You can smell his eau de cologne from a hundred yards away, but nobody tells him. He's taken out his clean shirt and pants. She's wearing matching garments.

I drag my feet behind them, sulking. They don't care, which really bugs me. Zé forced me to go to the hairdresser. My hair was down over my ears, now it's almost shaved off. Shorter over the temples. It's the fashion for boys, but it doesn't suit me at all. It stops me from peering out at people from under my hair, the way I used to.

They're walking in front, on the sidewalk, side by side. They're not touching, but their shoulders brush against each other from time to time and they don't move apart when another pedestrian tries to pass between them.

It's raining. This bloody endless November. I want it to be Christmas. Not for the gifts or the nice meals, just for a little snow at least. And the time off school.

"Mattia, speed up a bit!" the poetry lover yells at me.

I obey, whether I like it or not. Today's a big day. We're due to meet with my mother in the park. We don't see her often. Six times a year tops. She isn't in great shape. Not enough anyway to want to find out how I'm doing with my guardian. Zé might be a filthy pedophile and she wouldn't even know.

The court doesn't insist on Zé and Gabrielle being with me. Mom can see me or get in touch with me whenever she likes. It's just that she doesn't really want to (I'm not extrapolating, simply making an observation). Sometimes Gabrielle urges me to call her. She says she may be embarrassed by the fact that she can't live with me (but what does *can't* mean?). I don't do it. I have my pride.

"Mattia! Are you coming or what?"

I run to catch up with them.

The park is empty. At least, empty of my mother. There are little old men sitting on benches commenting on the activities around them, there are pigeons, there are groups of young guys hanging about for want of anywhere else to go. People walking their dogs. In other words, everyone's passing though. Nobody's waiting for anyone or anything. Nobody has anything much to hope for.

I look gloomily around this pale imitation of life and greenery. The smell of exhaust fumes catches me by the throat. I feel the tears coming. It's the smells, I've always been sensitive to smells.

A hand closes over mine. I look up at Zé.

"We're early," he lies.

He knows as well as I do that she won't come. We wait anyway. Stuck there in the middle of the park, we wait. Boys my age are playing soccer with a basketball. The old guys raise their voices when the ball hits the oldest of them in the ankles. The half-hearted feel of a Sunday that will turn into Monday all too soon.

After an hour, Zé himself admits he was deluded. Gabrielle tries to comfort me by stroking my cheek, but I dodge her hand.

We go back to the apartment. Once again, she hasn't come.

* * *

They call it an "educational meeting." It's a nice name for your parents getting bawled out because you aren't doing a damned thing at school.

Zé has been summoned by the principal. My teacher, Madame Sivrieux, is there, too, and so am I. Gabrielle didn't come.

Already November and only the first meeting. I haven't beaten my own record, far from it. Last year, it only took me ten days to prompt a meeting.

The principal is wearing tiny glasses that barely cover her blue eyes. Fifty-something, a beige suit, a cheerful face even though she's trying to look stern. She loves children too much to be doing this job. You should never work in something you feel passionate about. Zé says work kills all passion, that's why he works in a supermarket rather than in a library.

The two women wait opposite us in a small, well-heated office. The wind bangs against the windows, a long way from these educational realities. I hate school because it steals my time from me—a whole lot of time. There are much more interesting things to do than sit on a chair waiting stupidly for your head to be filled with useless knowledge while all the important stuff gets pushed out to make room for it.

They wait, curious to see what we'll say. But what else can the two of us give them but silence? Our eyes dart about the room, coming to rest anywhere but on them. There are ghosts in our eyes. He's thinking about Gabrielle, and I think about everything I'm missing out on in this prison.

"Please understand, monsieur," the teacher resumes. "I'm not saying this child can't learn, I'm saying he doesn't want to. He withdraws into himself and resists any kind of teaching."

Zé taps me on the shoulder as if to say, "Fine, keep up the good work."

"At least he doesn't disturb the rest of the class. He sits there in his corner by the window, in his own head . . . That's the problem, he's always in his own head." She throws me a sad look, then a sympathetic little smile.

"A lot of things must be happening in there, mustn't they, Mattia?"

The principal loses patience. She turns to Zé.

"If he continues like this, he may have to repeat a grade. You do want him to go into sixth grade, don't you?"

"Of course."

"We can't force him to work."

What she's saying is: You're a bad father. Zé shifts on his chair. I assume he's trying to get a poem by Verlaine out of his head so that he can concentrate on what's happening. He's sensed the accusation, too. He knows it only too well. The same lecture every year. The same weariness when we leave. The same emptiness. The same nausea caused by other people's judgements, people who don't know, who will never know anything, and who still see fit to judge in spite of everything because they think they belong to the same reality, live on the same level, but we live parallel lives, madame, and our paths will never meet.

Zé clears his throat.

"I've been living with Mattia for four years now, madame. And in those four years I've never been able to force him to do anything."

The two women raise their eyebrows. The silence returns. I can visualize it, sitting on Zé's shoulder, with its nightmarish smile and its steely skin, its insidious mechanism so well oiled that the hinges never squeak.

"How old are you, monsieur?"

"Twenty-four."

"That's a little young to be taking care of an eleven-year-old. Especially one as complicated as Mattia."

Zé smiles.

"I think I do quite well."

"But his grades—"

"There are other things in life apart from school."

They look at each other. They think they understand. My teacher thinks twice about starting down that slippery slope. She changes the subject abruptly, venturing on much more hostile territory.

"How were you able to obtain guardianship of him at the age of twenty?"

"The judge simply made official a situation that already existed."

"A complicated family situation, you mean?"

Zé folds his arms and sits more firmly on his chair.

"As I said, there are other things in life apart from school. If there weren't, it'd be easy."

The principal gives me her sincerest smile.

"Would you mind waiting in the corridor, Mattia?"

Zé tenses. Fear passes over his usually impassive face.

I shake my head.

"I'd rather stay, madame."

The principal gives a start. It's the first time in the whole meeting that I've spoken. She looks to Zé for help. He avoids her gaze. He doesn't want me to abandon him, but he can't tell her that.

"Monsieur Palaisot," she insists.

The teacher looks from one to the other of us without saying a word. I know that silence, it's the kind that analyzes.

"I'd like to bring up a subject that, shall we say, isn't for a child's ears."

Zé hesitates. I'd like, through my silence, to give him the strength to tell them both to go to hell. I wish he'd take his courage or his fear—it doesn't matter which—in both hands and stand up, make a deep bow, tell them the truth—that he hates talking about subjects that children aren't supposed to hear (has he himself ever grown up?)—or else make up some last-minute appointment, and just turn and go. I don't care what he says, as long as he refuses, dammit, just as long as he refuses.

He looks at me and indicates the door.

"I'll see you outside."

I obey, mortified, while the principal looks on triumphantly. Is there a grown-up in this world capable of doing what he wants and not what he has to?

I immediately hide behind the door. It's an underhanded thing to do, I admit. But it's only because of that annoying adult habit of talking behind closed doors. I hide and I listen. If I didn't, I would never have understood much about the world around me. I mean, even less than I do now.

". . . none of our business, but all the same that makes two suicides, one successful and one attempted, among people close to him. He seems to be able to cope, but one of these days . . ."

The wind knocks against the window of the dark corridor where I'm huddled. The school is shrouded in semidarkness. The teachers and the students have gone home, back to their family situations, which may be complicated, maybe not, who knows? Sometimes I look at the other kids and wonder if they've ever had to mop up a woman's blood from the back seat of a car, or spend nights on end hidden under a hospital bed, or throw pebbles in a pond and count the number of times they bounce, begging the Ultimate Bastard or whatever is up there to grant them the benefit of a tiny reprieve—just a little bit more time with those who are sick, those who are absent, and those who are going to die.

I give up eavesdropping on the conversation. What's the point? They always talk the same bullshit in the same offices and the same corridors without windows worthy of the name, at the same time and with the same people.

Zé is inscrutable when he comes out some fifteen minutes later. He's silent on the ride home in his beat-up old car that seems to have lived through a world war and nuclear annihilation—not to mention the blood on the back seat that I imagine gleaming intermittently in the moonlight.

He sticks a cigarette between his lips. The front of the car fills with smoke. He was supposed to quit the day I came to live with him. He said it was a good opportunity because, after all, he didn't want to give me cancer, though he still wasn't entirely convinced about the dangers of passive smoking. He held out for two weeks. That's quite something, according to him.

"We have to do something," he says at last.

"What?"

"I don't know. Something."

I wait a moment. He can't make up his mind to continue. I notice that he's driving slowly, well below the allowed speed limit. He doesn't want to go home. He doesn't want to find an empty apartment, empty although it's lived in, although we've been living in it for four years without ever taking possession of it.

He doesn't want to find Gabrielle staring at the wall in the same position he left her in.

"About what?" I ask.

"Huh?"

"Do something about what?"

"All this."

He indicates the street, the buildings, the town, the world. That's quite a job. I smile to myself. I'm eleven years old and I've realized what he still hasn't grasped in twenty-four: nothing ever changes, everything is endlessly repeated. Nothing is lost, nothing is created. If things do change, it's always in the same way, and only for a while.

4
GABRIELLE

One day, on her way home from school, she was sixteen or seventeen, a perfectly ordinary day, neither more nor less trying than any other, she was walking beside a fence when she suddenly collapsed.

Just like that, her legs gave way, she collapsed, all her muscles locked, she fell in the dust, letting go of her school bag, whose contents scattered on the ground, and she started screaming.

People passing on the street rushed to her, she wouldn't let anyone touch her, help her to her feet, approach her, talk to her, she snapped at all the hands held out to her, she didn't want to stop screaming.

So they came in an ambulance, they took her to the emergency psychiatric ward—she was still screaming—they put her to sleep and when she woke up she was still screaming.

After three days tied to her bed in an isolation room, she at last fell silent.

They let her go even though they didn't understand—she never deigned to explain it to them, silence was already her rule. She resumed an apparently normal life but
nothing was ever
the same as
it had been before.

* * *

"Why?"

She doesn't reply. She's been hearing this question since she was a teenager. Why, always why, and she never has an answer to give. It's gone on so long that she's ended up choosing silence. No. Answers don't exist. That's what the people around her find so hard to understand.

Barefoot, dressed in her inevitable extra-extra-large sweatshirt and shorts, she watches the passers-by through the half-open window. A cool wind is blowing over the town. She was born in Paris but she left it as soon as she was old enough to study. Officially to escape the pollution, the traffic jams, the stress common to city dwellers. Unofficially to get away from her family. And especially to get away from that thing that stops her from just being here, happy in the present moment.

But—as was to be expected—the thing followed her.

"Why, Gabrielle?"

Zé is behind her. He's so tall that he always shrinks when he speaks to her. Maybe he's too young. She's older than him. Thirty-something, and with plenty of reasons to go.

"Don't you love me anymore?"

"That's not the question," Gabrielle says.

"Do you love me or don't you?"

"That's—not—the—question."

It's true. There's no hidden explanation. No buried child-hood trauma, or not much of one. No turbulent family history. Nothing that could justify her desire to go. She always has to *justify* everything. To her family. To her countless psychiatrists and psychologists. To Zé.

Only Mattia respects her silence. Gabrielle likes him. He's eleven years old, yet he's the only one who understands, who knows, that some questions can't even be asked.

She's not accountable to anyone. That's what she used to tell herself before she passed the blade across her veins, to reassure herself: she wasn't accountable to anyone, but it wasn't true.

Sometimes she would prefer to have nobody to apologize to. But there's Zé. And Mattia. *I hope you're not going to leave us on our own*, that's what Zé said to her one day, sensing that she was about to act on her impulse.

He's there, sitting behind her on the back of the couch, a cigarette in his mouth, anxious lines on his forehead. She doesn't see him but she can imagine him perfectly well. Two years together, sharing this nothing. Like everyone else perhaps, or perhaps not. She has withdrawn from the world. She's forgotten how other people live. She watches them through the window with a kind of polite astonishment.

"Gabrielle . . ."

Silence.

"I love you. That should count for something."

She smiles at the window pane. A rather grim smile.

"Stop making me feel guilty."

"You can't expect me to act as if nothing happened."

Actually, she doesn't expect anything of him. But telling him that would be to hurt him again. He's the one putting pressure on himself, stubbornly holding onto someone who wants to go. Just like her family. Her psychiatrists. Her psychologists.

All she wants is to be left alone. Zé knew perfectly well what to expect when they decided to spend time together. That's how she's always described a relationship: spending time together. Nothing more, nothing less. She doesn't make any promises. No vows of fidelity, eternal love, joint accounts. She did warn him. He chose, knowing full well what he was getting into, and now he doesn't have the strength to take responsibility for that decision.

How can she blame him?

Outside, there are people passing by. They are going somewhere. Far from the high walls of Charcot. Far from the hospitals. Far from "that thing" she can never shake off because it's part of her, it took her years to realize that. The anguish. The terrible anguish of not knowing if she is alive or not.

An eternity goes by. Mattia will be out of school soon. And Zé gives up. She senses it distinctly in his sigh.

"I have to pick up the kid."

She nods to show that she's heard him.

"They want to make him take some tests," he adds.

"What kind of tests?"

"IQ tests. They think he's gifted. They've asked my permission."

"What did you tell them?"

"That I'll have to talk to him first. What do you think of the idea?"

She shrugs. She doesn't think much of it.

"I don't think it'll change anything in our lives. He doesn't need an IQ test to know who he is and what he has to do."

The usual silence tells her that Zé hasn't understood. A pause, then the front door slams shut. Her eyes closed, Gabrielle savors her solitude.

5

My psychologist's name is Nouria.

She practices in a tiny office no bigger than a broom closet that she's somehow managed to fix up so that it looks huge and airy. No furniture apart from two chairs. No desk. No taking of notes, no computer. Just a telephone on the floor, plugged in only between sessions.

I've been seeing her for forty-five minutes every two weeks for the last four years. Like it or not, that creates a bond. She has an unusual smile. She smiles with every muscle in her face and her eyes shrink to two dark slits. She's special. As a person and especially as a shrink. I like her.

"How's Gabrielle?" she asks.

"Still silent."

"And Zé?"

"The same. He keeps saying that something has to change but he doesn't know what. The same old story."

"And what about you?"

"What about *you*?"

She smiles. That's always my answer and it's always hers.

It's dark outside. It's getting dark earlier and earlier. It's December 1. Just over a month since Gabrielle's suicide attempt. It's cold. Lots of things must be happening in the world but nothing, absolutely nothing, is happening here.

I'm bored. I sink into the silence to stop other people dragging me with them.

"Have you heard from your mother?"

At first she did what all shrinks do, waited for me to speak. But I didn't speak and so she started asking me questions. Which I answer, except that I don't have much to say. It's the same old problem. But she doesn't get discouraged. She's wonderful. She really is.

"No."

"Have you called her?"

"No."

"Why not?"

"I don't need her."

"You don't need anyone."

I don't know if it's a question or a statement. Not sure what to say, I turn away and look out the window. A murky fog has descended on the town. Zé must be waiting for me in the nearest bar. Between his job as a night watchman and Lamartine, he only socializes once every two weeks, during my session with Nouria.

"I don't know why," I say, "but I've been thinking a lot about Saïd lately."

"Who's Saïd?"

"The boy who got himself killed, you know, it was after that that my father was sent to Charcot."

Out of the corner of my eye, I sense her nodding her head. She's all ears. And I smile inside. It does me good to know that, whatever happens, if I have something to say, there's someone to hear me. It's just a pity that this someone is paid to do it.

"Saïd Zahidi, yes, I remember it well."

"He was fifteen," I say, not too sure of the point I'm making.

"Yes."

Silence. Headlights through the fog. A car skids on the street and straightens up at the last moment before it can hit anything. Pedestrians curse.

Her brown eyes are fixed on me. Nothing escapes her. With anybody else, that would make me uncomfortable.

"And you're thinking about him."

"Yes."

"And indirectly about your father's death?"

"No. Just about him. I've been wondering . . ."

"Yes?"

"Why nobody talks about it any more."

"I suppose it happens all too often, Mattia."

I don't know why she always says my name but it makes me feel good. She puts an unusual warmth into it. Neither my mother, nor my brother, nor my sister, nor Zé talk to me like that. Gabrielle sometimes, when she deigns to lower herself to the level of the living.

"That's what Zé says."

"It's hard to have enough empathy to mourn all those who die unjustly."

"I'm not talking about mourning. But at least remembering."

"Memory is silent sometimes."

Silent . . .

I have a flashback. My mother, my sister, and I, visiting Charcot a few months before the end. My father, looking thinner, his blue pajamas—he no longer bothers to take them off even though he's allowed outdoor clothes—much too large for him now. My father, a shattered man but smiling despite everything, and that gesture, his hand touching my hand, which I've put down without thinking next to his arm.

My hand that I withdraw in an inexplicable reflex, like a cry from the heart.

Mom's look of alarm.

My father's smile fading and my sister biting her lip—and me, aware of my mistake but too late.

My father's eyes pursuing me long after the end of the visit, planted like fish hooks in my head. So sad, his words: "See you again, Mattia," infinite regret in his voice made slow by the antipsychotics.

My sister: "He needs us, don't judge him." My mother silent as always. Me, too.

* * *

I come back to reality. I move away from the window and look at Nouria. Sometimes I can't bear the gaze from those dark eyes.

"What are you thinking about?" she says softly.

I shake my head.

"Saïd."

It's a lie. She knows it. She doesn't say anything. She makes a mental note. I change the subject.

"At school, they want me to take some IQ tests."

"Really?"

"They think I'm either a moron or gifted."

"What do you think of the idea?"

I shrug. "I'm afraid they'll make me change schools. I prefer not to take them. Do you think I'm allowed to refuse?"

"Of course."

Behind her smile, I sense that she's proud of me, and I feel better.

* * *

Mom lives on the other side of town, in Les Verrières, the neighborhood where I grew up, almost abandoned now and on the way to being redeveloped. Soon, these thirty-story blocks isolated from the rest of the world will be razed to the ground and replaced by apartment buildings that conform to European and environmental regulations, with rents to match. Here as elsewhere, the work has already started. Bulldozers, mechanical diggers, patches of waste ground, and huge real-estate posters showing gorgeous, happy young couples pushing strollers, their smiles overflowing with joy at the thought of at last finding the apartment of their dreams and the quiet life that automatically ensues.

Zé parks by a fence surrounding a deep crater. All that domestic happiness is due to come to fruition next year. The building where I used to live has withstood this flood of propaganda, the only one of its kind.

The stairwell is covered in graffiti about the police, unlikely nocturnal appointments, and telephone numbers flung there like offerings. We climb the five flights of stairs. Zé rings the bell, waits, then knocks at the door while I lean over the banister, wrapped in a winter coat. According to the weather forecast, it's going to snow next week. It'll be the Christmas holidays soon.

"Madame Lorozzi!" Zé calls out.

A sixty-something neighbor comes out onto the landing opposite.

"She hasn't been home in three weeks. Are you her sons?"

"He is, I'm not," Zé says, searching in his pockets for cigarettes.

"I haven't heard from Amélia for a while now," the neighbor says. "The last time I saw her, she told me she was having problems with the rent."

"Do you think she's been thrown out?"

"No, we would have heard. Everyone's having problems right now. They're rebuilding the neighborhood. Right now they're purchasing the building. In a few months they'll have rehoused everybody."

Zé nods politely. He doesn't really give a damn. Maybe a little. He's about to light a cigarette, then changes his mind when he sees the neighbor's outraged expression.

"If I leave you my telephone number, will you call me if you see her?"

She looks us up and down inquisitively, while Zé writes a

number on a piece of paper that he then slips into her hand. She peers at his spidery scrawl.

"You're not a cop by any chance?"

"Why, do you think I look like one?"

She puts the paper in her pocket.

"I'll tell her you're trying to reach her."

A little later, in the car, as I'm prematurely examining the clouds in search of the promised snow, I notice we aren't heading in the direction of home.

"Where are we going?"

Zé doesn't reply. I'm used to it, so I give up on the idea of asking any more questions and go back to gazing at the sky. Zé would be a terrific recruit for drug dealers. It's impossible to get anything out of him, and he doesn't even do it deliberately. He'd drive the Narcs crazy. Even after three days of questioning, he'd be reciting Baudelaire on loop.

We drive back halfway across town. Zé is heading for the ritzy neighborhood known to its friends as La Solaire because there, on top of the hill, you're closer to daylight, and life, so they say, looks more beautiful.

Personally, I doubt it. Zé grew up here, and look how he turned out. If the rich didn't take antidepressants, everybody would know about it.

"Are we going to see your parents?" I ask.

He laughs and throws his cigarette out the window. A crystal-clear laugh that doesn't match his inscrutable face. I like his laugh. It's become a lot less frequent since Gabrielle tried to kill herself.

We climb the long hillside leading to the sumptuous villas looking down on the city and its gray layer of diesel. The air is nicer to breathe here than elsewhere. Zé stops on a little street with a medieval look, its cobbles reproducing those of old.

I recognize the house on the left.

"Oh, no, I don't want to see him!"

He doesn't care. Like a chauffeur, he gets out of the car, walks around to the other side, opens the door for me, and gives a low bow.

"Come on, move your ass."

He takes me by the arm as if I'm likely to run away and drags me over to a thick gate with a videophone on the outside. The gold nameplate says: *Stefano Lorozzi, surgeon.*

"It's all right for some," Zé murmurs, which is hypocritical of him considering where he comes from, then says into the speaker, "Stefano, it's Zé. I'm with Mattia. Can we come in for a few minutes?"

Against all expectations, it's not a butler, but the master of the house himself who comes and opens the gate. He leads us onto the terrace for a little aperitif, grape juice for me and soda for Zé, who never drinks alcohol. I fiddle with the sleeves of my jacket as I look him over. He's short, pushing thirty, with glasses, a smile like a toothpaste commercial, a striped polo shirt with the collar of another, spotless shirt peering out.

He's my brother. My half-brother. The son of my mother and another guy before she met my father. Started his medical studies at fifteen, qualified as a doctor when he was Zé's age, gifted in every sense of the word.

He doesn't have much in common with either me or Zé. The conversation proves laborious and the silence threatens to spread throughout the villa, but because he's been well brought-up, he makes an effort to keep something of a conversation going.

"How's work? Everything okay?"

"Yes," Zé says.

Silence. My brother stirs his cappuccino and looks up at the sky, frowning slightly. "Still a night watchman?"

"Yes."

"And what about you, Mattia? How's school?"

"It's okay."

I cross my fingers, hoping that Zé won't say a word about the educational meeting. But my failures are his, too, so he keeps quiet.

"What class are you in?"

"Last year of elementary."

"Sixth grade soon."

"Yes."

Silence. His fake smile gradually fades, at the same time as the sun sets behind the hill. I sympathize. It isn't easy having us as guests. Which of us has infected the other, Zé or me? Which of us has established then maintained this systematic policy of silence? I guess we were made to live together.

"What about you?" Zé says at last, remembering the rules that govern social intercourse—it's as if he's trying to recall the different paragraphs of a manual.

"How do you mean?"

"The job, all that."

"Everything's fine."

* * *

I was five years old Mom was mourning his absence his illness, there were no tears in her eyes only a terrible emptiness but anyone could see it—and you didn't.

You would leave for the university every morning, your satchel across your back, and you'd pass Mom lying on the couch in front of the TV, which was switched off. Her eyes filled with nothing would come to rest on you, those imploring eyes, and you would go on your way.

You'd come back in the evening without a glance at her—at us—and shut yourself up in your room, Stefano, fleeing that atmosphere of brain death, you'd withdraw from the world, from our world, and immerse yourself in your precious anatomy books. Sometimes at midnight Mom would knock at your door on the pretext of seeing if you'd managed to study, and in a curt tone you'd tell her you didn't need anything, and she'd retreat, already a shadow, and you would close your eyes in order not to see her aimless wandering.

I was five years old, Stefano, I saw all that I wasn't asleep I couldn't sleep knowing that she was there, alone facing all that, in spite of your presence, you were there but you existed even less than Dad.

You said he wasn't your father—he was none of your business—she should move on, you were her son and she was your mother, it wasn't

    up to you
    to be there
    for her.

* * *

"I'm looking for your mother," Zé says.

"My mother?"

The word sounds alien in his mouth, just like "Dad" in mine.

"Have you been to her place?"

"Her neighbor says she hasn't been back in three weeks. Have you heard from her?"

The silence changes sides. Affected by it or by the dusk, the lines on the corners of Stefano's lips grow deeper and ghosts pass across his eyes. A magpie comes to rest on the grass a few yards from me. I hold out my hand toward it. It flies up and perches at the top of a pine.

"No," my brother says. "To be honest, I haven't seen her for several months."

Zé sighs. He drinks the rest of his soda in one go.

"Thanks for your help."

My brother walks us to the car, after first insisting on inviting us to dinner.

"You mustn't worry," he says. "This isn't the first time she's disappeared for a while. She must have needed a change of scenery."

"There are visits with Mattia scheduled," Zé said. "She usually warns us."

"It must have slipped her mind. I'll let you know if I have any news. Goodbye, Mattia."

"Bye . . ."

Zé lights a cigarette, switches on the car radio, which is permanently tuned to France Culture, and, the incorrigible fan that he is, he begins to listen enraptured to a reading of Homer's *Odyssey*.

6

I was seven and nothing was happening. I even got to wondering if the end of the world hadn't already taken place. I was never cold, never hungry, I didn't need anything, and I wasn't suffering. There was a lot I could have asked myself, but I didn't want to formulate the questions because they reverberated too deeply in my soul. I could hear their distant echo, words flung into a hopelessly empty cavity.

But it's true, I wasn't suffering, which meant I was doing better than everyone else. I somehow couldn't think of that as good luck.

* * *

The snow finally arrives on December 15.

I sit eating cereal out of the box and watch the snow falling on the other side of the window. Zé has forgotten to go shopping. He and Gabrielle have been in their room for hours. I don't think they're sleeping together. Not right now, with the scars still fresh on her wrists.

I don't know what they're doing and it's getting on my nerves. They've closed the door. They long ago blocked the keyhole with a piece of Scotch tape. They're paranoid but also sensible, aware of my habit of constantly observing (just as well, because although I always have the impression they're talking about me, when I listen at doors I realize it isn't true). Anyway, they don't seem able to express themselves except in whispers.

So I'm left to my own devices. That's fine by me, I'm used to it, and I try to fill my usual silence with little everyday beauties, like that blanket of snow covering the tar.

The street is empty. It's late. After midnight. I'm tired but I don't feel like sleeping. Nobody's asking me to go to bed. Nobody's asking me anything. I blink to get rid of the tiredness.

I think of my mother looking at the tracks of a solitary walker in the snow. That walker could quite easily be her. I make an effort to remember her features. I have a very good aural memory, but my visual memory is useless, so that I sometimes forget her face, and I often recognize people only when I hear the sound of their voice.

Once I think I've reconstructed her, I imagine her standing there, by the window—never mind that we're on the fifth floor—a smile on her lips, placing her hand flat on the window pane for me to put my hand on it. Simple physical contact to prove to me that she's still there, alive and tangible, a creature of flesh and blood, quite simply my mother.

I close my eyes to hide everyone's absence, and my solitude. I concentrate with all my might on thinking about her, about my father, about sad things, about the day we learned that he was dead, the day of the funeral, all those pointless and timeless visits to the hospital, the time I took my hand away when he tried to touch me, Saïd Zahidi, all my mistakes, all theirs.

I listen to the beating of my heart, the sound of my breathing, I try to locate my diaphragm, which moves lower each time I breathe in. The sound of my cells jostling together, the impulses constantly leaving my brain, the cereal decomposing under the onslaught of the gastric juices in my stomach.

All these mechanics, the noise of life, assures me that I'm genuinely in the here and now.

I feel better. I open my eyes.

"Mattia?"

Gabrielle is looking at the snow over my shoulder, her eyes

swollen, wrapped in the extra-extra-large sweatshirt she wears instead of a robe, barefoot, adult and child, lost.

"What are you doing?" she asks.

"Just looking."

She smiles. "Beautiful, isn't it? We've also been watching it falling for hours."

So that's what they've been doing in the secrecy of their room . . . Clearly worth letting me die of starvation.

"It'll be Christmas soon," she adds, strangely resistant to the silence, which gradually retreats. "Is there something you'd like?"

I shrug. She sits down next to me and puts her arm around my shoulders.

"Is Zé asleep?" I ask.

"Yes. It's his day off tomorrow. Shouldn't you be going to bed?"

"I don't feel like it."

"It's up to you."

A pause. She hugs me. The warmth of another body—that's something I haven't felt for a long time.

She speaks close to my ear.

"What do you need to be happy?"

"What about you?" I reply with a lump in my throat.

She responds by hugging me tighter. I bury my head in the folds of her sweatshirt, sealing the union of our two solitudes.

"I don't feel like going to school tomorrow."

"Then don't go," Gabrielle says.

"Or the other days."

"You'll have to go back sometime."

"Why?"

My voice is muffled by the weight of her clothes. She thinks out loud as she strokes my head.

"You have to learn to live with other people, even if it's not always much fun."

"Other people" . . . She talks about them as if they're from another world, extraterrestrials she feels she has nothing in common with.

"Do we really have to live with them?"

"Yes, otherwise you fall through their big net. Stop with your questions, Mattia." She laughs. "You're bumming me out."

I look at the scars on her bare arms, sleeves rolled back to the elbows. I want to ask her what happened to her—and to Zé, and to my father—if the fact of falling through the net inevitably leads to hospital rooms, if it's a sickness, if the only cure is either to die or to live confined within white or gray walls.

But I already know her answer.

* * *

I'm waiting for Zé on the corner of the street, as always. It's minus two degrees and that bastard has been letting me die of cold for the past hour. He must be in bed, all cozy and warm with Gabrielle, while my fingers and lips are turning blue.

I keep glancing at the post office. Those suspicious guys from the other time aren't there. I've been watching my back for a while now and they haven't showed themselves again. Zé may be right after all, it must have been a mistake. There's no reason for them to take an interest in us. We're as boring as everybody else, we're just trying to survive.

After he's an hour and a quarter late, I get tired of waiting. I set off, trudging through the brown muck that litters the streets, muck defeated by the town hall's salt and the citizens' relentless shuffle.

I walk the mile or so separating me from home. Zé and Gabrielle are curled up together on the couch, covered with a thick layer of blankets, sleeping peacefully. From what I can see, they fell asleep naked. I start to understand why they forgot to pick me up from school.

Under normal circumstances, I'd have gone to my room and sulked. But that's been my strategy for two years and it hasn't been very effective. So I grab the blankets and yank them off. There they both are, in their birthday suits. Zé is the first to wake up. He sees me, looks down at his completely exposed body, rushes to his clothes, then grabs the blanket from my hands in order to cover Gabrielle.

"What the hell are you doing?" he hisses.

"I waited for you outside school for an hour!"

I scream the words. I don't usually do that, and it leaves him rooted to the spot. Gabrielle stirs, waking up.

"It's minus five degrees but you don't give a damn as long as you're nice and warm with her! When you asked to have custody of me, you should have thought of the responsibility, but you're just a stupid kid, worse than me, plus you're a son of a bitch, but it's not too late to see the judge and tell him you don't want to look after me anymore, don't worry, I won't cry, I'm used to it."

He opens his mouth. I refuse to let him speak. Gabrielle grabs the armrest to sit up and gropes on the table for her cigarettes, dull-eyed.

"You can't even stop your girlfriend from trying to kill herself, so what makes you think you can take care of a child, you filthy bastard?"

The slap knocks me back a good six feet. I stagger on the carpet and manage to regain my balance by grabbing onto the curtains, which tear from top to bottom. Zé's hand has left red marks on my cheek, you can almost see the fingerprints. And here I was, dreaming of physical contact . . .

"Zé!" Gabrielle screams, jumping up from the couch, forgetting that she's naked.

Zé bows his head. His hands are shaking. He looks at me,

clearly already regretting what he did, but I don't care, Zé, if only you knew how little I care, I just want things to change, we have to do something, anything . . .

I turn my back on both of them and take refuge in my room, just to make a dramatic exit. I collapse on my bed. I'm shaking all over. I pull the blanket up over my face. I wait a few minutes but nobody comes.

Against all expectation, I fall asleep.

* * *

One day I was seven years old I took a knife from the kitchen and tried to cut my wrists with it. It hurt it drew blood but it didn't go right in, I couldn't do it, not sharp enough, cuts every-where as I stubbornly rooted about in the skin looking for the veins, not knowing it's the arteries dammit that you had to aim for.

It hurt but I kept going, I just wanted either to stop the silence or to let it take hold forever, it had become unbearable.

Bringing the knife down again and again with such ferocity I didn't notice that the blood was starting to gush I had it on my shoes it was spreading across the tiled floor I was succeeding in my task.

Worse still, I didn't hear the key in the lock and everything was spinning around me and there were white spots in front of my eyes and I looked down and saw the blood and I was scared I wanted to let go of the knife but it was too late, the harm was done, a scream and it was torn from my hands. Mom lifted me off the floor and hugged me to her crying Mattia Mattia Mattia

and it hurt and I didn't want to die anymore but somewhere deep down inside me I was smiling because

the silence was broken.

Then the emergency room and some time later Nouria.

And Mom

never
forgave me.
Maybe that's what I'd wanted.

* * *

I'm shivering with fever.

My sleep is populated with those nightmares peculiar to my sickness, half dream half delirium. My unconscious environment is superimposed on the reality of my room, a reality I seem to glimpse through closed eyelids.

Grinning figures follow one another at my bedside. Each time I blink, a different person is at the foot of my bed. There's no logic to the speed with which they appear.

Sometimes it's my father sadly watching me struggling with the fever, sometimes my mother, sometimes my sister, Nouria, Gabrielle, and even Saïd Zahidi who died at the age of fifteen, lying at the foot of the high-rises with his skull smashed in, *I know his face from seeing it so often, painted on the walls of my town, from Les Verrières to the pretty streets of La Solaire, along with words that weren't enough—that are never enough—to express all the anger, all the hatred, all the injustice of his death, words crying out for revenge, words telling us not to forget and not to forgive.*

I want to get up but the sickness confines me to the bed and I can only roll my eyes as I try to seize hold of these intangible ghosts.

Mom places a hand on my forehead and whispers inaudibly, I strain to hear her words but all I catch is her sympathetic silence.

In the middle of the night, voices buzz around me, saying my name, and arms lift me from my bed and carry me away. Barely conscious, I let them do it. They undress me and lay me down on a frozen surface filled with water. I no longer know if

I'm shaking with heat or cold. Figures loom above me, a man and a woman, the light hurts my eyes, the touch of something cold in my ear, a cry emerges from amid my confused thoughts, a number: 105, I hear that the duty doctor needs to be called, and I drift off.

* * *

Dad in his blue pajamas that are much too big for his scrawny, malnourished body, sitting on his hospital bed, his face buried in his palms. I want to call to him, to touch him, but I have no physical existence, I'm floating in the void like the draft of air I've always been.

Dad scratching his cheeks with his nails, tears rolling down his neck.

Dad unable to bear it any more.

The torn sheet around his throat, the cracking of bones.

I want to cry out.

My vocal cords express only silence and it hurts like hell when they give way, I hear the break distinctly, as if a guitar string was being cut with scissors.

But someone else screams instead of me.

Zé rushing to him and grabbing him by the legs to allow him to breathe—but it's too late, the cervical vertebrae have snapped, he calls for help and the room is overrun with white coats.

* * *

I open my eyes and see an unknown face. She's a woman of about fifty, with a stethoscope around her neck. My whole body is paralyzed by a terrible heat. Big drops of sweat run down my forehead. My throat is as dry as if it's been rubbed with sandpaper.

"Mattia?" It's Zé's voice. "Mattia, can you hear me?"

I can't speak: my vocal cords are gone. I blink to indicate that I'm conscious. Gradually my surroundings come into focus. I'm lying on the couch in the living room. Zé is leaning on the back of it, face drawn with fear, and Gabrielle is sitting on the armrest with her hand in my hair.

The other woman must be a doctor. She's talking to Zé and Gabrielle.

"The fever's going down."

A whole lot of medical equipment is strewn on the coffee table, including a syringe.

"The antibiotics will start to take effect in forty-eight hours. You should have called earlier."

The hint of reproach in her voice is obvious.

"It happened suddenly," Zé protests. "He was fine last night."

Oh, yes, that's right, you son of a bitch, I was fine . . .

"And what's this?"

This is my right cheek, and she's pointing an accusing finger at it.

"Did you hit him?"

Silence. Later, when I look in the mirror, I'll see the big bruise left by Zé's hand. Zé lowers his eyes, ready once again to assume the role of bad father.

"I'm sorry," the doctor says curtly as she disinfects her equipment, "but I'm obliged to inform social services."

"What?" Zé says.

His voice is shaking with anger. In a way, I'm pleased. He doesn't often get excited about anything that isn't a poem by Verlaine, plus it's about me. It must be a Christmas miracle.

"Do you think I mistreat him?"

"I don't think anything, I'm just applying the usual procedure when there's suspicion."

"Suspicion of what, dammit?"

"Be quiet," Gabrielle says.

"No, I'm not going to let her . . ." He loses his temper. "You just have to look at him. Check if he has any marks, you won't find a thing!"

"This kind of thing isn't necessarily visible to the naked eye, monsieur."

She closes her black bag and heads for the door of the apartment, pursued by Zé, while Gabrielle sits down at my side.

"What do you mean, you're going to have him see a shrink? He's already seeing one, they'd know if I was beating him!"

"You half admitted that you'd hit him."

"But that happens to everybody! I dare you to tell me you've never hit anyone."

"We're talking about an eleven-year-old child, monsieur," the doctor says as she opens the door. "Check his temperature every hour and inform us if the fever gets worse. Have a very good evening."

She slams the door. I feel as if the impact reverberates down my spine. A shiver goes through me. Gabrielle squeezes my hand with her moist fingers.

"Mattia, are you all right?"

I make a huge effort and point to my throat to make it clear to her that my larynx is in no state to do anybody any harm. I don't know if she understands but she doesn't insist. Zé's back, looming over me, a cigarette in his mouth. He takes huge, angry drags.

"That bitch—"

"Stop, she's doing it for Mattia's good. They'll see he hasn't been mistreated."

"Sure, but it isn't going to look good in family court."

"You think they'll pass it on?"

"Of course. It's the same people."

But I'm smiling. In spite of everything I'm touched that he's worried about keeping his guardianship of me. That isn't the impression he's been giving me lately, even though he fought to obtain it.

They spend the night taking turns watching over me. I drift off and wake up several times in the course of the following few hours. I see dawn come up. I realize that Zé didn't go to work last night. Once or twice he unwittingly wakes me when he applies arnica to my cheek, but I don't know if it's because he feels sorry for what he did or because the doctor's accusations have scared him. They follow instructions and take my temperature regularly, but I feel a little better and they don't get alarmed at any point. I'm almost disappointed. All the same, my temperature stays at 103. Not so far from an emergency.

Naturally, I miss school the next day. Needless to say, it's no great loss for me—and vice versa I imagine.

They let me sleep in the living room so that they can keep an eye on me. My temples are throbbing, I have the shivers, and my body aches all over. I must have caught a chill waiting outside the school. That's good. Maybe it'll teach Zé a sense of responsibility (grown-ups are always boring me to tears with that, so they might as well set a good example, it's the least you can expect).

Sometimes in my dreams I see my mother and try to ask her where she is, and if she's still angry with me, but I still can't speak.

The frustration makes me clench my fists in anger.

When Gabrielle holds my hand, I look at the scars on her wrists and compare them with mine, which are already white. I don't think hers will ever get to that stage. That must be the difference between someone who wants to die and someone who's trying desperately to come back to life, but I don't know, I've never known what I was really looking for when I picked up that knife.

The sickness lasts for several days. They say it's a raging flu.

Zé skips work, even though Gabrielle had offered to look after me. I sometimes hear them whispering near the couch. I don't know if they're talking about me.

To make it worse, it's still snowing. I hate being stuck in bed when the weather's so lovely. I haven't been ill in years. That's just like me. When I was little, I'd sometimes get high fevers with no other associated symptoms. They drove my mother crazy. They stopped not long after my father died. There must have been a connection, one way or another.

7
ZÉ

Aux lieux tranquilles où mon coeur te souhaitait, je respirais un éternel été . . .[3] He's looking after the boy, a book in his hand as always. This time, he's chosen Camus's *Les Justes*. That's just like Zé. Rebellion on the page, in ink and words. No other way to survive. The only time he tried to get out of the straitjacket he's put around himself, as an teenager, it earned him several months in Charcot—but that was the least of his worries.

He was always a quiet person. An infant prodigy, a model student, a perfect classmate. Up until that blackboard—he closes his eyes when he thinks about it and again sees the blood staining the chalk, then he opens a book and gets drunk on words until it passes, until he atones for his sin and is forgiven.

In the meantime, he reads.

Gabrielle is watching TV in the living room. He drops in to see her from time to time and check that she isn't dead. She vegetates in front of the bluish screen. If it was up to him, he'd throw it out the window, that fucking TV whose ever darker and more cynical news reports help keep Gabrielle in a state of terrifyingly calm despair. But he would have a rebellion on his

[3] In the quiet places where my heart longed for you, I breathed in an eternal summer.

hands. Mattia doesn't look like a rebel, but he's really fond of his cartoons on Sunday mornings.

Just a kid. Zé has to keep telling himself that, surprised, because he forgets it sometimes.

Aux lieux tranquilles où mon coeur te souhaitait . . .

He can't concentrate on his reading. The revolutionaries of the Russian Communist Party are debating good and evil, life and death and justice before carrying out an assassination. Today, such considerations strike him as quite pointless. To each his own life. To each his own shit. To each his own death, Gabrielle would add. And to each his own injustices. Zé finds it hard to take up a position with regard to all these everyday questions. He isn't really a player of the game. He's just trying to do his best. For himself. For those he loves. To survive, that's what it comes down to, to survive without waking one day with the simple desire to blow your brains out.

He hears the TV trotting out Nixon, Pinochet, and the coup of September 11, 1973. He closes his eyes in irritation. Just channel-hop, Gabrielle. He tells her that all the time: don't get sucked into the world's nightmares. Other people manage to overcome all the mess around them, picking up a little happiness here and there, in their own lives, they manage to extricate themselves from the shit surrounding them. But not Gabrielle. That's what's killing her. She won't be happy as long as there's still one unhappy person left on earth. Which means that nobody—not the psychiatrists, not the doctors, not Zé—will ever be able to convince her that things aren't so bad. Why would she accept such a lie?

Some people like that are doomed not to make it to old age.

So he gradually resigns himself to the thought that one morning he will wake up next to a cold corpse. There will only be Mattia left, which is the same as saying nobody, because

Mattia will also leave—not in the same way, no, he hopes not—but children always leave in the end, and if he were Mattia, Zé would already have left.

Even the TV falls silent now. The apartment fills with the silence and Zé feels the visceral need to hear his own voice. He closes his book and bends over the sleeping Mattia.

"Are you asleep?"

The boy's features remain still. Even in his sleep, he doesn't smile. Zé feels quite alone.

"I think about her, you know, the girl I killed . . ."

He swallows painfully. He thinks about it all the time and never talks about it.

"Émilie. Her name was Émilie."

No response.

"One day I'd like you to go with me when I visit her grave. Not so you can bear the weight of my mistakes. But so you can see what happens if you let yourself be swallowed up by the world. It's disgusting, the world, you know, it's so hard to resist it, everything's set up for you to lose your footing, and if you let go, if you leave hold of the edge of the skating rink for just one second, if you slip . . ."

He doesn't know how to finish. He's used to arguing with himself—in silence—but he seldom goes all the way with his arguments. That's because he can't find any meaning in them. With time, he's almost stopped looking.

He sighs and puts his hand on the boy's hand, which is warm but not burning hot.

"Stay away from the world. It may be cowardly, but it's the only way not to do any harm. At least, it's the only way I know, and I hope I'm wrong."

He leaves the book on the night table, stands up, and stretches. He looks around the room. Mattia doesn't have many things. A desk. A chair, a bed, a chest of drawers with some clothes. No books. Almost no toys. Nothing to suggest a particular interest, a hobby. He's another one who's not too sure how to survive.

"Get well soon," Zé adds as he heads for the door. "Without you, the only thing left is silence."

Gabrielle has fallen asleep on the couch. Zé switches off the TV and suppresses a sudden urge to cry.

8

The fever finally passes after a few days. I've missed a week of school and Zé a week's work. My head weighs two or three tons but I'm capable of getting up and eating, much to the relief of the other two, who've had to feed me.

Zé wakes up one morning, with sleep in his eyes, and opens his mouth when he sees me searching through the refrigerator.

"I've made coffee," I say nonchalantly.

"Why all this attention?"

"What attention?"

"You didn't seem so willing to please me the last time we spoke."

"Neither did you," I retort, pointing at the yellow bruise finally fading on my cheek.

He falls silent. So do I. He sits down at the kitchen table, pours a lot of coffee into a glass, and adds a splash of milk. Meanwhile, I make my breakfast, a bowl of cereal, then automatically head for the living room so that I can watch the cartoons as I eat. Zé catches me by the tail of my pajamas as I pass him.

"Where are you going?"

"To watch TV, why?"

"No way. You're going to school. We already have social services on our backs."

The bastard dresses me by force and bundles me into the car. Once he's managed to get me in, he locks the doors. I elbow him in revenge.

"If I'd known, I'd have thrown the hot coffee in your face."

We're outside the school and I already have my hand on the handle when he finally speaks.

"Do you want to end up in an institution, Mattia?"

"Excuse me?"

"An institution, with dormitories and supervisors, how would you like that? That's what'll happen if the judge decides that I'm not doing well as your guardian. So it's in both our interests to be on our best behavior from now on." He puts all the sternness he can summon into his expression. "Don't do anything stupid at school, okay? From now on, you apply yourself to your work."

I turn my back on him, leaving him to close the door after me, without showing the fear that's making my stomach churn.

Madame Sivrieux looks genuinely relieved to see me again. Just like the last time, she takes me aside before class. I tell her I was confined to bed with a bad fever. She seems delighted to learn that there haven't been any more suicide attempts among my nearest and dearest. She's nice. She's been a lot nicer to me since she heard about my "complicated family situation."

It's impossible to concentrate on the lessons. I'd gladly have a coughing fit so that they'd send me back home, but Zé would tear me to pieces. I think about what he told me in the car. His words haunt me. He doesn't talk much but he knows just what to say when it really matters.

I don't want to be sent to an institution.

It wouldn't be right. I still have family. Why should I have that Damocles sword hanging over me when my mother, my brother, and my sister are still around?

Because nobody wants to take care of me.

I feel a wave of self-pity, which is something I hate. Even if it means having bad thoughts, I'd rather concentrate on the litany of the French kings.

I manage not to fall asleep. They don't give out prizes for that. One more injustice, but at least this one's bearable.

* * *

Dad was dead and the emptiness kept growing in Mom's eyes.

I was seven. I was in the hospital. A student nurse was bandaging my cuts. I hadn't needed stitches. The wounds were superficial. The ones on my skin, anyway. But the knife had also lodged itself in Mom's heart and increased the emptiness.

She waited for the nurse to go then said:

"I can't live with you anymore, Mattia."

I felt a chasm open up somewhere inside me, beneath my feet, I opened my mouth, no sound came out.

"I can't live with you anymore."

A bird came to rest on the window ledge.

"I'm sorry. I just can't do it anymore. It's too difficult."

And she left.

The student nurse came back soon afterwards. I was still watching the bird. She smiled at me, I could see the reflection of her face in the window. There was something profoundly indecent in that smile. I swayed backwards and forwards, my fingers wrapped around my ankles, my mind elsewhere.

I couldn't even say to her "don't leave me alone."

The silence was both

outside

and inside.

* * *

That night, I pretend to go to bed early on the pretext that the disease is lingering. Gabrielle opens the door toward midnight to check if I'm asleep; I mime sleep. She's taken in. Zé probably wouldn't have been fooled. Too bad for him if he prefers to delegate.

After a few minutes, I get out of bed and creep along the narrow corridor.

A soft light is filtering from the living room door. I crouch down and stick an ear to the keyhole. At first, all I can hear are whispers, but my hearing, sharpened by a lifetime of silence, soon adjusts to their thin voices.

Gabrielle: ". . . his mother. Don't you think we should go to the cops?"

Zé: "What do you think she wants?"

Gabrielle: "It's not about her, or about us. It's about Mattia."

Zé: "The reason she didn't leave a forwarding address is because she doesn't want us to find her. I respect that."

Gabrielle: "And I say again this is about him, not about you."

Zé (after a silence): "Do you think I'm being selfish?"

Gabrielle: "I didn't say that."

Footsteps. I quickly get up, but nobody comes to the door and I realize that Zé is walking around in circles, as he tends to do when he's worried. Gabrielle must be sitting on the couch, a solemn look on her face. I know them only too well. I can imagine all their expressions. More than anything, I even know what their silences look like.

Gabrielle: "Zé."

Zé: "Yes."

Gabrielle: "Those guys Mattia mentioned when I was in the hospital, do you think they were after you?"

Zé: "What guys?"

Gabrielle: "The ones who asked him questions about you. Maybe there's some connection with his mother."

Zé: "I'm sure it's a mistake."

I wait several minutes, but their silence goes on forever and I start to get tired. In the end, I go back to bed.

The following Friday is a great day, because it's the last day of school. I'm itching with impatience all day. At recess, the others exchange tips on how best to get their parents to cough up and buy them the latest console or the little dog they've wanted for years. The only gift I want is for it to be four-thirty at last.

Father Christmas finally grants my wish. I'm the first out through the school gates. I spot Zé, double-parked. He's always on time now, ever since my attack of flu. I fling myself into the car like a diver swallowing his first mouthful of air. He smiles at my excitement. I'm in such a good mood that I fasten my seat belt without his needing to ask me.

I look out at the passing scene. That's how I notice the gray car that's been behind us since we left the school. I wouldn't have paid it any attention if it hadn't accelerated in such a dangerous fashion in order to stay behind us when the lights changed to yellow.

As usual, Zé doesn't see a thing. I tap him on the knee.

"We're being followed."

He looks where I'm looking in the rearview mirror.

"Where?"

"The gray car."

He shakes his head, as if to say I'm good for the funny farm.

"Check if you don't believe me!" I say irritably.

He heaves a deep sigh and again double-parks. All the cars pass him, but not this one, which stays where it is at a light. Zé's face clouds over. He lights a cigarette and sets off again. Our pursuers follow suit.

"Now that's strange," Zé mutters.

"It must be the weird guys who were waiting for me outside the school!"

"What did they look like?"

Up until now he hasn't been particularly worried about their existence. Maybe he's suspected me of making it all up for attention. In all honesty, I have sometimes lied to get him to take an interest in me.

I describe the two men, all the while keeping an eye on the other car in the rearview mirror.

"Cops or just weird guys?" he interrupts me.

"I'm not sure."

He nods as if it didn't matter anymore, but then accelerates abruptly at the next light—my head hits the seat as he does a U-turn and almost causes the pileup of the century.

There's some cursing from the other drivers, and some give us the finger, but we lose our pursuers. I'm white in the face. Focused on his driving, Zé doesn't even notice. I put a hand on my heart and try to swallow down the nausea. I hate speed.

He stops outside our building.

"Get out, I'll park a bit farther on."

I go up to the apartment. Gabrielle is dozing on the couch. The TV is off. I drop my school bag at my feet. My joy at the last day of school was stamped out in just a few minutes.

I wait for Zé in the kitchen. He takes a good fifteen minutes to get back. Through the open door I see him crouch by Gabrielle's head, stroke her hair, and whisper something in her ear. She's asleep. He puts his ear to her mouth, then stands up and takes off his blouson. Ignoring me, he opens the fridge and looks inside it indifferently.

I clear my throat.

"Who are those guys?"

Zé shrugs and doesn't turn.

"What do they want?" I insist.

"No idea."

He closes the fridge.

"Do you want cereal?"

I glare at him. He soon turns away. He lights another cigarette.

"You're hiding things from me," I venture.

"No, I'm not."

"Yes, you are."

He sighs and pulls up a chair to face me.

"I was totally honest with you when I suggested you come

and live with me, remember? I didn't hide anything. If I'd
wanted to lie to you, I would have done it when I told you why
I was in the hospital with your father. There was nothing forcing me to tell you the truth. Why would I hide it from you
now? You already know my . . . my worst side."

It's true. I bow my head. He pats me on the shoulder as if
to comfort me.

* * *

It's four by the alarm clock and I'm still not asleep. I toss
and turn in my sweat-drenched sheets. I can't stop getting up
to go take a leak. As I do, I take advantage to glance down at
the street, looking for a gray car parked outside the building,
but I don't recognize the one that was following us.

It'll be Christmas in a week. Some guys are trying to find
out where we live and nobody gives a damn except me. Mom
has been missing for more than a month. We haven't heard
from my sister for nearly a year. And nobody cares, nobody.

However hard I try, I can never figure out how it works—
Zé, grown-ups, the world. I don't know if it's because I haven't
lived enough yet or if everybody feels the same but doesn't talk
about it. When I was small, I thought grown-ups never cried.
I realized later that they hid in order to do so. Now I've
stopped trusting them. I've learned to look beyond what they
agree to show me, because grown-ups keep the most important
things to themselves.

It's snowing. I'm not interested anymore. With each year
that passes, I have the impression another piece of my interest
in the world is taken away from me. At this rate, in two years'
time, I'll be nothing more than an empty shell.

But I remember that male nurse.

I was alone in Dad's room, my mother and my sister had
gone to get hot drinks from the machine. Zé was also there,

sitting at his desk with headphones on his ears, but at the time I didn't even know his name. Zé who'd gained more than twenty pounds because of the drugs, Zé who was sixteen but looked ten years older than that, his hands shaking from the side effects, he kept correcting the letter he was writing and our silence was punctuated by his curses.

In theory, the secure section, Les Orchidées, was forbidden to anyone under fifteen, like many psychiatric departments, but Mom hadn't needed to insist for more than a few seconds for them to allow me to see my father. After all, he was destined to die there.

Dad, sitting on the edge of his bed, a forced smile at the corners of his lips, didn't show any symptoms. After five years in Charcot, he'd grown used to the doses he was administered with the full consent of Mom, who had no other solution to suggest.

Dad whose eyes never came to rest on me, but always a few inches to my left.

Dad whose voice came from limbo.

I didn't like coming here, didn't like being alone with him, I wanted to leave, I hated the place. Dad was staring into space without saying a word and all at once I couldn't stand it anymore, I left the room and walked down the corridor looking for Mom, but she was nowhere to be seen, and I ended up in the smokers' yard, which was deserted apart from two male nurses who were smoking with their backs to me, they didn't even hear me coming.

One of them was that nurse Mom always talked to behind closed doors at the end of her visits. I wanted to ask him if he knew where she was, but then he mentioned Dad's name and I fell silent.

". . . ran into Monsieur Younès's family," he was saying to his colleague. "They come quite often."

"How old are his children?"

"Five and eighteen, the younger ones. I don't know about the older one, he's his stepson."

"The girl's a bit strange, don't you think?"

"So's the boy. He's very inhibited, he doesn't communicate at all."

"Oh, dear."

"You're right, it doesn't look good."

There was a silence, and the nurse added these words which were to haunt my nights:

"It's always the same with schizophrenics. Find one in a family, it's the tip of the iceberg."

It took me years to understand exactly what that meant. But I think I grasped the fundamental point even then, because I still remember the strength of the vise that gripped my heart. I looked at the high walls around me, mute with fear, and thought: "This is where I'm going to end up." That's when I started building my own walls.

If you're going to end your days in a prison, you might as well choose the color of the bricks and the quality of the concrete yourself.

9

Zé thought he was doing the right thing bringing home a Christmas tree, but he's picked up an unsold one from his store and it's hardly the king of the forest with its twisted branches and its top leaning sadly to the right, like the tower of Pisa.

But I say nothing. I don't give a damn what the tree looks like. On the evening of the 24th, Gabrielle, Zé, and I decorate it without much conviction, before sitting down to a good meal: roast beef, roast potatoes, and an ice cream Yule log, if you're wondering. Zé is off work. The gifts are already waiting under the tree. We eat in silence, just for a change, while on the floor above they must have gathered all their family and friends, they're pounding the floor and singing their heads off. Part of me despises them.

I haven't seen the gray car again, although it may well have followed Zé without his noticing or without his telling me. We haven't talked about it again since the last day of school.

Zé uncorks a bottle of wine just before the dessert, even though he never drinks alcohol. Gabrielle and I raise our eyebrows. He pours a glass for Gabrielle, a glass for himself, and half a glass for me, but he signals to us to wait when we're about to drink. We both look at him questioningly. He's like an orchestra conductor, standing there with his glass in his hand, one finger up as if to freeze the moment.

"What?" I ask, irritably.

"Thirty seconds."

He stares at his watch. I turn to Gabrielle but she looks as puzzled as me. I put down my glass. After half a minute's wait, there's a knock at the door. Zé gives a triumphant smile.

"Who's that?" I ask in an urgent voice.

"Open the door if you're so curious."

I rush to the door. For a second, I think I'm going to see my mother, but the figure on the landing isn't Amélia. My jaw drops. The girl standing at the top of the stairs is carrying a backpack that's bigger than her, and is wearing gray jogging pants, a white sweatshirt, and a black fur hat; she has dark skin, brown hair in tufts, and black eyes, she looks like me, she's my sister, Gina.

"Gina?"

I need to say her name to make sure she isn't an illusion. Her response is to drop her bag—the noise echoes through the whole building—take me in her arms, lift me off the floor, and hug me so hard I feel I might choke. How long has it been since anyone touched me like this? It takes my breath away. She puts me down again after a few seconds, smooths a strand of my hair over my temple, and smiles.

"You haven't changed, Mattia. I'm so glad to see you." She glances inside the apartment. "Are you going to let me in?"

Before long, she's joined us in the living room and is sipping at the glass of wine that Zé has unhesitatingly poured for her. She's quickly introduced to Gabrielle, who she's never met. Am I the only one to notice that when she kisses her on the cheeks, her eyes move down her arms and come to rest on her scars? She won't say anything. She's like me, Gina. She notices everything. But she's inherited from my mother the art of keeping silent about important things, and from my father the art of escaping.

She's spent the last few months traveling along the Mediterranean coast, from Marseilles to Izmir, almost always on foot. Without a telephone and without the slightest contact with us. She doesn't tell us about the people, or about the landscapes. She doesn't tell us much about her travels at all. Her account is limited to names of cities. Maybe she hasn't experienced anything unusual during the trip, or maybe she has no desire to share its secrets with us. But I've never left this town, so I'm hungry for information that she won't give me.

"How about here?" she asks, after a long, pensive silence. She's looking at me. "Mom, Stefano?"

I shake my head. Zé tells her that Mom has disappeared. As usual, there's nothing to be said about my brother. He lives his life and doesn't care about ours. Everything is going well in the best of all possible worlds. Gina makes no comment. Staring into space, she rolls a cigarette and sticks it in the corner of her lips without lighting it. Gabrielle strokes the insides of her wrists, looking at Zé who's looking at my sister, and I look at all their reflections on the window pane.

It's snowing. It's Christmas eve.

Tomorrow is the anniversary of my father's death.

* * *

I get up at five in the morning, unable to sleep. I creep to the living room. As I suspected, Gina isn't asleep either. She's looking at the tree, her eyes wide open. A cigarette butt is burning down between her thumb and index finger. She hasn't even unpacked. She has her back to me, but she hears my steps, or my breathing. Like me, she's a child of silence, an expert in analyzing the different forms of it.

"Can't wait to open your presents, Mattia?" she asks under her breath.

I shake my head even though she can't see me. It's pointless. She knows me as well as I know her, and I sense that wry smile she has, a mixture of mischief and sadness.

"I'm watching the snow," she says. A pause. "How about going for a walk?"

Without a word, I put on my sneakers, which I left at the foot of the tree. She pulls her fur hat down over her ears and we leave. I'm wearing just a coat over my pajamas. Zé would never have let me go out like this. Gina doesn't give a damn. I don't blame her. Hers isn't the same kind of indifference.

The streets are empty on Christmas morning. Unexpectedly, she takes my hand. Her fingers are warm, mine frozen. We walk slowly, side by side, the untouched snow crunches under our feet. The snowflakes look huge in the light of the street lamps. Not a single bird singing. They've either migrated or they're hibernating. Gina isn't dressed for the season, she's still wearing the sweatshirt she's been across Europe in, but she doesn't complain of the cold.

"Take me to a place that matters to you," she says. "I don't know this town anymore."

She left soon after my father's death, on a whim. She was eighteen. She dropped the course she'd been doing and followed a girlfriend who was going to Russia. The two of them took the Trans-Siberian Railroad, and in Vladivostok she left her friend and set off for Japan. Since then, we've only seen her intermittently.

A place that matters to me . . .

I can't think of one. But then I look up. I see the giant cranes that mark where Les Verrières used to be and I head in that direction, holding her hand very tightly in mine. I'm a bit old for that, but there are moments when I don't want people to talk about how incredibly mature I am, given all the hard knocks that come with being mature.

Gina smiles to herself when she realizes where we're going. She says nothing. But her smile fades as we advance amid the ruins, the patches of waste ground, the billboards with their horrible, garish colors. She looks at every piece of rubble, and

I know she's trying to remember what used to be here, before the town gave this place up to the greed of the property developers. She lets go of my hand.

"What are they doing?" she whispers.

I point to the billboards, the inanimate young couples with their strollers. I don't need to say more. She doesn't speak either. Was she fond of this place after all?

Our steps lead us to the wilderness closest to our old building. Two cranes stand there, powerful, regal, unavoidable, stamped with the name of a big finance group. They're painted in three colors: blue, white, red—red for the blood of Saïd Zahidi, who died not far from here, blue for the uniform of the cop who killed him, white for the killer's skin.

We cross the waste ground in a strange, carefree, almost respectful silence. The snow is almost completely untouched here. Our steps impress themselves on the icy surface as we advance, solitary figures caught in the glue of their memories. We stop at the foot of one of the cranes. I strain my neck to see the top of it.

Suddenly, Gina nudges me with her elbow. "Shall we climb up?"

I look at her, astonished, but she's serious.

"Up there?"

"Yes. Haven't you ever climbed a crane?"

I shake my head.

"It's something you have to experience at least once."

She takes my hand and places it on one of the rungs.

"Go on, Mattia. It's Christmas."

"What's that got to do with it?"

She laughs: "I don't know. You're too well-behaved, and that scares me a little. You're allowed to be a child, Mattia. And children climb trees."

Trees maybe. Not cranes. But I can tell how much it means to her, and I don't want to disappoint her the way I've disappointed everyone else. So I bite the bullet, swallow my fear, and start climbing. She encourages me from the ground, then catches up with me in no time at all. It's easy for her. She's taller than me. These ladders are built for adult workers.

After a while, I look down and tell myself the nurse was right, my sister's crazy, there's no more doubt. We've already climbed thirty feet of girders. The icy metal sticks to my palms, a cold so biting that it burns me, and I'm seized with fear, but Gina murmurs that everything will be fine, we're almost there, the only thing I want to do is go back down, but again I bite the bullet, close my eyes, and continue. I force myself to look just at my fingers tirelessly clutching the rungs. And after a few more yards, the fear suddenly vanishes. I have the impression I'm climbing the bars of my own prison.

I don't know how long it takes us to make the ascent, but in the end we get to the top, to the relative safety of the cradle. My heart sinks at the thought that we'll have to go back down. Helped by Gina, I sit down on a girder, my legs hanging in the air, beside her. She puts her arm around my shoulders. She doesn't say anything. She shows me the town down there and I abruptly understand why she was so determined that we should get to the top.

All those lights seen from here look like a dance of fireflies. The neon store signs, the street lamps, the public lighting, the few lighted windows merge to form a single source repeated ad infinitum. Seen from above, even the ugliest things look beautiful.

"When things go beyond what you can stand, you have to change your angle of vision," Gina whispers, reading my thoughts.

I put my head on her shoulder. Gradually, I relax. I feel good.

And we stay there for a long time, watching dawn rise over the town.

Gina, do you remember Saïd?

I never knew him. I wasn't born yet, but you were. You

were ten when he died. Stefano told me you talked about him all the time after he'd been to the apartment with Dad, who liked him a lot.

But according to Stefano, Saïd was a terrible kid. He couldn't understand why you and Dad were so fond of him. He said he stole cars from the parking lot of the supermarket and it wasn't a good thing to upset poor people. Rich people's cars, he could understand, but not here, not our cars.

You, Gina, would reply that you didn't have a car and they were only objects, there was insurance, so who cares? Stefano said you loved him the way only children can love. I never understood what that meant, is love different depending on age?

You attended his trial when he was arrested in the parking lot, and like his family and his friends you sighed with relief when the judge gave him a suspended sentence, "it's your last chance, Monsieur Zahidi," but the judge didn't know, and neither did any of you, that he'd already had his last chance, because a few weeks later he was dead, his skull smashed in by a police baton.

Gina, did you cry, did you also want to go out on the streets with the others, did your anger make you want to see this whole place explode the way his head exploded? Did Dad stop you?

Do you still regret not going?

And what about that cop, do you think about him sometimes, is it because of him, the fact that he's free, is it because of that final injustice that you sleep so badly, that you left the country, that you never show your face here?

Have you forgotten us in all this time?

* * *

We get back to the apartment at ten in the morning. We spent hours at the top of the crane, dozing, unaware of the time passing. Gabrielle and Zé are already up. Zé gives Gina a dirty look when I have a coughing fit as I take off my jacket.

"Where were you?"

"On a crane," Gina says.

"On a . . . Are you serious?"

"It's all right, Zé, I know what I'm doing."

His eyes say he doesn't believe it for a second, but he doesn't object. He's too aware of my affection for my sister, the only member of my family who hasn't completely abandoned me.

The grown-ups drink Viennese coffee—Zé has bought whipped cream for the occasion—while I settle for a home-made orange juice. Then we turn to the Christmas tree and the packages beneath it. Two gifts for me: one from Zé and Gabrielle, one from Gina. Gina's is wrapped in newspaper covered in Arabic characters.

"It's Turkish," she says.

Very carefully, I open the package. Inside, a little knife with a curved blade, a mixture of a penknife and a dagger, the handle engraved in black and gold. I kiss my sister. I don't care about the nature of the gift. If there had been nothing inside the newspaper, or a relic worth heaps of money, it would have been the same. The important thing is that she thought of me, even in Turkey.

Zé and Gabrielle have given me a sound amplifier. It looks like a gun with a cone attached to it, the kind of cone they put around a dog's neck to stop it licking its wounds.

"For birds," Gabrielle says.

"Or people," Zé adds, half joking.

I look at him and smile. He suspects I might use this gift for disreputable purposes, in other words, eavesdropping on their conversations. I hadn't realized they'd noticed my interest in birds, and I'm touched. I kiss them, too. Zé smells of after-shave. He's given himself a thorough shave for the occasion.

All day long, I have a secret hope that my mother will show

up, that they're keeping her visit from me as a surprise, that she'll knock shyly at the door and say, "Do you really think I'd let you down on Christmas Day?" But she doesn't come.

Never mind. I have Gina. I have Zé, I have Gabrielle. That ought to be enough for me.

Why isn't it?

* * *

Nouria, my psychologist, doesn't take a vacation at Christmas time. She says that's often when her patients need her most. Three days after Christmas, there she is, at her post. It's Gina who takes me to her office. Zé wanted to go, but she insisted and I made it clear to Zé that I wanted to go with her. He goes into a sulk. I wonder if he's jealous.

"Social services paid me a little visit," Nouria says.

"Really? Shit."

"Apparently you're being mistreated?"

I give her a crooked smile. "What do you think?"

"No, Mattia, what do *you* think?"

"I've had one slap in four years. I think I'll survive."

She smiles, too, with that peculiar smile of hers that makes all the features of her face go up. If she has children, they must be happy. Everyone who meets her must be happy. Unless she reserves her smiles for her patients.

I'm curious, and move closer to the edge of my chair. "What did they ask you?"

"If you were unhappy with Zé."

"What did you reply?"

"That happiness doesn't depend only on the people we share our life with."

"Do you think I shouldn't be living with him?"

She shrugs. "What do *you* think, Mattia?"

"You first."

"I don't know him."

"Neither do I. Nobody knows him. He's weird."

"So are you."

"But I have time to change," I say, though I don't really believe it.

"Do you want to change?"

"I don't know."

"What would you change about your life so far if you could?"

A good question. I think about it. Really think about it. Where to start? First I'd make sure that the paths of Saïd and that cop had never crossed. Then I'd tell my father that illusions lead only to ruin, and that his had slowly but surely caused the madness sowed on the edges of his mind from early childhood to grow.

"From early childhood?" Nouria says.

"Apparently."

"Who told you that?"

"That's what everyone says about schizophrenia."

She smiles. "A complicated name for a disease that's equally complicated."

"I'm one of the few people who can spell it."

"That's not enough to understand it."

"Then explain it to me."

"I can't. I don't understand it. Not me, not any psychiatrist, not anyone who isn't directly concerned. Forget what you've been told, Mattia. Nobody knows how it starts. We just know that at a certain moment it manifests itself in some people and not in others. The rest is worthless. You probably wouldn't find two psychiatrists who'd give you the same definition of it."

I wonder whether or not to tell her about the fear that's been eating away at me ever since I overheard that conversation between the two male nurses in the yard of the Orchidées unit of Charcot Hospital at the age of five. But I already know her answer. She likes me too much; she wouldn't tell me the truth if it might hurt me.

"My sister's come back," I say.

"Gina?"

"Yes. We went up to the top of the cranes at Les Verrières. It was beautiful."

"You love your sister very much."

"Yes."

"Is she going to stay for a while?"

"I don't know. I hope so."

"Have you told her you want her to stay?"

"No."

"Tell her."

"I will."

But I'm lying, and she knows I am. She smiles sadly.

Once the hour is over, she walks me out into the lobby and I sense her watching us as I join Gina, who's waiting for me on a bench opposite the office, a cigarette between her lips, heedless of the surrounding cold.

* * *

My sister has brought up her love of sleeping late as an excuse to escape the noise of the living room and take advantage of the spare mattress in my room, much to my delight. Zé didn't seem very enthusiastic at first, but I convinced him.

That means we can share our insomnia when we can't get to sleep at night. Luckily, it's the holidays and I don't need to get up in the morning. I go to bed later with each day that passes. We don't talk. We merge into the same silence. That already makes a big difference.

The night after my session with Nouria, she's smoking by the window while I'm reading *A Season in Hell* by Rimbaud, which Zé has warmly recommended, when she says:

"Do you like it here?"

I nod, forgetting that she can't see me, but she doesn't ask the question again.

"Doesn't it scare you?"

"What?"

"You know what I mean."

Yes, I do know. Zé and his psychiatric record. Zé whom I call a murderer when I want to hurt him. Zé who's already killed once and who drowns himself in poetry to avoid thinking about it, the way others drown themselves in alcohol or heroin.

"No. How about you?"

She doesn't reply. There's no point. She isn't scared of anything, Gina. She's like Zé. She runs away from the past and the future, she tries not to ask herself any questions, she moves, she advances, she stagnates and regresses, she doesn't give a damn, she doesn't think about tomorrow. Not about her future or mine.

When I'm grown up I'd like to be like that.

I feel like an hour has gone by when she starts talking again. She long ago stubbed out her cigarette butt on the gutter, but she hasn't closed the window. The cold has swept into the room. I have goose pimples. Not her. Gina's invincible. That's what she told me once, when she was a teenager. *Invincible Mattia.* She said it with such conviction that I believed her. *You're invincible, too. A brick wall.* The same defenses. Except that she could leave and I couldn't. *Not like our parents. In-vin-ci-ble, repeat it.* Later, she ran away and I started to hate her. I only love her when she comes back. In other words, not often.

"I don't like him very much," she says.

"Zé? Why?"

"Because he doesn't like me either."

"Why?"

"I don't know."

I think about this. I've avoided paying any attention to it until now, but it's true, obviously, Zé doesn't like her. He accepts her presence because he knows I would leave the apartment if he got it into his head to throw my sister out.

"He's jealous," I say.

She laughs. "I know. That's not a reason."

"Talk to him."

"I don't know how to talk to people. Do you?"

"No."

She closes the window and slips under the blankets.

"Good night."

"Good night."

* * *

She didn't tell anyone before she left. Just a little note stuck to the fridge: "I'm going. Sorry. Gina." For the first time, I saw Mom angry with one of her children. A real anger that spilled over and flowed through the apartment, even into my room, and I hid under the blankets so that it wouldn't reach me, I could almost see the black waves engulf my bed. Something was trembling deep inside me but I didn't have any words for it. Mom didn't say anything. As usual, the anger was in her eyes. She wanted to keep it to herself but it was impossible, just as hiding her sadness from us never worked. There are things that are too big to be contained.

Stefano didn't say anything. Neither did I.

There was just one less place setting at the table in the days that followed and then we got used to it.

10

As usual, the holidays have gone by too fast.

There was New Year's Day, which we "celebrated" at home (actually just a little glass of cheap sparkling wine and smiles that were even less confident than the rest of the year, smiles that expressed all their pessimism about the year to come), and it was time to go back to school.

Zé shakes me at seven in the morning when he comes in from work.

"Time for school."

Just for the hell of it, I mutter that I don't want to go. But he's pitiless, he yanks the blanket away and the ambient cold freezes my lungs. Gina stirs under her blanket, her disheveled hair hiding her face.

"Leave him alone, he'll go this afternoon."

I open my eyes in anticipation of what's coming next.

"Hasn't anyone ever told you it's compulsory?" Zé says through gritted teeth.

"I gave up school, so did you, and we're not doing too badly."

"Stop talking bullshit, you didn't give it up in elementary school. When he's old enough, he'll decide whether or not he wants to continue. Until that day comes, I'm the one who decides."

Gina emerges from beneath the sheets. Her face looks weary, and not just from sleep.

I quietly get out of bed. "It's all right, I'm going."

"Just because you're his legal guardian doesn't mean you can order him about."

"He's a child," Zé says. "Would you like me to let him stay in bed all day? If you want to take over his upbringing, feel free. Just ask the judge, I'm sure he'll let you take custody, you're his sister. In the meantime, let me deal with it, thank you very much, because the reason I'm taking care of him is because you've only ever thought about yourself, just like your half-brother."

Oh, shit. She wasn't joking when she said he didn't like her. I hadn't realized how true that was. I choose to escape, and quickly take refuge in the kitchen, but my sister's voice carries beyond the walls of my room:

"Where do you get off judging me? What do you know about my life?"

"What do you know about mine?"

I hammer on the door of the other bedroom. "Gabrielle, Gabrielle!"

She opens immediately. The yelling has woken her. Without a word, she walks to the door of my bedroom. Gina has gotten up and the two of them are glaring at each other, it's obvious it wouldn't take much for them to come to blows. I stay out in the corridor, not knowing what to do, while Gabrielle announces her presence by tapping shyly on the door, but they ignore her. My sister looks tiny compared with Zé's height, but she doesn't give a damn.

"You're pretending to be a responsible adult, even though you killed someone," she says. "You think you have the right to preach to me? I may not be perfect but at least I'm not a murderer."

"Shut up," Zé says. "You have no idea what you're talking about. How come you're suddenly so worried about what I did? Shouldn't you have thought of that when the judge was making his decision? You should have mentioned it there, not here, it doesn't make any sense now, it's ancient history."

"Ancient history. That's easy for you to say."

He takes a step forward. They're almost up against each other now, both looking threatening. I wonder which of the two is going to strike first, and that's enough to send shivers down my spine.

"Easy?" he echoes.

She simply sustains his gaze. Fire versus ice.

"I'm sorry, but coming from a girl who takes off to the other side of the world as soon as anything unpleasant happens, I find that quite funny."

"Anything unpleasant? You bastard."

"You come back once every three years to ease your conscience and you think you can make comments about the way I take care of your brother? You think it's easy? You don't even know the boy anymore. You and the rest of your family messed him up and now I have to pick up the pieces. I do what I can with what you left me!"

Suddenly, Gabrielle bangs her fist against the wall. "You do realize Mattia can hear every word you say?"

They stop and turn to us. They look at me shamefaced.

Gabrielle takes me by the hand. "Get dressed, I'm taking you to school."

Zé is so surprised, he forgets his anger. Gina turns away, hiding her face with the help of an unruly lock of hair, and lights a cigarette at the window. A minute later—I'm relatively quick when it comes to running away—I'm in Zé's car, with Gabrielle at the wheel. I haven't seen her drive in months. She breathes deeply in and out as she tries to find her way across town.

"Are you all right?" she asks.

"How about you?"

She sounds her horn when a motorist cuts in front of her. It snowed last night but those bastards in the town hall have already put salt on the streets. There's no excuse not to go to school, apart from the fact that I'm wasting three quarters of my life there. If I died tomorrow, what would I be able to say about my life except that I was terribly proud I could do long division without a calculator?

"You mustn't react like that, Mattia."

"React like what?"

"When you came to get me. You were in such a panic, I thought there was a fire somewhere. It was just an argument. These things happen."

I don't say anything. She smiles to herself.

"It's true, you're not used to it. It's hard to see two people you love yelling at each other, even hitting each other. But sometimes violence is better than silence."

I ponder her words as she pulls up outside the school.

"Good luck," she says, with genuine compassion.

"Thanks."

I've flunked my history and geography test. It was on World War II. I couldn't give the names of the most famous concentration camps, or the date of the armistice, and I forgot where the French collaborationist government was based (Vichy, dammit, Vi-chy). The grade brings my general average even lower. By way of appreciation, my teacher seems to have given in to despair: "Why such a waste of intelligence?" That's pretty much what I ask myself every time I set foot in the classroom.

Try telling her, try telling all of them, that there are times in your life when you're really not interested in Hitler, or the Holocaust, or any of the wars their ancestors happily waged on each other. Try telling them that you prefer climbing to the top of a crane, visiting neighborhoods being redeveloped, counting the graffiti tags, and watching the crows. But it's already a struggle to take responsibility for your own mistakes.

Try telling them that if they're so interested in the need to remember, they don't need to go back three generations. They just have to go out on the streets. They'll see the face of a fifteen-year-old boy sprayed on the walls. But do they even remember his name? Did they ever know it?

* * *

Gina comes to pick me up from school, an extinguished cigarette between her lips, a grim look on her face, pretty much the way I expect her to be. She easily spots me in the crowd, takes me by the hand as soon as I've joined her, and drags me off in the direction of the apartment before she's even said a word. She walks so quickly, I'm almost forced to run to keep up with her. I don't dare ask her anything about this morning's quarrel. Suddenly, instead of turning left onto the avenue where the shops are, which is the shortest way home, she stops before the intersection and hurries us both into the public library.

"What are you—"

"There's a weird guy following us," she says. "I'd rather not lead him to your place."

The security guard comes toward us, squinting at her cigarette. Gina rushes past him.

"Don't worry, it's out."

She stuffs the cigarette butt in her pocket and walks even faster, leaving the guard to do an about-turn.

"Do you think he's keeping an eye on the books in case they decide to up sticks and leave?" she mutters, as if to herself.

I don't reply. She's holding my hand tight. I let her drag me along, all the while twisting my neck to see if they're following us, but I can't see anybody. We walk through the whole library to the back exit, which is between a row of buildings. I throw a last glance over my shoulder before coming out into the open air. And I see him. The man from the other time, the one who held back while his pal tried to get information from me. He's changed his clothes but I recognize him from his Goliath-like bulk. He pushes his way past the students, the old people, the idle who come to look at the books, craning his neck in order not to lose sight of us.

"He's still there," I say.

"I know."

That doesn't seem to bother her too much. Nothing about her betrays the slightest nervousness except that her features are drawn and her fingers are tight around mine. We turn into the first side street and there, without warning, Gina starts running. I struggle to keep up the same pace as her. She's still clutching my hand. We go all around the neighborhood three or four more times before she deigns to slow down. As a smoker, her lungs have suffered more than mine. At last she lets go of me. She looks around her as she catches her breath.

"I think we've lost him."

"Who is that guy?"

"I don't know. But I wasn't going to just let him follow us and do nothing."

"*You don't know?*"

I don't believe a word of it. I insist but she's adamant. We go back to the apartment as if nothing has happened. Gina doesn't give anything away to Gabrielle and Zé. The atmosphere is somber, a sure sign that this morning's argument hasn't been completely settled. I shut myself in my room with the excuse that I have homework to do. Gina doesn't join me. I wait a few minutes before creeping back out into the corridor. As I suspected, they've shut themselves in the kitchen. I stick my ear to the door.

Gina: ". . . lost him in the library."

Zé: "Did you see what he looked like?"

Gina (vaguely): "He's about forty, forty-five. Tall, broad shoulders. He reminded me of a bull. Apart from that . . ."

Zé: . . .

Gina: . . .

Gabrielle: . . .

Gina: "Do you think it's about—"

Zé: "Shhh."

Gina: "What?"

Zé: "The kid's gotten into the bad habit of listening at doors."

Gina: "Does it matter?"

Zé: "It matters because I don't think your father would have wanted him mixed up in all this shit."

Gina: "I forgot, you knew him better than I did."

Zé: "Stop it."

Gina: "If it starts again we'll have to . . ."

Zé: . . .

Gabrielle: . . .

Zé: "We'll have to what?"

Gina: "How the fuck should I know?"

Zé: "If you don't, neither do I."

Silence. I hold my breath. I'm so tense I can almost feel my eardrums expanding. I hear footsteps approach the door.

Zé: "Wait, you . . ."

I quickly move away. I just have time to rush to the toilet before Gabrielle flings open the kitchen door. Angrily, she puts on her coat and disappears down the stairs. Zé runs after her. Incomprehensible shouting from the lobby, then silence.

Zé comes back up after a few minutes and rejoins my sister in the kitchen. I've lost all desire to eavesdrop on them. I collapse on my bed, feeling immensely weary. I soon fall asleep.

Nobody comes and wakes me up to eat.

* * *

When I open my eyes a few hours later, I first glance at Gina's mattress. She isn't there. Her sleeping bag has disappeared, and so has her traveling bag. There's light in the living room. I walk barefoot, my steps light and undetectable.

"*. . . Mais la Voix me console et dit: 'Garde tes songes, Les sages n'en ont pas d'aussi beaux que les fous!'*"[4]

Zé is reciting Baudelaire. By this time, he should be in the store. The door is ajar, and I push it open. Standing at the window, without a book, his eyes half-closed, absorbed in the poetry, he hasn't seen me. There's no sign of Gina or Gabrielle. Magnanimously, I let him finish his poem before coughing to let him know I'm here.

He glances at his watch and glowers at me.

"You have to get up in two hours. Go back to bed."

"I went to bed early. Where is she?"

"Who?"

"Gina."

His annoyed expression confirms my suspicions. I turn away, raising my hand to cut short his explanations. I don't want to hear them. I go to the kitchen and drink a carton of orange juice. I was planning to have breakfast, but I'm not hungry.

With enormous reluctance, Zé comes in after me.

"She asked me to say goodbye to you from her."

I say nothing.

"You mustn't blame her. That's how she is. She never stays long. You should be used to it."

"It's all right, I didn't say anything!"

He sits down opposite me and lights a cigarette. I look away, but don't leave, accepting his silent presence. He says nothing for a long while.

---

[4] But the Voice consoled me, saying "Keep your dreams./The wise don't have such beautiful ones as the mad."

"Gabrielle . . . isn't back," he says at last.

"Is that why you aren't at work?"

He nods.

"I'm waiting for her."

I snigger.

He glares at me. "That makes you laugh, does it?"

I stand up. "My mother told me once that you should never get attached to people because everyone leaves you in the end."

"That's a horrible way of thinking."

"It's what parents ought to do, prepare you for how horrible the world is. If your mother had warned you, you might not be in this situation."

And I leave him there, sitting alone in the kitchen, his only company Gabrielle's future ghost. Because I'm not a good person. Because for once I don't want to listen. Because we're always alone and we might as well get used to it.

Some time later, he knocks at the door of my room. I don't reply. He comes in, wearing his coat.

"I'm going to look for her."

"Okay."

"I'll be back to take you to school."

"Don't feel obliged."

He leaves. Through the window, I watch him get in his car and disappear around the corner. Nobody sets off after him. Either the two weird guys have lost us, or they've already found us.

I keep standing there at the window, perfectly inert and motionless, watching the dawn come up. On the stroke of seven, I see a thin figure enter the lobby. I count the footsteps coming upstairs. The key in the lock, the squeak of the door, almost inaudible steps in the living room. A deafening silence. Minutes pass, very long minutes. The sound of curtains being opened wide. I close my eyes. I can almost feel the cold flooding into the apartment. I stick my nose up against the pane so that I can see the window of the living room. And I see her, Gabrielle, translucent, dressed only in a huge brown sweatshirt, the hood pulled down over her forehead, sitting in the window frame, legs dangling in space, leaning forward, her eyes caught up in the dizziness, visually measuring the five floors separating her from death. There's a kind of relief on her face.

I stare at her so hard, my eyes hurt. I think about Zé looking for her somewhere outside. About Mom when she told me my father had hanged himself. I can't breathe and I can't move. I know I have to do something, call someone, just cry her name to keep her in this reality, but I *can't move* and Gina's words echo in my head: "When things go beyond what you can stand, you have to change your angle of vision." Isn't that what Gabrielle is doing right now?

I know all I'd have to do would be to open the window and say just one word, it wouldn't matter what. She wouldn't do it in front of me. She'd put it off until later. And Zé, once alerted, might be able to stop her—but how? By sending her to Charcot, where people use sheets to hang themselves from the lights? Gabrielle is too light. No piece of furniture would yield under her weight.

And that unchanging question arises, how the hell are you supposed to keep hold of someone who refuses to stay? That's something they don't teach you at school—or anywhere.

Her breathing produces a little steam between her lips. She leans forward more and more, already liberated. I wonder if I'll be able to close my eyes.

And then it comes—the yell.

"GABRIELLE!"

Like the voice of God. But it's only Zé.

"GABRIELLE!"

Zé, one leg out of his car, which he's stopped right in the

middle of the street. Zé, literally flying to under the window. Zé yelling so loudly his vocal chords might snap. Zé at last emerging from the silence.

"GABRIELLE!"

The strength contained in those three syllables . . .

Lights come on in the apartments opposite. Shutters half open. Angry faces appear, ready to throw any object that might silence this disturber of the peace, but Gabrielle is quite visible, such a pale stain on such a gray facade, and they all shut their mouths. Fingers dial a two-digit number, once, twice, ten times, it doesn't matter, they're alone—Zé and Gabrielle, always alone even in the middle of a whole lot of people.

She looks at him, she hesitates, he implores her with his eyes, he's shaking all over, searching inside himself for the words to convince her. If they existed, they would have been uttered a long time ago. And none of the poets among your loyal friends from days gone by, Zé, has ever been able to write them.

What are you going to do now? Do you realize how alone you are? I was right.

"Gabrielle . . ."

The street is hopelessly empty. Nobody uses it much outside peak times. And they're taking their time coming, the cops, the firefighters, anyone.

She says nothing. She looks at him. He looks at her. Nothing else exists.

And all at once Zé's eyes spot me at the window. His face lights up. Still looking at her, he points at me.

"Mattia's looking at you."

She turns her head. Our eyes meet. She sets her lips as tight as they'll go. There's apology in her eyes.

"*He's looking at you*, Gabrielle. You can't do this in front of him."

Silence.

"You can't do this in front of him . . ."

I have the impression that he's whispering, but if he was, his voice wouldn't reach me from such a great distance. Yet I also seem to hear the incessant ticking of his watch, calculating and recalculating every second before the end of the world.

She folds her legs under her buttocks and cautiously stands. She disappears inside, first one leg, then the other.

All the way down there, Zé's shoulders relax.

A siren shatters the silence of the street. Flashing blue lights.

The cavalry always arrives too late.

I grab my bag to go to school.

11

We spend the day reading a play by Marivaux full of aristocrats discussing their romantic problems with their servants. The discrepancy between real life and what they force you to listen to all day long in a stifling classroom grabs me by the throat as never before.

At four-thirty, I'm getting ready to walk home when a car honks its horn at me. Zé has come to pick me up. He doesn't say anything during the ride. I notice that he's keeping an eye on the traffic in the rearview mirror. Nobody is following us. He stops outside our building and rolls a cigarette. The car fills with smoke. It tickles my throat, but I don't say anything. He doesn't move.

"They want to have her committed again," he says. "They've been hassling me all morning to sign their damned paper. There's no point. You can't hold someone who wants to die. If they have to put her on meds to stop her killing herself, it isn't worth it. What do they want? What's the point of keeping someone alive with pills? If that's the case, we might as well let her go."

But you can't.

"They want to find the members of her family and get them to sign a request to put her in Charcot. She hasn't seen them in years. What the hell does it mean anyway? I live with her. I know her better than anyone. I know it wouldn't make any difference putting her in that place. But they don't trust me. They know."

"Know what?"

"That I was in Charcot. The shrink who came used to work there, I recognized him, and vice versa, I imagine. Because of that, they don't think I can be objective. Or they remember what I did and that gives me zero credibility. Nobody listens to you when you've been in a psychiatric hospital."

He falls abruptly silent as if he's exhausted all his available vocabulary. I'm not sure what to say. We sit for a while in the car, breathing in the smoke from his cigarette. At last, he stubs it out in the ashtray.

"I really have to start smoking menthols."

* * *

Gabrielle's asleep and the silence has gained ground.

I promise Zé I'll keep an eye on her while he's at the store. What with my fever that other time and last night, he can't afford to miss any more work. I settle in the kitchen, right opposite their bedroom so that I'll know if she ventures out of bed. I get down to my homework. I have a conjugation test tomorrow. How fortunate that someone invented the imperfect subjunctive to distract us from how lousy things really are!

At midnight, I drink a can of that energy drink that Zé left for me. He drinks gallons of it at work. It's not bad. I take a couple more from the fridge. By two in the morning, I'm on my fourth and feeling quite weird. My heart is pounding in my temples and my fingertips. I put down my pen; my hand is shaking. The sound of my own breathing seems to fill the room.

And everything
gets mixed up
in my head.
I'm walking.
I don't know what time it is, I don't care, my head is spin-

ning, I feel sick I want to throw up but I walk, I should call Zé at the store and say, "Sorry, I'm still sick," but something stronger keeps me going. I know if I stop something horrible will happen, and besides I don't feel good in the apartment, the air was becoming unbreathable, that silence that silence, that silence was crushing me.

I get to the cemetery that Les Verrières has become, I'm ready to barf at the sight of the developers' billboard, but to my surprise, *when the curfew came, wandering fingers* covered it in blood-red paint and wrote on it HERE THE POLICE KILLED SAÏD, *and the grim mornings were quite transformed.*

I stop in front of this now magnificent poster, stars in my eyes. The nausea fades a little. My heart leaps into my throat.

* * *

GINA. On the third day of the riots, the cops managed to wedge about twenty people into a dead-end street. Vans arrived to take them all away. I went out on the street with Dad. Almost everyone was outside watching them but nobody could stop them. The only people with the guts to oppose the cops were either already in prison or in that dead-end street.

There were reporters there, too. A cameraman and a guy talking into a microphone. I can't remember what channel they were working for. I was on my own, Dad was trying to negotiate with the cops. They aimed the camera at me and held out the microphone, smiling like idiots while a few yards away twenty people were being arrested.

They said: "What's your name?"

I didn't reply. They said: "Do you live here?" I said yes, they asked me if I was afraid, I said yes, they asked if it was because of the rioters, I said "No, it's because of the cops," they looked at each other strangely, they asked me why I was afraid of them, I showed them the people being forced into the van and those standing with their arms outspread and gloved hands pinning them to the wall, there was one who was gushing blood from his temple, he'd been hit with a tonfa, but these small details were too subtle to be caught in the beam of that camera.

I said into the microphone: "Why should I be afraid of them, I'm afraid of people who kill, and around here the people who kill are cops."

They recorded it all, but they didn't answer me and it was never shown on TV. What they did show was the footage they'd filmed before they spoke to me, the reflections of the flames on my angelic little face, and the fear in my eyes, a cute little girl terrified by the anger of those rioters.

Never trust images, Mattia. Never trust them. These people don't live in the same world. They have no idea of the extent of their ignorance.

It was seeing that footage that made me realize, at the age of ten, Mattia, that the only solution is to burn it all down. Dad was wrong. That's what killed him: the immensity of his errors. There shouldn't have been any appeal to calm, it was an insult, I'm not even talking about Saïd's memory, Mattia, it was an insult to all of us.

You'll understand one day, when you've lived some more. I'll keep telling you until you understand. I won't let you become like them.

Everything's going around and around.

I bend double at the foot of that huge construction site and throw up everything that's in my belly. After that I feel a bit better. I lie down on the ground, my knees drawn up to my chest in a fetal position. I think I call for my mother under my breath.

And I fall asleep.

* * *

I open my eyes to a blinding light.

"Hey, boy, can you hear me?"

"Put your torch down, you're scaring him."

"Did you do that, you little scumbag?"

"Drop it, he's just a kid."

"Trust me, I've seen plenty like him. When you've had a few more years on the job under your belt, you won't fall for it again."

"Oh, so he climbed onto that billboard all by himself, did his thing, climbed back down, went and got rid of his spray cans, came back here, and fell asleep? Plus, he threw up, look, it's disgusting."

Clearly two guys who don't understand the subtle art of silence. My dizziness gradually fades. A gloved hand is held out to me and I refuse it instinctively, because at the end of the hand is a navy blue uniform with a number and the words "National Police," and where I come from that's not exactly promising.

I have specks of vomit on my chin and between my teeth. I get up by myself, my legs unsteady, and spit on the ground, taking care to avoid the cops' boots. I almost fall back down and one of them grabs me by the arm.

"Hey, easy does it!"

I don't want him to touch me but I don't say anything. With my sleeve I wipe away the acrid liquid that's all over my cheeks. I think I even have some in my hair.

A police car is parked a few yards away. The second cop shines his torch at the billboard. The graffiti's still there, majestic, looking down on the rubble that's replaced the buildings, the last touch of beauty amid the ruins. How did they manage to climb up there? There had to have been several of them. They must have used a ladder. There's almost nobody living around here now, so there won't be anyone to snitch.

I immediately think of my sister but it isn't her handwriting.

"How old are you?" the first cop asks, the one who defended me to his colleague.

I respond grudgingly. He asks me for my name. I don't reply. He repeats the question, articulating the words. I shake my head. I think about Zé and Gabrielle and social services. I should be in bed. What will happen if the family judge finds out that the cops discovered me miles from home, all on my own, lying in my own vomit?

"Are you sick? Have you been drinking?"

"Sick," I say, exaggerating my weak state.

"What about your parents?"

". . ."

"Where are your parents?"

"Do you live there?" they ask, pointing to the one surviving building—my mother's building.

I don't know what else I can say to get out of this mess. So they put me in the car and take me to the police station. I don't try to protest. Pretending to be a moron is the only defense I've come up with so far.

My clothes stink of vomit. They don't make any comment, but they do open the windows.

At the station, they sit me down in a waiting room that's empty apart from a couple arguing loudly. One of the cops stays with me while the other one disappears into a corridor. The man and the woman are bawling each other out about their son who's been arrested for burglary. I listen to them to distract myself from my own situation, before realizing that I'd do better to find an explanation, and fast.

I ask to go to the toilet. The cop consents but goes with me all the way there. I don't even take a leak. It was an excuse to try to get out of here before they find out my name. It's obvious they weren't born yesterday.

The couple quiets down when they see me with the cop clinging to me. They look at me curiously, not daring to ask the question they're dying to ask. The woman gives me a smile that's encouraging, stern, and sympathetic, all at the same time.

I don't belong here, dammit, I'm only eleven.

Facing me, a poster of a little girl with her arm in a sling and a bruise on her cheek, followed by a telephone number: an abuse hotline. There's also a hot drinks dispenser and a big clock. Six in the morning. Zé will be home in an hour. Not to mention my conjugation test. If I fail it, they'll summon us to another meeting.

At last, the cop comes back and takes me into an office where another cop is waiting, this one in plainclothes. He smiles at me and motions me to a chair. He has a coffee stain on the collar of his striped shirt. He taps at a computer keyboard as he asks:

"What's your name?"

I keep silent. I should have done that from the start, pretended to be deaf or foreign. I wasn't quick enough on my feet. He leans toward me.

"Do you understand what I'm saying?"

And then immediately:

"Are you even French?"

In the end, he takes me back to the waiting room, delegates a cop who was hanging around the station to keep an eye on me, and goes off to look for some kind of help.

Through a large window, I see a room with desks. It was empty earlier, but there's been a shift change, and now it's full of cops talking among themselves, holding paper cups of coffee. It reminds me of the treatment room in the hospital, where they pretend to be busy in order not to be disturbed.

I spot the officer with the striped shirt talking with his colleagues. Several of them look at me now through the window, intrigued—I've rarely felt so uncomfortable—and eventually the striped shirt comes back out to fetch me and leads me inside.

"Yeah, I'm pretty sure that's him," a man in plainclothes with prominent incisors says, although I've never seen him before.

"What's his name?"

"Can't remember, an Arab name. Hey, Bertrand, remember the surname of the teacher at the community center in Les Verrières?"

It must still be a sensitive subject here because the talk breaks off for a moment and all the cops look at me. I'd give anything to be somewhere else.

"Younès," the guy called Bertrand replies.

The striped shirt leans toward me.

"Younès, is that your surname?'

"No," I say without even lying.

"Ah, suddenly you can speak French. All right, what's your mother's phone number?"

"He has a legal guardian," the cop who somehow recognized me says. "Just look up a guy named Zéphyr Palaisot."

The striped shirt laughs. "Zéphyr? Are you kidding?"

Yes, that's Zé. Hardly surprising nobody uses his real name.

"Palaisot like the prosecutor?" the same cop continues.

"Yep, same family. And Palaisot like the kid who was almost sentenced for the murder of one of his classmates in Paris, remember?"

And suddenly they're all around us. I have the impression I'm in the zoo, but they're not interested in me, they're interested in the cop with the incisors, anxious to hear a juicy story.

I listen, too. The cop says he knew the family of the girl who died. He followed the case closely, including when Zé applied for custody of me, which is why he identified me so easily.

"Why is that bastard still at large?" someone calls out.

"Because his name's Palaisot," the cop sneers. "It's useful to have a father who's a prosecutor and a mother in the court of appeals. That's also how he was able to become this kid's legal guardian even though he's a murderer."

I feel like insulting all of them, spitting at their feet, setting fire to this fucking police station, and just taking off. I'll never criticise you again, Zé, but please come and get me out of here. I hate him being called a murderer. I do it when he really gets on my nerves, because I know it wounds him, but he hasn't done anything to them, so why don't they mind their own business, dammit?

Burn it all down, Gina told me once. *You'll understand when you've lived some more*. She may have meant *when you've crossed swords with them*, because now I'm starting to understand.

"Good," the striped shirt says, and turns to me. "Will you give me his number now?"

What can I do? Given where I am . . . I recite the ten figures, feeling as I do so that I'm betraying Zé. The cop goes into an adjoining office to call and I wait with his colleagues, who at least are kind enough to stop mentioning either my guardian's past or my father's, but they're still looking at me out of the corners of their eyes and I keep praying that they'll let me go as soon as possible. I can't even imagine what it must be like when they hold you for questioning.

The striped shirt doesn't come back. After a while, a woman takes me into a corner of the room and offers me a seat. She has blond hair streaked with gray, a narrow and strangely sympathetic face, she's quite nice and that makes me feel better, but I don't answer any of her questions. She starts telling me jokes. I manage to smile, and I relax a little.

I don't know how much time goes by before there's a knock at the window. I turn my head and find myself face to face with Zé, who smiles at me—the first sincere smile I've seen in ages, it seems to me, even though I've only been here two hours tops. I'm exhausted.

Before long, Zé and I are sitting facing the cop in the striped shirt and the cop with the incisors in the first one's office, letting him finally finish his statement. Zé is a tad more talkative than me, but only a tad. He isn't smiling anymore. In fact, he's actually sulking.

Striped Shirt: "Name?"

Zé: "Zé Palaisot."

Striped Shirt: "Occupation?"

Zé: "Night watchman."

Incisors: "And the boy?"

Zé: "Last year of elementary school."

Incisors: "I meant his name."

Zé: "Mattia Lorozzi."

Striped Shirt: "Isn't it Younès?"

Zé: "He has his mother's surname."

Striped Shirt: "Mattia. Isn't that a girl's name?"

Zé: . . .

Striped Shirt: . . .

Incisors: . . .

Zé: "No, are you really going to put that in the statement?"

Incisors: "Your ward was picked up at four forty-five in the morning, out on the streets, almost unconscious and clearly sick."

Zé: . . .

Incisors: "Don't you have school tomorrow, boy?"

Me: . . .

Zé: "We still have time to get there."

Striped Shirt: "And apart from school, how do you account for the fact that he wasn't in bed?"

Zé: "I don't know."

Striped Shirt: "When you work nights, who looks after him?"

Zé: "My girlfriend."

Striped Shirt: "What's her name?"

Zé: "Gabrielle Dubreuil."

* * *

I turn my head slightly. That isn't her real surname. Instinctively, I don't show my surprise. Striped Shirt takes this down without any reaction, but Incisors stares at Zé in a way I really don't like.

For the address, Zé gives the right street, but not the right number. I'm more and more puzzled. I jump when the cop with the incisors asks me why I wasn't in bed. I'd almost forgotten I was in the room, seeing how nobody has been saying a word to me. I look to Zé for help, but he's impassive, as if to say, "You sort it out." I assume he's asking himself the same question.

And so am I, to be honest. I shift in my chair, my eyes lowered. When it comes to grown-ups in positions of authority, whether it's the school principal or the cops, I always find it hard to look them in the face.

"I was sick."

"You were sick," Striped Shirt says. "And when you're sick you wander the streets by yourself at five o'clock in the morning."

"I wasn't . . . I . . . I drank one of those things that stops you sleeping."

"One of those things that stops you sleeping."

"I forget the brand."

"I drink it for my job," Zé cuts in, coming to my rescue (not soon enough, you traitor!). "There are cans of it in the fridge, but this is the first time he's helped himself. I thought you were more sensible, Mattia."

I glare back at him. Imperturbably, Striped Shirt takes this down. His colleague is sitting on the radiator, arms folded over his chest in a pose clearly meant to suggest power. Zé looks quite small compared to them, in spite of his height.

There's a short silence, soon broken by the cop who recognized me.

"Were you trying to run away from something?"

He peers at me. He has disturbingly clear eyes.

I turn away. "No, why?"

"From someone, then?"

"No."

I have no idea what he's getting at. My eyes meet Zé's and he lowers his. His fists are clenched on his thighs, his back and shoulders tenser than they've ever been.

"It can't be easy, living with a murderer," the cop finally says.

Striped Shirt throws him an inscrutable look.

Zé looks up abruptly. "I beg your pardon?" he says in a low voice.

"You heard me. You'd be inside if your Ma and Pa weren't in the law."

"That's not what we're here for, or is it?" Zé retorts, surprisingly calm.

Striped Shirt evidently agrees with him. He pretends to concentrate on his computer screen in order to hide his unease, but the sidelong glance he gives his colleague betrays his disapproval.

"We're here because your ward does whatever he likes and you're responsible for him," the cop with the incisors replies. "But what can we expect from a degenerate who should never have been let out of the funny farm? Trust me, this is going to get back to the family judge. This kid would be much better off in a foster family."

"Okay," Zé says. He turns to Striped Shirt with a forced smile. "Are we done? I wouldn't like Mattia to miss school today."

* * *

Once outside, he slaps me on the back of my neck. It's more humiliating than violent.

"Thanks a lot for that magic moment."

"It isn't my fault you're not in their good books," I mutter, rubbing my neck.

We get in his car. He rolls a cigarette with shaking fingers. He's getting ready to start the engine when I stop him.

"I left my coat in the station."

"There's no way I'm going back in there."

The bastard lets me go back on my own. Fortunately, I don't pass any cops in the waiting room. My coat is lying on the back of the chair I sat down on when I came in. I wedge it under my arm and get ready to finally take my leave . . . but then I stop dead, knocked back by a face in profile beyond the window.

A man with a cup of coffee in his hand is talking with the woman who told me jokes. He's dressed in plainclothes, a black sweater and all-purpose brown pants. He's about forty, with a head and muscles like a bull. I've seen him before, he's the guy who followed me and Gina into the library, who was waiting for me outside school, and was probably the one at the wheel of the car that was tailing us.

So he's a cop. Yesterday, that might have reassured me. Today, I'd frankly have preferred him to be a gangster.

I hide my head under my coat, bend double, and almost crawl across the waiting room so that I can get out without being seen. Once outside, I jump into the car without knowing if he's spotted me.

"Do I have to go to school?" I ask Zé.

"Just to annoy you, yes. You were supposed to be keeping an eye on Gabrielle."

"The guys following us are cops."

He doesn't react. He doesn't ask me how I found out and I realize he's known all along.

Frankly, I'm sick of being kept in the dark about everything that's important.

Murderer. The word echoes in his head. He barely heard Mattia tell him about the two cops who are following him. At this point, he doesn't care. He drives to the school, smoking one cigarette after another.

How many more years is it going to be before he's allowed to forget?

He can't help it, the girl's features take shape and superimpose themselves on his vision. An oval face, thick eyebrows, a turned-up nose, and bright blue eyes. Émilie Vauquier, seventeen, rests in a family vault somewhere in Alsace.

He can't even remember if he thought she was pretty. In those days, he didn't look at anybody, and certainly not girls. His nose was always stuck in his school books. He has hardly any memories of that time. From ten to sixteen, he didn't live much. He preferred to study.

From very early on, he was predicted to be a great success. His parents expected a lot of him and he didn't disappoint them. His school grades soon lived up to his family's expectations, but there was a price to pay.

Sent to a famous high school in Paris, then put on a preparatory course for the advanced math exam, Zéphyr Palaisot, son of a deputy prosecutor and an appeals court judge, gifted with an above average IQ and an unequaled sense of logic, could easily see himself doing equations all his life.

But then came the incident in his second year.

Émilie Vauquier, those five syllables still keep him from

sleeping on those nights when he listens to Gabrielle's breathing.

They were in the same class but had never spoken. Zé didn't speak to many people. He was self-sufficient. All he needed to be happy were figures. He was all set for a radiant future.

Émilie, on the other hand, wasn't happy, and nobody knew it. She couldn't keep up. She often ended up at the bottom of the class. She held back her tears whenever she got a bad grade. None of the students and none of the teachers noticed. Certainly not Zé. He wasn't interested in his peers.

Between noon and two, the school would leave its classrooms open to students on the preparatory course, so that they could study during the lunch break. One day—it was in March—he finds himself alone in the room with Émilie.

She writes various series of numbers on the blackboard. She curses between her teeth whenever she makes a mistake. Engrossed in his own work, Zé barely hears her. After a while she calls over to him, her cheeks turning pink.

"I've finished."

"Okay," Zé says, just to be left in peace.

"Can you tell me if it's correct?"

He heaves a deep sigh and looks up at the blackboard. It only takes him a second to spot a basic error. He holds back a smile. How could she ever have been accepted on the course? She's really not good enough. Even a third-year student in junior high wouldn't have got it wrong.

"You've made mistakes in carrying over. There, there, and there."

"Where?"

There's panic in Émilie's eyes—but Zé doesn't see it. He heaves a deep sigh and stands up to show her where she went wrong. Engrossed in his demonstration, he doesn't notice that she isn't listening to him.

What happens next he still doesn't understand eight years

later. At the trial, the experts called by the defense will say it was an anxiety attack.

She moves away while he's speaking and leans out the open window. He thinks at first she wants to get some fresh air, but then she gets up onto the sill. He only has time to break off what he's doing. A moment later, she's no longer there and cries of horror can be heard from down on the street.

He stands there, frozen to the spot, beside the blackboard and the failed equation. He looks at the window, at the spot where she was and isn't anymore. *Tell them I tried.* These words enter his thoughts in Émilie's voice, did she say them or did he make it up in the confusion of the moment?

The door is flung open. People rush in. Pupils, teachers, monitors with chalk-white faces, some in tears, others in a rage, some talk to him gently, others yell at him, he's asked for some reaction at least, but although even a minute earlier he had an answer for everything and was never wrong, he has no reaction to give them.

Then he closes his right hand, that hand that has only ever been used to raise a finger to answer the teachers, and with all his might brings his fist down on the blackboard.

The wounds on his fingers leave a red trail over the chalk.

He would like to strike out again, but they grab him and move him away from the walls, he tries to run away, he has no more energy, and they hem him in on all sides until the police arrive.

What happens next is just a long series of questions. The most frequent haunts his nights. *Did you push her?*

The answer is no—but in a way, yes.

He's held for forty-eight hours then referred to an examining magistrate who decides, in the absence of sufficient evidence, to release him until he appears in court. Preventive custody would have ruined all his efforts to get the top grade and hampered his promising future. "Concentrate on your studies until the trial."

The next day Zé returns to school. For the first time in his life he looks at other people and doesn't like what he sees in their eyes. Doubt. The terrible smell of doubt.

The blood has been washed off the asphalt, but nobody can ignore Émilie's empty chair, and the principal, having declared himself convinced of Zé's innocence, addresses the whole class.

"It was suicide. I'm sorry things turned out this way, but nobody is responsible."

It isn't true, Zé thinks. They were all responsible. There must have been signs. *There must have been something to see* that they didn't see.

During the days that follow, he doesn't work. He still goes to class but doesn't even take notes. He looks at the others, that's all he does, for the first time in his life, and he sees. The rings under their eyes. The tiredness. The meals many of them skip so they can study. The false gaiety in their conversations. The depression in some cases. The pressure in others, and that constant fear of not being good enough. The lack of mutual aid: it's every man for himself, each of them torn between the desire to be first and the dread of being last.

Zé founders.

He stops eating. He stops studying. He stops speaking. He doesn't answer his lawyer's calls, or his parents'. The day he receives a summons to go to court, he tears up the letter. He burns all his school exercise books, all his math books, everything that used to keep him alive, there's a fever in his eyes, in his head, everywhere, he slams the door of his tiny studio apartment behind him and sets off, his pockets empty, dressed only in jeans and a T-shirt—he walks aimlessly, for a long, long time.

A police car picks him up from the side of the beltway in the middle of the night, thinking he's some crazy hobo. Zé just has to say a few words for the machine to be set into motion.

He's taken to Sainte-Anne Hospital, then transferred

behind the high walls of Charcot at his parents' insistence. He refuses to eat, to see his parents, to talk to the psychiatrist.

And one day he finds himself sharing a double room with Monsieur Younès—Mattia's father. The former teacher keeps telling him it's not his fault. Perhaps Émilie knew perfectly well what she was doing. She'd made a conscious decision. Nobody could have made that decision in her place, or blamed her for making it.

Sometimes you can't hold back someone who wants to die.

These words make him feel better. Gradually, very gradually, he starts to appreciate the daylight again, his own company, and above all, he's able to bear the sight of his own reflection in the mirror.

When he thinks about it now, he realizes that Younès wasn't talking specifically about Émilie. That in a sense, he was preparing him for his own suicide.

After Younès dies, Zé is taken directly from the hospital to the court, where it is soon determined that it was indeed a suicide. Zé greets the verdict with a degree of astonishment: *innocent*. He may not have killed anyone but he isn't innocent either. A prison sentence would almost have been a relief.

To the few reporters waiting for him outside, he makes the mistake of admitting that he's not pleased with his acquittal. That he deserved to be punished, and that he's been finding it hard to sleep since it happened. That's all it takes to instill doubt, a doubt that will never be completely dispelled.

And when people call him "murderer" to his face, he doesn't deny it, in a way it soothes him.

Exhausted after the trial and the hospital, Zé quits his studies for good and vows never again to do any equations. He gets a job as a night watchman and moves into social housing in Les Verrières.

One day, Amélia Lorozzi, the partner of the late Monsieur Younès, who grew fond of him during her visits to Charcot, knocks at the door of his apartment with a bottle of sparkling wine and tells him about her youngest child. *"You need to redeem yourself and I need you to look after Mattia. Deal?"*

Deal.

But a spoken agreement wasn't enough. Amélia really wanted him to become the boy's legal guardian. *I don't want to be responsible for him anymore.* She'd told him about Mattia's suicide attempt, and he knew only too well what she must be feeling—and the power that terrible word "responsible" had to keep you awake at night.

He told his parents about the plan, and they immediately approved, conscious that he needed something to take his mind off things. Monsieur and Madame Palaisot gave him a helping hand to speed up the process, and Zé found himself officially the legal guardian of a seven-year-old boy.

And as he vowed the day after the decision was handed down, Zé would never let this one throw himself out the window.

* * *

There are days when he wonders if he'll be able to keep his vow. He thinks about this as, with a pang in his heart, he watches Mattia disappear beneath the roof of the school's covered playground.

Stopping at the red light, he briefly closes his eyes and immediately sees again the image of the bloodstained blackboard.

13

My eyes jolt open. Something's wrong. It's so obvious that it takes me an insane amount of time to realize what it is. I'm lying in my bed, at home, in the dark, everything seems normal in the room, except that *I can't breathe*. There's a huge weight on my chest. I'm suffocating. I try to sit up but I can't move. It's impossible to make the slightest movement.

A feeling of déjà vu . . .

I look for air, but can't find it, all my muscles take part in this unlikely search, I emit strangled sounds that end in something like a death rattle, my throat is dry, the weight on my chest is too heavy, dammit, what's happening to me?

I try to call Zé—it's impossible to speak.

It's starting to become clearer.

The outline of a figure on top of me, perched on my chest. I open my eyes wide to get a better glimpse of it. It has the shape of a man but it isn't a man. It seems made out of darkness, as if it wasn't tangible, *and yet it's so heavy that it's stopping me from breathing.*

Terror grabs hold of me. I open my mouth wide in a silent scream. Zé help me Gabrielle Gina Mom anyone dammit *help me I'm going to die.*

The truth of my imminent death is like a blow to the heart. I contract all my muscles to get rid of that thing, that presence, whatever it is, I'm tangled up in the sheets, too small to resist this thing pressing on my ribs and stomach, I gather all the strength I have in me and manage to produce a tiny sigh, so soft that nobody could hear it, but there must be a God somewhere and I've forgotten that I've been living within the walls of silence, where whispers shatter your eardrums.

The door opens.

"Mattia?"

The presence vanishes in a hundredth of a second. All at once I can breathe. I swallow a huge mouthful of air. I raise myself up on my elbows, breathing in deeply, and look around the room, searching for traces of *that thing* that tried to kill me.

Everything's normal. Everything's quiet. Everything's fine. And once again that familiar sensation I can't put a name to . . .

Gabrielle slowly approaches and sits down at the foot of the bed, dressed as always in that sweatshirt that hides her spidery hands. My breathing is still halting. She waits politely until I get back into a reasonable rhythm.

"Where's Zé?" I mutter.

"At the store. What's the matter? Been having a nightmare?"

I shake my head. I don't know how to explain. I try anyway. She listens to me, no expression on her face. Two nights earlier, she almost threw herself out the window. There's no sign of it in her eyes. I've never asked her what goes through her mind when she's so close to death. She wouldn't tell me. Zé has already asked her all the questions you could think of.

"Are you sure it wasn't a dream?"

"I was awake! I saw you come in, it took me two minutes to call you."

"You didn't call me. I just heard a noise. I think you were asleep."

"I swear I wasn't, Gabrielle."

She can probably hear a vestige of panic in my voice, or

indignation at not being believed, because she nods her head and ruffles my hair.

"All right, you weren't asleep. But it's late. Try to get back to sleep. We'll see about it in the morning."

See about what? I pretend to agree but I can't hide my fear. I'm still shaking because what do I do if that *thing* comes back? Gabrielle reads my thoughts. She lies down next to me.

"I'll sleep with you if you like. If it starts again, it'll be easier for me to hear you."

"Okay."

I'm too old to sleep with my parents, but Gabrielle isn't my mother. I stretch out next to her. I close my eyes. I try to get to sleep, focusing on the noise of her breathing, but she doesn't make any sound and that makes me even more anxious. I open my eyes at regular intervals to check that her chest is rising and falling in time with her breathing. It's an old fear that's come back. When I was little, the first thing I did when I got up was to go and check that my mother hadn't died in her sleep.

Somehow I manage to fall asleep at dawn. The thing doesn't reappear, and yet when I wake up, I know that I wasn't dreaming.

* * *

Zé is waiting for me outside school. I thought he'd be up to his old tricks, given what happened last night, being forced to go to a police station and be reminded that he was a murderer, but Gabrielle has already brought him up to speed. For the first time since we've been living together, he takes me to a bar not far from the school and buys me a soda.

"I hear you had some problems last night?"

I look at him in amazement. He's never been more like a real parent—or how I imagine one. I don't say anything. He insists.

"Tell me about it."

I do as he says, still incredulous. Usually he ignores me for at least a month after Gabrielle has tried to kill herself. He doesn't really care what happens to me. Let's say he has his priorities.

When I've finished, he laughs.

"Not you too, please . . ."

"What do you mean?"

"You were the only one of the three of us not to have been in Charcot, but now I think you're going to be eligible."

I feel a cold sweat at the back of my neck and all the blood drains from my face. Zé's expression changes, and he puts his hand on mine.

"Hey, I'm kidding. Mattia! It was a joke. I'm sorry. I'm never going to send you to Charcot, you know that."

Yes, I know that. But it doesn't make me laugh. I can still hear the nurse's words: "the tip of the iceberg." I can still see the articles I read on the sly in the library about the sickness that swallowed up my father, in the days when I was searching desperately for a single psychiatrist to refute the theory that there's a genetic factor.

So that's it, is it? It's coming. I, too, am going to . . . just like him.

Zé heaves a deep sigh and sinks into his armchair.

"Me and my big mouth."

You said it, you son of a bitch.

* * *

GINA. *The day of the trial they pulled out all the stops. Metal detectors on the way into the courtroom, cops in groups of ten. I'd never seen so many, except during the riots.*

I was thirteen. I went there with Dad. Mom stayed at home with Stefano, she was in her seventh month but they were afraid you would be premature. We couldn't get in. The place was packed. Reporters, sociologists, all kinds of people who had no reason to be there, it was almost indecent. Even Saïd's family had to force their way through.

Lots of people from Les Verrières had come with photographs of Saïd, and other people who didn't know him but were sick of cops who killed. It made for quite a gathering outside the courthouse. There were a whole lot of CRS trucks.

We had to stay outside, waiting for the verdict. Hours on end in the cold, it was December, just before Christmas. Dad was looking vacantly around him. He smiled to those who came up to talk to him. He hadn't left home in months.

It's the only time in my life I tried to pray. I wanted him to pay. Dad had given me this whole spiel about justice and I believed in it, but I had an excuse, I was young, I didn't know how things worked.

Most of the people around us didn't believe in it. They knew what was at stake. They said the justice system couldn't afford to get on the wrong side of the police. That the police unions had too much influence. That it was always the same anyway, that there were never any surprises.

I'd left Dad and was listening to them. Their words seemed to me more plausible than my father's, because there were no illusions in them.

It lasted three days.

On the third evening we heard booing, cries of anger. The CRS brought out their shields. Saïd's sister Siham appeared on the courtroom steps. Behind her, her parents were doing their best not to cry in front of the cameras. I knew Siham a little. She was a year older than me. Sometimes she helped me with my homework. She wasn't crying. She had that kind of hatred in her eyes.

She said: "Acquitted."

Those three syllables, I swear . . . "Acquitted." What did it mean? That Saïd hadn't died, or that he had never existed? I turned to my father. I saw a light go out in him. Completely. As if a candle had been blown out in his head. For the first time, I was afraid of losing him. For a moment I stopped thinking about Saïd.

But people started yelling, they tried to force their way

through the cordon and get inside the courthouse, and the CRS
threw their tear gas grenades. I was caught in the crowd. At first
I tried to move back, but the surge kept pushing me closer to the
cops, people were refusing to retreat in spite of the gas, so I
moved forward with them. There was jostling at the front, I saw
someone fall with his head covered in blood. I was pulled back-
wards, all at once I was outside the crowd.

I looked around for Dad. I couldn't see him through the
clouds of smoke. Anyone would have thought it was a civil war,
but it was merely one more confrontation on a relentless chess-
board where there had been thousands of others.

And there, opposite the courthouse, I saw that bus stop.
There was a poster for perfume, you know how horrible they
always are, that one was the worst. There was this stunning
woman with a big smile, in black and white, and beneath it were
the words "Life is beautiful."

I looked behind me at the last foolhardy spirits scattering as
the CRS charged. People were running in all directions to escape
the tear gas and the blows, then came back armed with loose
stones, throwing them wildly, but the stones were powerless,
they bounced off the helmets, the visors, the shields, the CRS
seemed invincible.

And on the other side, the poster at the bus stop: "Life is beau-
tiful." That was the name of the perfume. I said to myself "How
could those dumb advertising people do something like that?"
And even now that's a question I ask myself. You have to be blind
not to see the discrepancy between the name of that perfume and
reality, but that advertisement was on the street, at a bus stop, the
very place where you see the misery of this world, it's not as if it
was on TV where you can see it snug and warm in your living
room without thinking about all the crap around you.

I felt like screaming, like taking an iron bar and smashing up
that advertisement until the shards sank into the asphalt. I don't
know if you understand how strong that feeling was. I was

*thinking of those cretins up there in their nice clean buildings,
racking their brains to figure out what might appeal to the people and make them want to buy their fucking perfume. Life is
beautiful. Of course, my friend. Come down and see us, check
your theory, there may be something off.*

*But in the meantime, the demonstrators had dispersed. I
found Dad leaning against a tree, not far from the courthouse, he
hadn't moved even when the cops had charged. No anger in him.
Just an infinite sense of resignation, and I knew he would never
again be the way he'd been before.*

*The Zahidis helped me take him back to Les Verrières. I
looked at the high-rises, I told myself that this place was done
for. I didn't want to die here. If I stayed I knew I would end up
like Saïd, or worse still, like my father.*

*I vowed to go somewhere where nobody would try to make
me believe there's still something to be saved in this dying world.*

* * *

I'm doing my homework in my room when Zé comes in
with a sachet of fine-crystal sea salt. He already has his coat on,
and is getting ready to go to work. I stare at him questioningly
as he traces a circle around my bed with the salt.

He sees my stunned expression. "It's salt," he says.

"Great. And then you're going to complain that my room is
dirty."

"It protects against demons! Christians do it for exorcisms.
It's a protective circle. Nobody can touch you while you're
inside it."

I look at him until he lowers his head.

"Okay, I agree, I tried something psychological, it didn't
work, I'm sorry."

He pretends to sweep away the salt. I stop him with a gesture. I don't suppose it can do any harm. He gives a victorious

smile, then says good night and reminds me that I can reach him on the store's landline if anything's wrong.

I go to bed just before midnight. To feel safe, I pull the blanket up over my head. I try to fall asleep without thinking about that thing.

I open my eyes again just before dawn. I've turned over onto my back in my sleep, and again I feel the complete absence of air in my lungs. I'm suffocating. The thing has returned. I can distinctly feel the weight of its body on mine. Like the last time, it's impossible to move or cry out. I try to see its eyes, its face, an expression, something, but all I see is darkness. It has a human shape, that's the most precise I can be.

I see little black dots as death seems to come closer. I breathe with my mouth wide open but the air refuses to go into my lungs. Life is gradually ebbing away—and suddenly, without any external intervention, the thing fades away like a draft.

Trying to get up, I fall out of bed. I have just one idea in my head: to leave my room before it comes back. I hurt myself as I hit the floor. I get to my feet, massaging my painful elbows, tears in my eyes.

I find Gabrielle in the living room, asleep on the couch. She wakes up when she hears my footsteps. I burst into tears before she can ask me any questions. She takes me in her arms and strokes my hair, whispering "What happened?" and between sobs I manage to tell her that I'm having hallucinations, that I'm crazy and, what's more, they're trying to kill me.

"Who's trying to kill you?"

"The hallucinations."

Dad held on for more than thirty years before he died of his madness. At this rate, I'd be surprised if I reached fifteen.

As for the protective circle of salt, Zé, forget it.

14

Nobody's followed us since we went to the police station. I don't suppose it's necessary anymore. They have our address—not the exact building, but nearly—and our names. Zé deftly changes the subject whenever I try to ask him questions about the cops.

Gradually, I stop sleeping at night. I'm too scared of getting a visit from the thing. I'm the only one who's seen it. They think it's a recurring nightmare, but I know it isn't. I can tell the difference between dreams and reality, or at least I know when I'm awake.

They suggest I sleep with them. I refuse. I'm not a kid anymore. Even when I was very small I never slept in my parents' bed, and I'm not going to start now.

I spend my nights watching TV in the living room with Gabrielle. Her vaguely reassuring presence helps me get a couple of hours' sleep a night. I nod off at school. Every hour of class is torture when you're trying to stay awake, but I somehow hold out. I'm too scared of the family judge.

Zé and Gabrielle are ultra-kind to me. She spends a lot of time asking me questions about what I feel when the *thing* comes. But I don't want to talk about it anymore and I don't answer her. In the end she gives up.

Zé keeps asking me if I need anything. I have the extremely unpleasant feeling that they think I'm trying to worry them deliberately so that they'll take better care of me. As if the terror I feel as soon as night falls was a laughing matter . . .

Mom used to say that problems hate solitude. Whenever one of them shows up, you can be sure that before long he'll bring all this friends over, too. And like almost everything she says, her theory is soon proved right.

It takes the form of a letter from the county court. Zé finds it when we come in from school, two weeks after the thing first appeared. I get myself a bowl of cereal from the kitchen while he looks through his mail with his usual expression, the expression a hen would have if given a knife and fork—he's never quite figured out how the bureaucracy works.

He throws me an alarmed glance as he unfolds the paper. I raise an eyebrow. He pretends to lose himself in his reading, all the while hiding the envelope with a supposedly casual hand. If he's trying not to worry me, he isn't succeeding.

When he's finished reading, he screws the paper into a compact ball and tries to throw it in the trash, but it lands three feet short of its target.

"What is it?" I sigh.

He doesn't reply. I smooth out the paper. The letter is only a few sentences long. Zé and I are summoned to appear before the family judge in a month. Between now and then, we should expect a short visit from social services, who will deliver their report to the court before the hearing.

I turn to Zé. He looks at me through his half-open palms, a question in his eyes. We should have expected this, but the fact is, neither of us knows what to do.

"We need to contact your mother," he says.

I jut out my chin in agreement. I know this whole thing stinks, but I can't bring myself to worry about it too much. All I want is to sleep.

"You already saw that judge when you asked for custody of me," I remind him. "How did you manage it then?"

He answers in such a low voice that I have to go closer to hear him.

"My parents helped me."

I laugh to myself. Zé is just a rich man's kid, he's never had to handle anything alone.

* * *

The thing comes back in force that night, but then goes as mysteriously as it came. I get up after its departure, on the stroke of two, gulp down a portion of last night's gratin in the kitchen, and spend the rest of the night trying to make a pencil drawing of the entity that's stopping my breathing. I close my eyes to help me concentrate, but I still can't remember its face. It's as if at the crucial moment I can see it, but then it fades, like the memory of a bad dream.

Gabrielle's asleep. Zé's at work. The apartment is more silent than ever. Even the neighbors don't deign to make the slightest noise. That's when you know how terrifying the night can be.

The next morning, Zé finds me exhausted, my bulging eyes fixed on the paper, the kitchen table strewn with other sheets of paper covered in fearsome scribblings. He comes to a standstill when he sees me, and his cigarette falls from his half-open lips. He bends down to pick it up and heaves a deep sigh.

"Get dressed. Let's go."

I'm so tired, I don't have the strength to ask him where exactly we're going. It's too early for school. While I put on some decent clothes, Zé goes to check that Gabrielle is still alive before bundling me in his car. We drive to La Solaire. I think we're going to see his parents, but once again he pulls up outside my brother's villa.

Stefano greets us over a coffee in his vast residence. He looks at his electronic organizer while listening attentively to what Zé is saying. Zé hasn't bothered with any preamble. He blurts out the key words: hearing, family judge, guardianship, your mother's missing.

Stefano soon interrupts him.

"What do you expect me to do?"

"It's impossible to get ahold of your mother and I need character witnesses. People who know Mattia and can say that I'm bringing him up well. I want to keep custody of him."

"Why is your custody being questioned?"

Zé grimaces. "It'd take too long to explain. But it's not my fault."

"Not your fault?"

"Not my fault."

"Character witness?" My brother at last looks up from his organizer. "And how do you want me to do that?"

"Eh?"

"It's not as if I've observed much of you in your role as a guardian."

Zé gives him his widest smile.

"That's hardly surprising, when you don't give a damn about Mattia's upbringing. If I lose custody of him, where do you think he'll go? To an institution. Or to perfect strangers if nobody in your family wants to take care of him, which is clearly the case."

"In other words, you're asking me to make things up."

"I need you because you're a surgeon, which sounds impressive. Everyone trusts doctors."

"That's true."

"So it's a deal?"

A pause.

"It's a deal," Stefano says, shaking Zé's hand across the table. "More coffee?"

"Sure, why not?"

They fall silent. It's time for school but I don't say anything. I sip my grape juice while the grown-ups lose themselves in their thoughts. A flock of crows caws from the top of a nearby pine.

"I'll mail it to you tomorrow," Stefano resumes. "Do you have a lawyer?"

"Not yet."

"Do you want me to find you one?"

"I can manage, thanks."

"And how are you, Mattia?"

I don't reply. I don't even look at him. I try to make out the crows in the branches of the tree. Zé answers for me.

"He's not so good. He doesn't sleep well. He has the impression—"

"That's nothing to do with him!" I cut in.

Zé lapses into silence.

Stefano looks at me for a long time, gulps down the rest of his espresso, and stands up. "I have to be at the hospital in half an hour."

He walks us back to the car. He and Zé shake hands, but then he holds us back.

"About Mattia's sleep problem, I think I know what it is."

"What?" Zé asks.

"He can't breathe, he can't move, and he sees a shadowy figure on top of him, is that it?"

Zé nods in amazement. I suddenly emerge from my two weeks of lethargy. My brother looks at me with a sad smile. I think he's pleased to have grabbed my attention.

"You had the same problem when you were little. Don't you remember? You always slept with the door open so that Mom could hear you. You called it 'the thing.' It stopped when your father died. Mom had already made an appointment for you to see a shrink but you refused to go."

He's waiting for my reaction. I think hard, but I can't remember, even though that time hasn't gone from my memory: I still recall the visits to the hospital. Although come to

think of it, the first time the thing came it was a strangely familiar feeling.

"Did you ever find out what it was?" Zé asks, disconcerted.

"No. But with everything that was happening to us, it was
obviously a psychological problem. Is he still seeing his psychologist?"

"She's on vacation."

"Make an appointment with her as soon as possible. I'm
sure she can deal with it better than we could. See you soon,
Mattia."

"'Bye."

I get to school thirty minutes late. The teacher doesn't ask
me any questions. With these rings under my eyes, I probably
don't look as if I could handle an interrogation. If social services question her, which they're sure to do, I doubt she'd be
able to serve as a character witness.

* * *

There's something in the air.

Everybody in town knows this graffiti. It hadn't been
around for years. But everyone knows that face. For the last
three months—ever since I saw it opposite the hospital, to be
precise—it's been reappearing on the walls. You see it on the
way into and out of town. On the railroad bridges. On the
front of the town hall, from which it's quickly erased. And
even—get this—on the window of the police station.

I didn't see those. But Youcef did. He's a boy in my class. He
knew Les Verrières before it was demolished. His father is in
municipal maintenance, and was given the task of erasing the
graffiti from the town hall; he says there have been lots of others.

"They do it at night, there are a whole lot of them but they
get cleaned up in the morning before anyone's up," Youcef
says.

He's talking at recess, surrounded by a small group, including me in the front row.

"I saw one near where I live," someone says, "but I didn't get it. Who is that guy?"

Youcef stares at him as if he came from Alpha Centauri. In Les Verrières, everyone knows who that face belongs to.

"He's Saïd Zahidi!"

"Who?"

"Saïd, fuck it! Haven't you ever heard of him?"

Our school is very close to Les Verrieres. Most of the people around here were relocated not far from the old high-rises. In fact about half of us come from the same place. Youcef soon loses interest in those who don't know the story and only addresses the others.

"Apparently they've doubled the patrols to try to get whoever's doing it, but they haven't caught them yet."

"What's the point?" a girl asks. "There was already a trial, so what's the point? Do you think that cop can be tried again?"

"The point is to remember."

"Remember what? Saïd?"

"Not just Saïd. The point is to remember that the cops can kill whoever they like and nothing happens to them."

Silence. Everyone's trying to think about what that means.

"And what's the point of that?" the same girl insists. "It's not going to bring Saïd back."

Youcef thinks about this for a while. It's a question I hadn't asked myself, and I suspect he hasn't either. When he finally replies, the bell covers the last few syllables:

"Well, it's still better than not doing anything at all."

* * *

Zé and Gabrielle are sitting in the bluish haze of the LED lights. The TV is off. I'm crouching behind the door. I'm supposed to be asleep. It's seven in the morning. He's just got back from the store, he'll soon come to wake me. He came into my room just now to see if I was asleep, and I pretended I was so as not to worry him. I'm starting to think it's best to stop telling grown-ups about the thing. To end up in Charcot, you have to be sent there by someone. If I'm the only one who knows I'm crazy, there's no reason for me to end up there. I'm not going to certify myself.

It's yesterday morning that we got the letter. I haven't slept all night. I don't dare lie down for fear of attracting the thing.

Zé: "I swung by Amélia's again. She still isn't back. Her neighbor hasn't seen her in two months."

Gabrielle: . . .

Zé: "If she doesn't come back before the hearing, they might take custody away from me. She's the one who convinced them the first time. She and my parents. With my history, there's no chance they . . ."

Gabrielle: . . .

Zé: . . .

Gabrielle: . . .

Zé: "Gabrielle."

Gabrielle: "Yes."

Zé: "Why do you want to go away?"

Long silence. He's there, huddled in patches of shadow, and she's half slumped against the back of the couch, her left shoulder bearing the weight of Zé's head. He has his eyes closed, not daring to look her in the face for fear of the answer he'll see in it.

I get the feeling hours have gone by before she finally speaks up.

Gabrielle: "Why should I stay?"

When he comes to my room, which I ran back to as fast as my legs would carry me, he looks as if he hasn't slept much. He hasn't shaved for days even though he hates having "itchy cheeks" (he always uses childish terms). There are new lines at the corners of his dry lips.

"Mattia . . . It's time to go to school."

He leaves the room before I can pretend to wake up. He knows I wasn't asleep. I don't know if he's realized that I was listening to their conversation.

"You have an appointment with Nouria at 4:45," he informs me as we pull up outside the school.

"Really?"

"Yes, she's back from her vacation. Can you go on your own? I have an appointment with a lawyer but I'll pick you up afterwards."

"Okay."

At first, a bright smile lights up my face and my day. That soon fades when I remember that a psychologist's first duty is to make a diagnosis. All through the hours separating me from the session, I weigh up the pros and cons, wondering if it's worth taking the risk of telling her about the thing. Then I reason with myself: she's never played any tricks on me, she likes me, and she knows what happened to my father. If there's any grown-up I can trust, it's her.

I'm pathetically happy to see her broom-closet office again, the fake leather armchair into which she sinks up to her elbows, the few books in her empty bookcase, put there as if not to offend preconceived ideas. Nouria, thirty-six years old, small and upright in an old gray sweater, greets me as if I'm an old friend she hasn't seen in far too long.

I'd planned to wait for her to ask me questions. But as soon as I sit down, I crack and let it all out. The thing, the sleepless nights, the tip of the iceberg, Zé who's going to lose custody of me—Zé who implied earlier, in an apparently casual remark, that she might be able to help us with the hearing if I asked her.

She hears me out and then homes in on the most important point.

"You're not going crazy. No more than anyone else, anyway."

"How do you know?" I retort, almost aggressively, my hands moving frantically.

"I know because you're not the only person to feel that. Far from it—it even has a name."

"Yes: madness."

"No, Mattia, sleep paralysis."

She's articulated each syllable in a sharper voice than usual, almost as if she's annoyed. I sink back in my chair. It's unusual for her to lose even one iota of her composure.

"Sleep paralysis," she repeats with a strange kind of weariness. "It's a classic sleep disorder. Lots of people have it at some time in their lives, but nobody talks about it, for fear of being thought crazy."

I stare at her with round, almost mistrustful eyes. She deigns to explain.

"Let me make it brief. When you fall asleep, a neurological mechanism blocks your movements so that you don't hurt yourself in your sleep, especially when you dream. But sometimes there's a kind of bug in the brain that doesn't take in the fact that you're awake, and it takes it a few seconds or a few minutes to put an end to the paralysis. That's what produces that feeling of suffocation that stops you from breathing and moving."

I think about this. So far it doesn't seem stupid at all. But she's forgotten an essential element: the thing. She smiles, stands up, and goes to stand by the narrow window, looking out at the town and all the crap that comes with it. I look at her square-cut brown hair, carefully smoothed as if to reflect the perfect order there's supposed to be in her head. *No crazier than anyone else . . .* When I look around me, I don't know if that's really reassuring. The others, those in my immediate circle, Zé and Gabrielle, my father, my mother and her absurd love of silence, my brother and his inflexibility, my sister and her constant, headlong flight.

"This thing, as you call it. The doctors who've examined the question say it's a creation of the mind."

"In other words, a hallucination!"

She bursts out laughing.

"You seem almost triumphant. Anyone would think it's what you wanted."

I fall back into silence. She gives me a sidelong glance before she continues:

"Yes, if you like, a hallucination. But having hallucinations doesn't mean you're going crazy. They can happen to anyone, including sane people, in so far as anyone is sane, in so far as it's even possible to be completely sane. We can't breathe or move anymore, we have no explanation for what's happening to us. The human mind is conditioned in such a way that we can't bear not understanding a phenomenon. We always have to reason, to justify, to explain. In sleep paralysis, the brain takes it upon itself to invent images that correspond to what we're feeling; in your case, someone sitting on you, stopping you from moving and breathing. It's very common, in cases of sleep paralysis. Most people affected by it suffer from the same visions, although they vary from one individual to another depending on what embodies our deepest fears. Do you understand?"

"Yes," I say after a moment's reflection.

She smiles and again turns to the window.

"Did you see that?"

"What?"

"They're just removing some graffiti from the front of the bar across the street."

I rush to her side. The word JUSTICE is there, beneath a half-erased stencil of Saïd's face. We both stand there, motionless for a while, watching someone from the bar slogging away in an attempt to get rid of the red paint with detergent.

"Do you want to continue living with Zé and Gabrielle?" she asks after what seems like forever, just as the graffiti is starting to give up the ghost.

I nod. Tiny as the movement is, she catches it, and it's enough for her.

"Tell Zé or his lawyer to call me this week, I'll see what I can do for the hearing."

"Thank you."

"Thank *you*, Mattia."

As she's walking me to the door, I come to a halt and ask, "What can I do to stop the paralysis?"

"Just avoid sleeping on your back, that's what sets it off, apart from insomnia and anxiety, which are harder to deal with. Get someone to sew a ping-pong ball cut in half on the back of your pajamas, that'll stop you from turning around in your sleep. But, Mattia . . ."

"Yes?"

"The more obsessed you are by the absurd idea that your father's sickness has been transmitted to you in your genes, the more evidence you'll see of your own madness. Auto-suggestion can go a long way, you know."

* * *

Zé and Gabrielle are waiting for me outside the building. She went with him to see the lawyer, knowing that he needed support to face the legal establishment. This is the man who represented him when he applied for custody of me the first time. The meeting went very well until the lawyer brought up the question of fees. Zé almost had a heart attack. "I see," he said, thought about it, then suggested one less zero. The lawyer suggested he should use someone appointed by the court.

"You should ask your parents for financial help," Gabrielle says. "I'm sure they'd agree."

"No," Zé replies.

"It's been years since you last asked them for anything. There wouldn't be any shame in it."

"No."

"You could at least do it for Mattia."

Zé gives her a black look, which I catch in the rearview mirror. I say nothing. I don't think one lawyer or another would make much difference. Without the legal support of his parents, there's no way it's going to work, and that's it. There's a black mark on his medical record, a mark that covers all the rest and will never be wiped out.

I go ahead of them into the lobby, almost running. The only thing I want is for them to sew on that damned half a tennis ball or whatever it is so that at last I can sleep. But I stop dead on the landing, mouth half open. Zé and Gabrielle soon join me and freeze simultaneously.

The door has been broken open. Wood shavings are strewn over the linoleum just inside. From here you can see part of the living room, the cushions on the couch ripped open, their fluffy contents scattered over the floor.

Gabrielle goes in first. Zé tries to hold her back.

"Wait, they may still be in there!"

She proudly ignores him. I try to follow her, but Zé grabs me by the collar. Gabrielle disappears into the corridor. Her voice soon reaches us.

"There's nobody here."

We go in after her. I run to the TV set, driven by an uncontrollable protective instinct. It hasn't been stolen, no, it's much worse. It's lying, dismantled, at the foot of the low table on which it stood in all its glory just a few hours ago. It's been taken apart without much expertise, apparently with just a hammer and chisel. Circuits exposed. Wires torn out. Screen smashed in. Faced with such cruelty, I'm mute with horror. Gabrielle puts a sympathetic hand on my shoulder.

"Well, at least that's one good thing," Zé whispers triumphantly behind us.

We don't bother to respond to his insult. I weep silently, remembering my morning cartoons—gone forever now, because I know that Zé, all too pleased with this stroke of luck, will never buy another TV.

I turn away from the tragedy and examine the rest of the damage. At first glance, nothing is missing. Not Zé's camera, which has been gathering dust in a closet for the past two years, not Gabrielle's old LPs, collectors' items all of them.

They've turned over all the carpets, torn down all the posters, ransacked every last corner, but they haven't taken anything.

That can only mean one thing.

"The cops," I say.

"No," Zé replies.

"Yes."

"No. It's a burglary."

"Stop messing with me! They haven't taken anything!"

"We don't have anything worth taking."

"What were they looking for in the TV, gold ingots?"

"People hide things in all kinds of places."

I glare at him for a good long time. He doesn't lower his eyes. That's what's crazy about him, his ability to spout the worst bullshit without having the decency to look embarrassed. Gabrielle turns away as if this argument has nothing to do with her.

As for me, I'm tired. Really, really tired. I give up. I slam the door of my room and collapse onto the bed. With the help of a belt, I tie my left arm to the base of the bed. That way, I'm sure I won't be able to turn over into the wrong position without waking up.

The thing doesn't come. I sleep like a log for hours. I wish I could wake up on my eighteenth birthday.

15

The odd thing is that nobody goes to the police station to report the burglary. I wonder why. Zé repairs the door at his own expense and they spend several days cleaning the whole apartment. I keep well out of it. There are heated arguments about the new TV that Gabrielle plans to buy. She likes watching news and documentaries. Zé retorts that there's always the radio, she says it doesn't distract her as much. He says it's bad for her, when there are items about war it makes her sad. She replies that closing your eyes to what's going on in the world doesn't wipe it out. He says that if they let me I'd spend my whole life watching cartoons. She says he thinks I'm more stupid than I am.

In the end, she waits for him to take me to school and then sneaks out, and by the evening a new secondhand TV has replaced the old one. Zé sulks but gives in. We celebrate this victory with grape juice.

Having heard Nouria's recommendations, Zé undertakes to sew on that half ping-pong ball. I'm able to sleep again. It's as if I'm getting a second life, a second chance, but there are too many murky things going on around me for the enthusiasm to be more than half-hearted. One evening, a few days after the burglary, while I'm watching the news with Gabrielle, I again tackle the question of who was responsible.

"It's very unusual for there to be nobody in. You were both out for an hour, seeing the lawyer, and then you came to pick me up. It can't have been chance, they must have been watching the building."

She nods as if it doesn't concern her. I know she's pretending. I look at her and she looks at the screen.

"The two of you are hiding things from me."

"Yes," she says.

"Yes?"

"Of course. You have enough problems as it is."

"It's my problem, too, when they wait for me outside school and rummage through my toys."

"Maybe. But you can't do anything to stop what's happening. It's more than we can handle either."

I keep insisting, but she refuses to say another word.

The following evening, Zé drives straight to Les Verrières, just a few blocks from the school. The hearing will be soon, and he still has no evidence that my mother is on his side. Her letterbox is overflowing with leaflets. Zé keeps a lookout, nervously smoking a cigarette in the lobby of the building, while I slip my hand inside. I pull out a handful of envelopes. Bills, fines, and a letter from the court, a summons to the same hearing. She doesn't even know about it. The last letter goes back to October 16, three months ago.

"Okay," Zé says, "I've had enough of this. Wait for me here."

He returns with a backpack that jingles metallically as he moves. I follow him to the fifth floor. He peers in through the keyhole, but the apartment is too dark to see anything. He hesitates for a moment then rings the neighbor's bell. She opens almost immediately. She'd already heard us from behind her door.

"Still not heard from your mother?" she asks me with a sheepish little smile.

"We're starting to get worried," Zé says. "She's been missing for three months." He opens his backpack and takes out a crowbar. "Will you cover me?"

She hesitates for about ten seconds before reluctantly agreeing. There are only two apartments on this landing. She puts on some music, leaves the door open in order to cover the noise, and keeps an eye on the stairwell while Zé slides the crowbar into the thin gap between the door and its frame. He has to start again several times to get it far enough in, tapping on it with a hammer. The noise echoes on the stairs. I'm scared but I don't say a word.

At last, after a lot of sweating and grimacing, Zé manages to snap the lock. For a rich kid, he's quite resourceful . . . The door opens wide. We wait in deathly silence, but no neighbor comes down to see what's going on. Zé shines his torch into the corridor. The neighbor and I jostle each other to get a better view.

My heart skips a beat. Mom's apartment is in the same state as ours a few days ago. We enter in single file, as silent as people always are when they expect the worst. The neighbor switches on the light. No blood on the walls. Just a methodical illegal search, which has left nothing to chance. The work of cops or hardened gangsters. And we know perfectly well which one it is.

All we have to figure out is what they're looking for.

We visit each of the rooms. None have been spared. They've even dismantled the toilet and ripped open my mother's mattress. I hold my breath each time we walk through a door, but the suspense is short-lived in such a small apartment, and my mother's body is nowhere to be seen.

In the kitchen, Zé sighs and turns to the neighbor.

"Thanks for your help."

She gets the message, bites her lip, then does an about-turn.

"Shouldn't we . . . call the police?"

"Trust me, it wouldn't get us very far."

Surprisingly, she does trust him. He can seem very sure of himself when he wants to, and my being there helps to make him worthy of trust. Anyone who has a child with him can't be all bad.

Once we're alone, Zé launches into another search. I realize he's looking for a letter, a clue, anything that would explain Mom's disappearance. I help him reluctantly, not very eager to pry into my mother's private life, given that she's kept me at arm's length for years. I don't find anything, which depresses me more than anything else. There's something unusual here, which is the total absence of photographs. There are none of me, or of my brother and sister, or my father, or anybody.

We leave empty-handed after searching for an hour or two. In the car, we don't talk. There's nothing to say. Except that my mother has disappeared and nobody wants to tell me why.

* * *

When we get back, Gabrielle comes out to greet us when Zé opens the door, which has a brand-new lock. From her pursed lips, I gather that something's going on.

"You have visitors," she says.

"What are you talking about?"

"Your parents."

His face freezes in a comical grimace. He doesn't have time to run away. A man and a woman in their sixties come out of the living room into the corridor. They aren't wearing their robes but they don't need to, what they are is obvious from their stern features. They both have the wrinkled faces of people who've spent their lives frowning, him as a prosecutor, her as an appeals court judge.

Zé, who's so tall, shrinks in comparison. Sensing that he's on the verge of running away, Madame Palaisot makes the first move and walks up to him. Monsieur Palaisot looks at me without any hint of an expression. Madame examines her son's face, opens her mouth, and says nothing. For a few seconds nobody knows how to react. Then inspiration comes to her.

Madame: "Wait before you insult us, Zé."

Monsieur (interrupting her): "We heard you've been having a few little problems."

Madame: "You cut me off again."

Monsieur: "I beg your pardon?"

Madame: "That's exactly what I was telling you earlier."

Monsieur: "I cut you off?"

Madame: "You cut me off. It's incredible. You don't even notice."

Monsieur: "I'm sorry."

Madame: "Thank you. May I continue?"

Monsieur: "Of course."

Madame: "Thank you."

Gabrielle and I look at each other in amazement. But the scene seems familiar to Zé, who gives an almost tender smile. He doesn't have time to say anything, though.

Madame: "You're appearing before the family judge in two weeks' time. You know as well as we do they won't let you keep custody of the child."

"The child": that's how his parents have always referred to me. They're too accustomed to reports from institutions that take away even your name, or use it only in order not to confuse their countless files.

Madame: "I know how much it means to you. Let us help you."

Zé: "No."

Monsieur: "Zé—"

Zé: "Get out of here."

He points to the door. Behind him, Gabrielle has a strange gleam in her eyes. The couple doesn't move.

Monsieur: "Your old resentments are meaningless now. A lot of water has passed under the bridge."

Zé: "My old resentments? You—"

Gabrielle: "Stop being such a pain in the ass."

Zé: . . .

Madame: . . .

Monsieur: . . .

Zé: "What?"

Gabrielle: "You know they're right."

Monsieur: "Thank you, mademoiselle."

Gabrielle: "Zé, this isn't just your problem, it's mine, too, and Mattia's. Now we're all going to sit down and discuss it, and you are going to stop thinking only about yourself."

She has spoken. And when she speaks he doesn't argue. It doesn't happen often, so when it does you have to pay attention. Zé gives in, with a last look of hate addressed to his parents, who look questioningly at each other, alarmed by Gabrielle's stance, and everyone moves into the living room, even me. Nobody offers our guests a drink.

Monsieur: "Does the child have to be present?"

Zé: "After all that's happened, you still haven't realized that a child mustn't be excluded from his own life. You astonish me."

Gabrielle: "And the child's name is Mattia."

Thank you, Gabrielle. Out of the corner of my eye, I see that the prosecutor can't take his eyes off her wrists. She must have noticed, because she keeps pulling down the sleeves of her sweatshirt to hide the scars, blushing slightly as if it was something to be ashamed of.

The negotiations have been going on for five minutes when I realize that I haven't listened to a word. As usual, I observe. And what I see should have been blindingly obvious as soon as I set eyes on Zé's parents. It's something in the air. In their expressions. The way Madame keeps tucking a lock of black hair behind her ear. The shifty way Monsieur looks at him through screwed-up eyes. If they didn't have such self-control, I'd have seen it right away.

They hate being here. They're as uncomfortable as it's possible to be, although they hide it well. When they look at him, it's not their son they're seeing, or even a person, but a verdict and a diagnosis. They're seeing an empty classroom and a blood-stained blackboard. They're seeing the high walls of Charcot. They're seeing the isolation room and the bed, the straps, the brace, they're seeing boxes of pills and trembling hands, they're seeing his incoherent words whenever his psychiatrist was trying to find the right dosage and testing on him all kinds of antipsychotics with barbaric names in order to adjust the delicate balance governing the chemical molecules in his brain.

They're seeing "madness" and they're seeing "defendant." It doesn't matter which: what they don't see is him. And for a moment, I imagine what an accused man must feel when confronted with them and their infinite ignorance of the world and of people.

* * *

And names pass through my head.

June 15. Ossama Yabrir, 17, five years for repeated car theft. August 18. Mourad Kettani, 19, three years for criminal damage. August 29. Nasser Bellamine, 22, ten years for armed robbery. October 10. Clément Dechaveaux and Kamel Ahardane, 19 and 18, four years for burglary. December 31. Nesrine Othmani, 16, one year for setting fire to a container for glass. January 8. David Zuma, 21, six months for threatening behavior. January 24. Michaël Da Pojan, 17, eight years for assault on a police officer in the exercise of his duties.

February 1. Saïd Zahidi, 15, death for resisting the police during an identity check.

December 17, three years later. Thomas Ross, 29, acquitted for bodily harm leading to unintended death.

* * *

I know their names and their sentences because my father wrote them on a sheet of paper pinned to the wall near his hospital bed. Whenever I visited him, I would read them over and over again. My mother taught me to read before I was even in first grade. It filled our silences.

All these names belong to inhabitants of Les Verrières sentenced in the months before the death of Saïd. Many of these sentences were demanded by this same man on behalf of the prosecutor's department: Olivier Palaisot, deputy prosecutor at the county court.

My father hated him.

I stand up. All eyes turn to me. I look at them, that man, that woman, contempt blazing inside me, and without a word I leave the room, I can't bear their presence anymore. I slam the door of my bedroom and wait for them to leave.

I don't want them to help us either. But Gabrielle's right. It's that or an institution. And I hate them for being so indispensable to us.

* * *

Zé comes to see me just before leaving for the store. I'm hidden under the quilt. He sits down at the foot of the bed. His hand on my shoulder through the blanket. He clears his throat.

"They've gone."

Silence. A dreadful silence all down my throat.

"They're going to pay for a lawyer and do what they can to see that it works out. Mattia? What are you thinking?"

I emerge from under the quilt. He hasn't switched the light on, but the light from the street lamps is enough to illuminate the weary lines on his face.

"Explain," I say.

"Explain what?"

"How things work, I don't understand."

"What things?"

"How come your father jailed so many people from Les Verrières who hadn't done much, while the cop who killed Saïd got off scot-free."

Zé looks out the window. He lights a cigarette. He's either thinking it over or working out a strategy to avoid having to give me an answer. He's really embarrassed by my question. Because he was born in the right place at the right time. In the right country and with the right skin color. Because you don't talk about class war with children. You prefer to warble on about equal opportunity. But I'm tired of it, it's a nursery rhyme even kids don't believe in anymore. You have no idea how tired of it I am.

Finally he stands up.

"I have to go to work. Good night."

* * *

I'm dreaming.

A body at the foot of the high-rises. It's night. Everything is silent, motionless. No light visible on the horizon. Just that of the moon struggling to break through the fog over the town. Everyone's asleep. I walk, alone, toward the lying figure, which I can barely make out through the misty darkness. I walk but I don't seem to get any closer.

Suddenly, a fire.

It takes possession of the buildings, one after the other, they burn down like candle wicks. Nobody cries for help and I know instinctively that they're all already dead. I continue moving forward. I'm not afraid. I don't feel anything. I finally manage to distinguish the features of the person lying on the concrete. It's a woman. It's Mom, her hair soaked in blood.

She's alive. She points to something on the left. I look in that direction. The community center. Beyond the window, another figure is visible, swinging slowly at the end of a rope.

I'm overcome with nausea but I can't vomit. Someone grabs me by the shoulders. I turn. It's Gina. She's watching the buildings burn. The fire is reflected in her dark eyes.

"We have to go," she says.

"Go where?"

"They're coming."

"Who?"

"The people who started the fire."

"Who are they?"

She doesn't reply, as if the question was a minor one. But she doesn't move and neither do I. We can't tear ourselves away from the sight of the flames engulfing the concrete.

A flash, and then darkness.

I wake up with the feeling that I'm more alone than I've ever been.

It's two in the morning. Zé is at the store. Gabrielle must be asleep or watching the ins and outs of yet another anonymous war on TV. I'm not sleepy anymore. I get up with the firm intention of eating a bowl of cereal in front of the TV, but voices stop me, coming from the living room. Gabrielle's voice. And a man's voice—but not Zé's.

Heart pounding, I creep to the door. It's ajar. I quickly glance in. Gabrielle has her back to the window and is facing a man of about forty. A man I've seen before. He's the one who came and spoke to me outside the school and asked me for Zé's address. His companion was at the police station.

I hide behind the door, one hand over my mouth. The telephone is in the living room, out of my reach, and Zé won't be back until five. I start to feel panic but I control myself because I want to listen.

Gabrielle doesn't seem too afraid.

". . . for years. You never even thought about us," the man says.

"You're right," Gabrielle says.

"After all we did for you. All we had to put up with, dammit! I'm forced to come and see you in the middle of the night if I want to know how you are. You think that's normal? And that guy . . . a degenerate who's been in the funny farm."

"Like me," Gabrielle says.

"That's different. You just need someone to take care of you."

"Is that so?"

"Yes."

"No, thanks. I can take care of myself."

A scornful exclamation. Heavy footsteps move closer to her.

"Oh, really? Then what are these scars?"

"That's one way of taking care of yourself. Now you'd better go. You'll wake Mattia."

Silence.

I listen. I hear everything. The sound of their breathing. The rustle of fabric betraying their movements. The footsteps. His sighs and her silences.

"What is it you want?" she says.

"For you to leave here. You're never going to get better with a weirdo and an eleven-year-old boy."

"I don't need to get better."

"You know what I could do?"

Another silence creeping across the carpet. The voice turns threatening.

"I could have you committed, Gabrielle."

She laughs, but there's terror in her laughter.

"On what basis?"

"Your multiple suicide attempts."

"And you think they'll fix that in the hospital? They'll just deaden me with meds until I lose any sense that I'm even alive, so that I won't want to die."

"At least we'll know where you are."

"And where will I be? Trapped somewhere in my own head? You won't even recognize me. And Zé will find a way to get me out of there. He knows hospitals. He knows how these things work."

"Maybe so. But he's not a member of your family. Officially, you don't even live with him. He has no say in the matter."

"I'm not necessarily talking about getting out officially."

"I can also make sure he gets in trouble with the law."

Silence.

"I don't want to go that far," the man continues. "But if the only way you'll agree to be helped is if you have nobody else to rely on, then I'll do what it takes."

"His parents are judges themselves. You and your lousy cop friends can't touch him, he's protected."

"My lousy cop friends are after just one thing. I'm worried about you. I don't want you to die, and I don't care what I have to do to get you to accept help. Sometimes people have to be protected against their will."

"You come here in the middle of the night, you force open the door, you make me listen to your bullshit, you threaten me, you threaten someone I love, and you expect me to greet you with open arms? I told the family when I left, I don't want to have anything more to do with any of you. You all protected me against my will so much that it destroyed me. There's no life behind the walls of a hospital."

"And where is your life? In this apartment you never leave?"

"But I'm free to leave it if I want to."

"You never do, which is worse."

She suddenly raises her voice.

"Is your life any better than mine? Ever since you entered

the Police Academy, the only people you've spent time with are your cop friends. You've forgotten how the world works beyond your little circle of colleagues whose idea of social reality doesn't go any farther than the tops of their helmets! You disgust me. Get out of here."

"I'm not like that. Maybe I was once, but I've been forced to change."

"That's not exactly obvious. Just get out!"

"Gabrielle, I beg you. Come with me. Let me help you. I can't stand it anymore, waking up in the morning wondering if you've thrown yourself out the window during the night."

"Leave me your number. I'll tell Zé to let you know if I've killed myself."

A deathly silence like the kind that follows the news of a declaration of war. I stick my eye to the keyhole. They're standing face to face in the middle of the living room, she with her arms crossed, her hands lost in the folds of her sweatshirt, looking so thin and spectral, and he in his suede jacket, his mouth half open, frowning in anger and fear. He's wearing a big belt with a gun in a holster.

He stands there a while longer, looking at her, trying to get her to lower her eyes. He doesn't succeed. He's the one who turns away.

"Now get out," she says in a weary voice.

He doesn't react. She tries to take him by the arm to push him out. He pulls away violently.

"Come with me," he says again, more loudly than before.

I open the door and cough to let them know I'm here. The cop has his back to me. He turns, letting go of Gabrielle, whom he'd taken by the hand. Gabrielle looks at me without any surprise. She's used to seeing me stay up late to spy on them.

"Congratulations," she says. "You've woken Mattia."

I play my part well. My lips tremble and I blink to hold back sleep. I put all the tiredness in the world into my voice.

"Who's this? Why's he bothering you?"

"He's my brother," she replies. "He was just about to leave. Weren't you, Thomas?"

Thomas hesitates for a while before finally agreeing. As he throws Gabrielle one last look and walks around me to leave the room, I struggle to register the information. Her brother is a cop. *Her brother is a cop* . . . I run after him as he's about to disappear down the stairs.

"Was it you who burglarized us?" I ask, grabbing hold of his sleeve. "What were you looking for?"

He jerks his arm away.

"You must be confusing me with someone else."

He hurtles down the stairs. I rush to the window to watch him get in a car, start it, and set off in the direction of the town center. Nobody seemed to be waiting for him in the vehicle. His colleague hasn't come with him.

Gabrielle has sat down on the couch, her knees drawn up to her forehead. She's breathing hard, the way you do when recovering from a fit of anger. I stand in the doorway for a while, waiting to see if she wants to speak, but she's ignoring me now. She's withdrawn into herself and all I can do is respect her silence. I've been well trained.

16
SIHAM

S he says "hello" to every customer at the checkout. Her lips smile, but her eyes don't follow suit. The Christmas period is over, but now the sales are on. The store stays open late. She works until eight o'clock every weekday. She just has time to get back home between noon and two. The days seem endless . . .

But outside, this morning, at dawn, someone wrote JUSTICE FOR SAÏD on the windows of the police station for the second time this week. She saw it on her way to work. She passes the station every morning. Going the long way around to avoid it would take too much time. Every day the hate is still there, undying, unquestionable. It makes her feel better. She'd like to find the strength to get up every morning elsewhere, but for the moment that's what keeps her going.

An old man is looking for small change in his wallet. The customers get impatient. Nobody says anything. She says "hello" to the next customer, checks the items one by one, never seeing the end of the conveyor belt. She announces a total with a decimal point. When it's a round number, she tells herself that something unusual will happen. It's stupid but it works every time. Just a small event to break the routine. A shoplifter arguing with the security guard. A gang of kids testing the slipperiness of different brands of ketchup by sliding down the aisles, pursued by weary assistants.

She says "goodbye have a nice day." And "hello" to the next customer.

At noon, she finally gets a round number. She readies herself, and smiles at the man on his own who's placing his items on the conveyor belt. But her smile immediately fades.

She knows who he is, this forty-something guy with a suede jacket and rings under his eyes, she's seen him before. Everybody knew him over there in Les Verrières, before they demolished the high-rises. Sometimes he had a bright orange armband, sometimes not. He kept a low profile among his colleagues. He yelled less than most cops. Nobody mistrusted him.

The last time she saw him was in the dock in court, a strange twist of fate that didn't lead to the hoped-for outcome.

Their eyes meet. He smiles at her.

She doesn't smile back.

She scans the barcodes mechanically while he moves to the other side of the checkout. She looks down at the items. A pack of tagliatelle, some onions, a pot of crème fraîche, diced bacon. He's going to make himself pasta carbonara. *Pasta carbonara*, she repeats absurdly. She looks up again. He looks back at her, questioningly. He's realized that something isn't right. He doesn't know what. He hasn't recognized her.

An assistant is called to the stationery aisle.

"How much is that?" he asks after a few seconds.

"Eight euros 27."

He searches in his billfold. Inserts a credit card in the machine. Types in the four figures. Makes a mistake. Clears it. Types it in again, cursing. He's clearly nervous.

"I'm always forgetting my PIN," he says by way of apology in a cheerful but absolutely unnatural voice, the voice of a citizen attempting to start a conversation with his peers.

She looks at him. He stops laughing when he sees her expression. She hands him the receipt.

"Thank you, have a nice day."

"You, too, good luck."

She doesn't repeat "thank you" as she usually does. She twists her neck to watch him leave the store. He disappears into the parking lot.

His name is Thomas Ross. He's a cop. One day, a long time ago, he killed Saïd Zahidi near the community center. He's free but he was transferred. He couldn't keep working in this town after the riots that followed the murder and the acquittal. He was moved away for his own safety.

And yet here he is.

She types a quick text on her cell phone, bending low to hide from the security camera aimed at her. Then Siham Zahidi turns, smiles, and says "hello" to the next customer.

17

Zé has started to look for a new apartment.

He says he wants a change of scenery, we've been living here for four years and he needs to move. But I know it's because of the visit from Gabrielle's brother. When he got home from work they shut themselves in there, talking in such low voices that I couldn't understand their whispering even with the sound amplifier. That same evening he told me we were moving.

He's afraid for her. He's afraid the cop will send her to Charcot because he has the power to do so. Maybe he's afraid for himself, too. Afraid of the guy's threats. His original idea was to move to another town, but Gabrielle and I strongly objected.

As with our current apartment, the lease will be in Zé's name only. Gabrielle's name won't appear on the letterbox. She has her mail sent to an organization that finds accommodation for the homeless. She hasn't had an official address in years. Not because she's on the run, but to put her family off the scent and stop them from sending her back to Charcot. They've done it before. Zé says he won't allow her back there even if he has to cut off his own arm to get her out.

* * *

And you both remember how it was behind the high walls. No lobotomies, no electric shock treatment, no straitjackets, but the brace, the therapies, above all else the confinement.

You hadn't come of your own free will. And suddenly your body no longer belonged to you. Worse, your own emotions had been torn from you, stuffed willy-nilly into the mixer of clinical psychopathology, and had become unrecognizable to you, forced down your throats with a funnel as the interviews progressed, fifteen minutes a week with your respective psychiatrists.

Everything you said they interpreted through a frame of reference you knew nothing about. They sized you up with a look, pleased with their own analytical skills, they thought they understood you from those few minutes a week when you said what you had to say in order to get out.

The painfully slow days spent waiting for something to happen, punctuated by the comings and goings of the nurses. The days spent listening to footsteps in the corridor, people crying out or falling silent. The hope of a visit that didn't come, or only rarely. The meals. The pills. A colorful cocktail that a nurse brought you three times a day.

They watched you to make sure you swallowed everything they gave you. Everything they told you. They kept precise records of when you progressed, when you regressed, when you plateaued.

Antidepressants. Anxiolytics. Antipsychotics. Mood stabilizers. Sleeping pills. A paradise for junkies. A drug cartel, but perfectly legal.

And every day, the paper cup with the pills. Once or twice at the beginning you protested, weary of the side effects, the shaking in your hands, the difficulties you had in expressing yourself or even thinking or feeling. Weary of their language, the same words repeated over and over, words like "readjust." One treatment ended only to be followed by another. So you refused to take them. And they would put you in the isolation room for days and days and days, give you your treatment intravenously, sometimes strapped to the bed but always for your own good, they tied you up very humanely.

They would talk to you about the patient-doctor contract, a contract you had never signed. Someone else had done it in your place. The family or the prefect, because, apparently, you were not capable of giving your "informed consent."

They were full of talk.

And after two weeks of isolation, spent pounding your fists on the walls and screaming to be let out, you did what everybody else did, you became docile. You accepted the treatments, the schedule, the locked doors and the security cameras, all the constraints.

Gradually, the treatments worked. A nameless fog in your head. After that, the idea of escaping or dying was a long way from your daily concerns. As long as you could drink a cup of coffee without spilling it on your pajamas.

Your family would come and say that you looked better. You weren't aggressive anymore. Or unhappy. Simple, you weren't much of yourself anymore. You were interchangeable with the other patients. And unrecognizable. And yet your nearest and dearest seemed to recognize you, which you thought was quite a feat, given that sometimes you didn't even recognize yourself in the mirror.

So you broke the mirror and they put you back in isolation. And so it went on, until they decided you could leave.

Free at last, but on borrowed time. Until the next breakdown and the next spell in hospital. Thanks to them, you were again ready to live in society. You were normal. Were you happy? Nobody cared about that. The important thing was to make you capable of living outside, no matter in what state. No matter if the world around you hadn't changed. They said it was up to you to adapt. They haven't yet invented antipsychotics that can modify reality.

The problem lay with you, not with the world. And you wondered how normal people managed to put up with the surrounding crap that caught you by the throat the minute you opened your eyes.

And now? Have you found the answer? Because I don't have it either. I'm part of the iceberg hidden below the tip.

* * *

Zé and his high-powered lawyer gather character testimonies intended to prove that he's capable of looking after a child. My brother and Nouria have fulfilled their roles to perfection, handing in reports full of imaginary praise. If they're to be believed, Zé is the ideal parent, halfway between a benevolent, protective father and a sympathetic and understanding big brother. It's complete bullshit. But if that's what they want to hear, that's what they'll get.

They arrive unannounced one Saturday, ten days before the hearing. It's six in the evening. Gabrielle and I are slouched in front of the TV while Zé is reciting poetry, all alone in his room. All three of us quite frankly look like zombies.

The doorbell makes me jump. I rush to the door and get up on tiptoe to see through the peephole Zé installed just after Gabrielle's brother's surprise visit. The man and woman waiting impatiently outside the door don't really look as if they're here for a friendly visit, nobody here has any friends anyway, so I easily guess who they are.

I zoom back to the living room. "Watch out, social services!"

Gabrielle is dressed as usual in a huge sweatshirt with the sleeves rolled up to the elbows. She rushes into the bedroom to warn Zé and put on more respectable clothes. When she comes back, she's wearing quite a chic-looking black sweater whose tight sleeves are effective at hiding her wrists. Zé splashes water on his face in the bathroom and inspects the two of us critically. He tucks a lock of hair back behind my ear and proclaims himself satisfied.

They ring again. Gabrielle quickly grabs a vase filled with

cigarette butts—the flowers died a long time ago, they're dry and black—and hides it behind the couch. She switches off the TV. I open my math textbook, we sit down side by side, and she bends over my book as if explaining the lesson. Zé takes a deep breath and opens the door.

They shake his hand after checking his identity, then walk into the living room where Gabrielle and I present a really touching family scene. All it needs to add the finishing touch is classical music. We look up simultaneously, pretending we're emerging from intense concentration, and both give the same smile.

"Hello," we say in unison.

"Hello."

They greet Gabrielle without asking who she is, then introduce themselves to me. She's a pediatric nurse and he's a social worker. They're here to "see how things are going with my foster family."

Gabrielle goes off to make dinner while Zé helps me with my homework. Fortunately, I've chosen math so he can easily cope. He gets caught up in the game, going so far as to explain Pythagoras's and Thales's theorems when all we have to do is draw a rectangular parallelepiped. My head is spinning but I don't let it show: the social services people are carefully following our every word.

It's the first time Zé has helped me with my homework, and I enjoy the experience even with the two intruders here. We should have a hearing more often. He is really good at explaining things. He could be a teacher. Although he wouldn't last two minutes in a classroom, he'd be back in Charcot in less time than it takes to sign his committal papers.

Meanwhile, Gabrielle, who never cooks, plays the role of substitute mother, confined to the kitchen. She even overdoes it, humming an old tune as she puts a pan in the oven. She's making pancakes instead of the usual frozen dishes or pasta with tomato sauce. I really think I'm going to start making regular anonymous phone calls to social services in order to be treated like a king every day.

At seven o'clock, we sit down to eat. Gabrielle invites the social workers to join us. Title of the documentary: "The Daily Life of a Dysfunctional Family." It could even make a good reality TV show. I imagine the pitch: "A poetry-loving murderer, a suicidal depressive, and a disturbed child try to live together despite their differences, but social services intervene. Will Zé, Gabrielle, and Mattia be able to play their parts well enough to avert the threat?"

For the first time in my life for as far back as I can remember, I'm present at a meal where people actually talk. I feel more and more as if I'm in a sitcom.

Zé: "How were things at school today?"

Me: "I scored a goal in soccer and got an A in English."

Zé: "Fantastic, keep up the good work."

Gabrielle: "Who wants jam on their pancakes?"

It's both funny and pathetic. We're like one of those perfect families you see in coffee commercials on TV, where everyone's happy and communicative and nobody yells at anybody else. Mom is the ideal housewife and Dad devotes time to his son even though he works hard all day.

Suddenly, I feel nauseous.

I've never known that kind of family. I don't even know if it exists outside American movies and advertising posters. But with all this playacting, I have the impression I'm betraying my own family, the one that imploded before I was born and spent years falling apart a little more every day, slowly, surely, methodically.

I think about my mother. I know she would hate to see this. So would Gina. But we don't have a choice. We can't tell them that in reality we never talk to each other. That Gabrielle spends her days gazing at the TV screen, trying to find another reason to stay. That every other day, Zé forgets to pick me up from school, lets me go to bed at three o'clock in the morning, and asks me to miss classes in order to make sure that Gabrielle isn't trying to kill herself. That a faceless entity tries to kill me at night if I get it into my head to sleep in the wrong position. That I spend my time eavesdropping on conversations and listening to the silence. And that, just maybe, it isn't as bad as it seems.

They wouldn't believe us. And maybe they'd be right. But they would decide that I'd be better off in another foster family, and there they'd be wrong.

So I grit my teeth and swallow down a mouthful of pancake with strawberry jam even though I want to throw up. And I smile, on top of everything else—I smile.

It works so well that by the time they leave, at ten, they have the reassured expressions of people who've done their job and haven't found anything.

Gabrielle puts her head around the door of my room. I pretend to sleep, just as Zé pretended to send me to bed.

"It's all right, they've gone."

I immediately get up. Zé opens a bottle of wine to celebrate the coming of the perfect family, and I'm allowed to watch cartoons until one o'clock in the morning while they do God knows what in their room.

* * *

Another dream tonight.

I'm alone in a park or a forest. As I walk, the snow crunches under my feet. I'm in a T-shirt but I don't feel cold. I look calmly around me. I know there's someone there, somewhere, but I can't see him. I hear breathing behind me. I turn. The rustle of fabric. A shadowy figure that immediately disappears. I continue on my way. I don't know where I'm going but that doesn't bother me.

Somebody says my name. *Mattia*, like a sigh. I turn right

around. Nobody there. It doesn't worry me. I keep going. Everywhere, trees around me. I walk. My hair falls in front of my eyes and I keep pushing it back but it still keeps falling.

Someone runs past, a few yards from me. All I recognize in the dim moonlight is her clothes. I cry out: *Gina!* I run. She's going too fast. I lose her. I find her again a little farther on. I keep on after her but never catch up with her. My throat is hoarse from saying her name.

I finally get to the end of the woods. A shadowy figure is waiting for me, its back up against a fir tree. I approach slowly for fear it'll run away, but it watches me coming. It isn't my sister. It's my mother. Something's wrong. Her eyes are staring at me but there's no feeling in them. Drawing level with her, I realize that she's tied to the tree and that there's a terrible wound in her neck. I don't need to take her pulse to know she is dead.

I scream.

Gina laughs somewhere in the distance.

* * *

I wake up bathed in sweat, unable to breathe. My lungs have turned to water inside my rib cage, which seems to weigh a ton. I can't move. Remembering Nouria's advice, I close my eyes and count to thirty. My one thought is not to see that thing sitting on me.

When I get to twenty-nine, I try to close my fist. My body obeys me again. On the verge of suffocating, I breathe in air. I risk opening my eyes. I'm alone in my room. Everything's fine. No monster, no shadowy figure has its eye on me, at least as far as I can see.

A hard object against my leg. I sit up. It's the ping-pong ball. Zé isn't very good at sewing. Apart from reading poetry and solving equations, he's not good at much of anything.

This time there's nobody in the living room. I try to settle in front of the TV, but I can't concentrate. The images from my dream keep coming back to me. After half an hour like this, exhausted, almost falling from lack of sleep, I get up again. I put on my jacket and a pair of shoes, take my keys, and go out.

It's the first time I've ever really walked completely alone at night in a deserted town. At least, the first time without an energy drink inside me. I stay close to the walls and avoid the main streets, because I don't want to end up in the police station. If Zé was forced to come and get me once again, I think he'd tell the family judge that he'd be happy to give up custody of me to anybody who wanted me, in other words, nobody.

Dammit, I really can't wait to be eighteen and no longer subject to the whims of grown-ups!

Just as I'm having this thought, a police car turns onto the street, about thirty feet away. I jump into a doorway that casts a shadow on the asphalt. I hold my breath, but they drive past without slowing down.

"Are you hiding, too?" says an amused voice behind me.

I almost have a heart attack. Except that I don't, I just give a perfectly ridiculous little yelp of fright. In a flash, all those news items about missing children in the last five years come back into my mind. I see my body hurriedly buried under some bridge or other while my hands and my head are thrown in a river to make identification difficult.

Summoning all my courage, I turn and find myself face to face with two guys my sister's age. Their faces are hidden under hoods and I can't quite make them out. One of them is carrying a backpack that emits a metallic noise as he moves. He's looking at me. The other one is standing on tiptoe, watching the cops disappear at the other end of the street.

"You're not Gina's brother, are you?" the guy with the backpack asks.

Thrown, I tell him I am and shake the hand he holds out, while the other guy turns to look at me.

. "Are you from Les Verrières?" I ask, just to make them forget my initial reaction.

"I was. Don't you remember me? I was always at your mother's place."

"Karim?" I venture.

He confirms this with a smile. Of course I remember him. I think he used to go out with Gina. I'm not sure, because she didn't confide in me, but anyway they spent a lot of time together before she left.

"Shit, you have a good memory," Karim says. "How old were you the last time we met, six?"

His friend interrupts him. "We have to go."

"Just a second. Why are you hiding, are you in trouble?"

"No," I say very quickly. "I'm just afraid of being picked up. They don't like kids who walk around on their own. What about you?"

He shakes his head.

"We have to go. They're still driving around, so watch your back. See you later."

"'Bye."

They walk off in the same direction as the cops. I watch them going, my head filled with questions. I should have asked them if they'd heard from my sister. Then I feel a dampness in my right hand and look down. My heart skips a beat when I see the red stuff that's there. I'm not bleeding: it must have come from Karim when we shook hands. For a second or two, I imagine all the possible scenarios, before realizing that it's just red paint.

I smile to myself in the dark, and resume walking. A few minutes later, as I turn a corner, on a white wall, I see brand-new graffiti: JUSTICE FOR SAÏD.

It isn't much. But as Youcef would say, it's still better than not doing anything at all.

* * *

Flights and flights of steps. By the time I get to the top, my calves are killing me. I guess you have to make an effort to get to paradise, or at least to what comes closest to paradise in this world. Most of the villas in La Solaire have movement detectors that light up as I approach. But I keep moving forward in this neighborhood that's lit up as if it's broad daylight, and I have the impression I'm walking in a parallel universe.

I press the button on the videophone. A window lights up inside.

A face appears, then my brother's tired voice echoes in the loudspeaker:

"Mattia, are you crazy or what?"

"I'm sorry to wake you."

"Don't stand outside, come in."

Stefano looks more worried than angry when I join him halfway to his house. He takes me by the hand in an absurd protective reflex, given our relationship, and doesn't ask me any questions until he's dragged me into the kitchen, where he makes himself an espresso. He's in his pajamas. He rubs his eyes for a long time before putting on his glasses. He sits down opposite me.

"Want an orange juice?"

"Sure."

He pours me some juice, rubs his eyes again, and heaves a deep sigh.

"I'm sorry I woke you," I repeat.

"It doesn't matter. I'd have been getting up quite soon anyway. What's up?"

I open my mouth but I can't speak. I'm not in the habit of confiding in anybody, especially not this son of a bitch who's never had anything to do with me. And I see again Mom's apartment and our apartment, turned upside down with the same meticulousness. Zé and Gabrielle's muttered conversations. The graffiti appearing everywhere in town. Gina, who's vanished into thin air. The thing that stops me breathing, and the dreams.

I start crying. All at once, without any warning, I break down and burst into tears. In a last burst of dignity, I hide my face in my hands, I wipe the snot running from my nostrils and try to pull myself together, but my shoulders are shaken by the force of my tears and I have the impression that everything is coming out in one go—everything, Dad's death, the tip of the iceberg, Mom refusing to live with me, Gabrielle's suicide attempts, Zé's indifference, Gina's constant escaping, school, all the shit around and inside me, everything.

I fold my arms on the table and bury my head in them, bent beneath the weight of my failure. I don't know how much time has gone by when my brother places a hesitant hand on my head.

"Mattia . . . What's going on?"

His surprise is audible. He's never seen me cry like this, not even when I was very small. I was born in a context where tears were superfluous. You can't allow yourself to blubber like this when you can sense that everyone around you is on the edge of an abyss, ready to topple over at the slightest inattention. A wire stretched above the precipice, as Gabrielle said . . .

* * *

And you move forward, a puppet of yourself, of your nearest and dearest, of your world, you move forward one step at a time, always very upright, you can't support anybody because you have to hold out your arms to balance yourself, there are lots of people behind you, in front of you, you can't slow down or speed up, it's the whole of mankind moving forward on this wire and the slightest false move could be fatal, to you, but also to those in front of you and those behind you, that's the big dilemma.

* * *

I calm down after a very long time. Stefano is standing next to me, arms dangling, not sure how to act. I wipe my tears. I smile.

"It's passed."

"Great, maybe now you can tell me what you're doing here at five in the morning."

It's true. I drink a gulp of orange juice. He sits down again opposite me, all ears, chin between his palms, aware how serious I am, he hasn't touched his coffee, he listens.

I tell him. The burglaries. Mom missing and nobody giving a damn. The cops tailing us. Evrything that stops me breathing at night because it weighs too much and there are too many secrets, too many silences that grow heavier every day.

His expression doesn't change while I'm telling him all this. He's like Mom, imperturbable. At the end he knocks back his cold coffee in one go. The sun is rising. Zé will be home soon.

"To start with, you're going to call your guardian and tell him where you are."

"No. I want you to explain."

We look at each other. He must sense my determination because he's the one who gives in.

"Okay," he says. "But don't expect any incredible revelations or any sordid family secrets, because I don't know much about this business."

I nod. He thinks for a moment before he starts speaking again. His long surgeon's fingers tap an unknown rhythm on the wood. He stares at a point somewhere over my shoulder, like my father in Charcot.

"I was deep into my studies at the time, so I don't know

everything. And you know Mom. She never shared anything with us. But this isn't the first time she's been burglarized, or the first time I've heard about the police tailing us."

I encourage him to continue, drinking a little orange juice to occupy my hands. A ray of sunshine filters shyly into the kitchen.

"When that teenager was killed . . ."

"Saïd."

"Saïd, yes. The Internal Affairs section of the police investigated in the neighborhood, looking for witnesses. But nobody had seen what happened except for the colleagues of the cop responsible for the killing, which allowed them to claim it was self-defense. And to get him acquitted."

* * *

GINA. Saïd had hash on him when the police stopped him. They said he refused to allow them to search him, that they had to immobilize him by force, but without putting handcuffs on him. And when they found the bars he tried to run away. It was a guy named Ross who caught up with him. Saïd struggled "like a maniac" and he was "obliged to use force." And the blows didn't affect Saïd, as if he was numb. He kept hitting him. It was four against one, but that wasn't sufficient apparently, because this cop smashed his skull to calm him down.

Apparently he was trying to hit his shoulder and missed his target because Saïd was moving too much. It's funny, this tendency they have always to strike where they can kill by mistake. Especially as the postmortem confirmed that there had been several blows.

It also determined that Saïd was "under the influence of THC" when he died, which according to them, would explain the fact that he struggled until he was killed.

Apparently neither the judge nor the jurors had ever smoked even one joint because they all believed this bullshit.
And you still ask me why I left?

* * *

"But your father," Stefano says, "your father must have witnessed something."

It happened very close to the community center, around eight in the evening. According to the investigation, Dad was inside when it happened. He said he saw nothing.

I shake my head.

"It's not possible. He loved Saïd and would never have let anyone get killed without stepping in."

"How do you know? You hardly knew him."

"You always hated my father."

Much to my surprise, he agrees.

"Mom left my father for him, and he never really recovered from the breakup. I had good reasons to hate him. I was young. But I'm not saying he was a bad man. I never made the effort to get to know him."

"So what makes you say he might have seen what happened?"

"I don't know what he saw or didn't see. What's certain is that the police thought he knew something. Sometime after the death of Saïd Zahidi, our door was forced open and the whole apartment thoroughly searched. Nobody wanted to report it. They said it was pointless. As if they already knew why they'd broken in and what they were looking for."

"The cops . . ."

Stefano shrugs his shoulders. "It's quite likely. Later, Mom said that a weird guy had followed her all day and your father said that he'd been tailed ever since the murder. He was summoned to the police station several times, but I don't know what they wanted from him."

I wait for a moment or two, but it seems like this is the end of the story. He falls silent as if everything has been said. A cold anger makes my jaws tense. I massage my temples with my fingertips. I'm tired.

"Why hasn't anybody ever told me this?"

"You weren't even born yet. And the case was settled a long time ago."

"It isn't settled. The cop is free."

"It's settled from a legal point of view. And that's all that matters. Don't look at me like that. I didn't say it was right. I'm just stating a fact."

I've stopped listening to him. I remember Gina's words that I overheard in the kitchen. *If it ever starts again . . .* It's all this that she was referring to, these events that happened before I was born and that nobody deigned to tell me about. Dammit, it's part of my history. After all, it's because of all this shit that my father hanged himself.

Being followed into the library. She wasn't surprised because she'd already experienced that. And Zé? He swore to me he didn't know anything about these guys. Has he also known everything from the start?

"Did you ever talk about this with Dad or Mom?" I ask, overcoming my anger.

"No. I didn't want anything to do with it."

"It happened virtually outside your door. A kid died, cops broke into your apartment and turned everything upside down, they followed your mother on the street, and you weren't curious enough to ask?"

He gives a strange laugh.

"From the moment he was killed and your father went crazy, I didn't exist anymore as far as Mom was concerned. Not me, not Gina. Only your father mattered. She was completely devoted to helping him get back on his feet, and you know the result. I blamed both of them. I was a teenager. I had my problems, too, but the only thing that mattered was that damned trial, and that kid who wasn't even theirs. You can't imagine the atmosphere at home at the time. I felt as if Saïd Zahidi, or his ghost, was sitting down with us every evening for dinner. He was always there. I didn't want to hear about him anymore. That was their story. Not mine."

He falls silent before he says too much. I look away. So does he. I could tell him that I can imagine it very well, because I've experienced exactly the same thing, except that I didn't have the luxury of being able to withdraw into myself and pretend that none of this existed.

It wouldn't get us anywhere if I said that.

"I don't want to be dragged back into all that, Mattia. It's in the past. I'm going to call Zé and tell him where you are before he calls the police."

"But it's starting again," I protest as he heads toward the telephone. "How can you say it's over?"

"Talk about it with Gina, with Mom, or with your guardian. I can't help you any more than I have."

As if he'd ever helped me even once in our lives. I give up, a bitter taste in my throat, and he looks up the number of our landline in an address book. He doesn't even ask me directly, as if he didn't trust me.

18

So, to sum it all up.

Saïd gets himself killed near the community center. My father is there at the time. When he's questioned by Internal Affairs, he denies having seen anything. Instead of a search, he's burglarized. I don't think those are the methods of Internal Affairs. Especially since it's starting again thirteen years after the events and the people following us are cops. They were looking for something. Could it be that they were afraid my father wrote down what he saw, something that didn't tally with their statement?

But I find it hard to believe that Dad could have witnessed the scene without stepping in, or without coming forward as a witness, knowing that the acquittal of the murderer sent him to Charcot.

Fifteen years later, my mother disappears. Her apartment is burglarized. Ours, too, and some cops try to find out Zé's address. And one of the cops is Gabrielle's brother. If it hadn't been for that unauthorized search, I would have thought it was directly connected to her, but in light of my brother's story, I think that's pure coincidence.

Last but not least, some former inhabitants of Les Verrières are restless again, reintroducing the graffiti that covered the whole town at the time of Saïd's death. There has to be a connection between the fact that both they and the police have reappeared at the same time.

The question is: Why now? Why keep searching even

though Dad is dead? Even though the trial ended without the Zahidi family trying to appeal, knowing perfectly well that they wouldn't win the case?

"Are you listening to what I'm saying?"

"No," I say.

Back to reality. I'm in the car with Zé, who came to get me from my brother's. Stefano called him a few minutes after Zé got back from work. He didn't have time to panic but claims he had the fright of his life, and he's been yelling at me for ten minutes as we drive to the apartment. He's been smoking one cigarette after another just to demonstrate his anger.

"Going out alone, barely dressed, at four o'clock in the morning when we're seeing the judge next week! What would have happened if the police had picked you up? Shit, if you want me to lose custody, then tell me straight out, it'll avoid a lot of paperwork!"

I don't reply. Stefano's words are going around and around in my head. I'm like a detective in a book, I'm trying to put all the clues together, but not everybody can do that, and I don't understand what's going on.

"What the hell were you doing at your brother's? I thought you couldn't stand him."

I shrug my shoulders. I'm annoyed. With him, Gabrielle, Gina, everyone who knew and didn't say anything. But I have school in an hour and I'm too exhausted to settle scores. I'll talk about it tonight if I can summon up the courage. As soon as I open my mouth, the only things that come into my mind are insults.

And when we arrive, just to make this perfect night even better, there they are.

Who are they? Them. They've been quicker than we thought and Zé's mouth opens wide as he slams on the brakes. An ambulance is parked outside the building. It bears the logo of Charcot Hospital. With it is a police car.

"Gabrielle," he whispers.

He literally leaps out of the car and rushes into the lobby. I hurry to catch up with him, immediately forgetting that I hate him for lying to me, and we climb the stairs separating us from the apartment four steps at a time. There they are, in the corridor, two uniformed cops, a man in a white coat, and another man in everyday clothes. They're waiting outside the door. The only one not wearing a uniform is practically glued to the lock, and I guess that he's talking to Gabrielle through the wall.

Our stampede doesn't pass unnoticed. Everyone swivels to look at us, except for the guy talking to the door. Fearlessly, Zé walks straight up to them.

"What are you doing?"

"Are you Monsieur Palaisot?" the man in the white coat asks.

"Yes. What's this about?"

They exchange embarrassed glances. The man who's been talking to Gabrielle takes it upon himself to bring him up to date.

"We've been explaining to Mademoiselle Gabrielle Ross that her psychiatric state necessitates hospitalization, but she doesn't seem to accept that."

"What do you know about it?" he almost yells. "You haven't even spoken to her!"

"I'd be happy to do that if she'd agree to open the door. But we have a request from a third party and the opinions of two psychiatrists who observed her during her last hospitalization, after a suicide attempt."

For the first time since I've known him, Zé rises to his full height. He's very tall when he wants to be and the doctor doesn't seem too self-assured, but the two cops are approaching surreptitiously.

I see the disaster coming: Gabrielle in Charcot, Zé in prison, me in an institution.

"A request from a third party," he echoes.

"Yes."

"Her brother. You're making a really big mistake."

His voice is trembling even though he's speaking very softly. One of the cops has his hand on the grip of his gun and I suddenly freak out, thinking again about Saïd lying with a fractured skull at the foot of the high-rises, his face in red on all the walls, that word that no longer means anything if it ever did mean anything, "justice," and I'm afraid it'll happen to Zé.

"They can't bear the fact that she's chosen to break off with her family," he continues. "He hasn't seen her in years, except once when he forced his way in. But I live with her and I—"

"And you really didn't enjoy your own stay in Charcot," the psychiatrist says without lowering his eyes. "But Mademoiselle Ross has twice tried to kill herself in the last four months. We don't need her brother's opinion to consider that her condition requires medical supervision. So I beg you not to oppose her hospitalization. Don't make things more complicated than they already are."

Zé looks at him despondently, and I realize, at the same time as he does, that his words are worth nothing in the eyes of these people—or in anybody's eyes. A potential murderer. A former patient of Charcot. Theoretically cured but capable at any moment of having another crisis. He doesn't have a say in the matter. His distrust of psychiatric hospitals can only be explained by his being a former inmate. It's pointless listening to his recriminations. They're just paranoia.

The cops leap into the breech and position themselves on either side of Zé.

"You may be able to persuade Mademoiselle Ross to open the door," the psychiatrist says.

"Go fuck yourself."

The doctor takes a step back, creating a space immediately monopolized by the cops, who form a human barricade between them. The nurse and the psychiatrist turn back to the door.

"Mademoiselle Ross, please open up, so that we can talk."

"I'm not going to that place," Gabrielle's voice replies, barely muted by the wafer-thin walls.

"Please. I'm Dr. Amaris, do you remember me?"

"I'M NOT GOING TO THAT PLACE!"

She's screamed in a child's voice. I move away. I have no desire to watch this because I know that nobody can stop it, not me, not Zé. I turn to the stairs, wanting to put my fingers in my ears and close my eyes, and open them again to another reality where nobody wants to die because life is so amazing—and where nobody can force you to live. Right now, that strikes me as being crueler than killing someone.

"The child," the psychiatrist says.

A few seconds later, the nurse takes me by the hand and beckons me to come downstairs with him. I don't resist. Together, in the most measured silence, we walk down the flights of stairs that separate us from the open air. He takes me to the ambulance. He, too, seems relieved to have escaped the scene. I wonder if he disapproves. If he's one of those countless people who obey the prerogatives of their work without questioning them in spite of any disgust they might feel.

He smiles at me.

"Do you want to see what an ambulance is like?"

I stare at him until he lowers his eyes.

"No."

He tells me his name and asks me for mine, which I give him the way you'd throw a dog a bone. I hate him, even though I know it's not really his fault. So we stay there, silent, by the curb, watching the town wake up, the workers set off for their work, the school children for school, each person in his place, each on his wire, and for all of us, the abyss.

I'd like to tell him about Gabrielle. What little I know of

her. Tell him about her silences, her gestures, her expressions, her intonations, her breathing, how she is today so that he'll be able to compare her with how she will be tomorrow, when the drugs have done their work.

* * *

GINA. *It's true that something had to be done.*

Dad was becoming increasingly strange. There were times when he wasn't interested in anything, and others when he paid attention to the smallest details. He started being unable to bear certain colors, patterns, or materials. Once, I put on a pair of green pants, and he slapped me, even though he had never hit me before.

He would say things that made no sense at all. He became paranoid. He thought he was being followed on the street. Mom and I took turns going out after him, and we could see there was nobody. He said they'd put microphones and cameras in the apartment. That they were watching us all the time. He could never say who "they" were. By the end, he believed they were talking to him in his sleep, talking directly into his brain with the help of a microchip.

Mom was tired, and so was I. It was too hard to handle. After a few months like this, he went to emergency for food poisoning. The doctors thought he was strange. They sent for my mother. They asked her to sign his committal. She thought about it, she asked if he wanted to go there, he agreed and so did she.

We didn't know what else to do. It was driving us both crazy. I think we could already see ourselves having to be nurses for life, and we couldn't do it.

They put him in Charcot, in the secure section, Les Orchidées. At first, he wasn't allowed visitors. By the time we were able to see him, he had changed. He'd stopped saying those crazy things, but now he didn't say much at all. He didn't seem to feel much either.

Mom spoke to his psychiatrist. He told her it was normal, that it was important to find the right dosage, but it always took time. So we waited. And waited. And waited. Until he hanged himself.

With hindsight, I still don't know what we could have done. I think his suicide was inevitable. But we let him go because we couldn't stand it anymore, and it should have been different. We had nothing else to suggest. That's what we should have changed . . .

That's how things work, Mattia. Justice for the judges. Violence for the cops. Health for the doctors. The mad in asylums, and don't even think of claiming a place that isn't yours.

* * *

And they bring Gabrielle out.

She isn't struggling. She's walking by herself. The cops by her side, the psychiatrist in front, Zé behind. They lead her to the ambulance while Zé looks on, powerless to intervene. The nurse attempts an encouraging smile to which I don't respond. He leaves me and gets into the ambulance after the psychiatrist and Gabrielle. She waves goodbye at me. Her smile is meant to be confident, but I'm not fooled.

Standing next to the vehicle, the cops on either side of him in case he attempts a last-minute escape, Zé calls out:

"Don't worry, we'll get you out of that shithole!"

She nods. The doors slam shut. The seriousness of the situation is so tangible that I feel as if I'm witnessing a final farewell.

The ambulance sets off in the direction of Charcot. I join Zé as he watches them go, his face totally inscrutable. The cops are still there. One of them lingers beside us and says to Zé:

"Is this child Mademoiselle Ross's son? Are you able to take care of him?"

"Since when have the police become social workers?" Zé growls at him. Then, fearing a likely insult, he adds, "He's my ward. And I'm perfectly capable of taking care of him, thank you."

The cop looks at the two of us in turn, not very convinced thanks to Zé's youth and especially his psychiatric record, which the doctor mentioned earlier with a certain disregard for medical confidentiality. Zé lights a cigarette. He takes me by the hand—to pull the wool over the cops' eyes?—and drags me to the car: it's time for school.

"Monsieur Palaisot," the cop calls out behind us.

"We already have a hearing lined up with the family judge," Zé retorts without turning around. "Your pals got here before you did, thank you very much."

I look up at our building as he starts the car. Lots of neighbors are at their windows, wreathed in an ordinary silence. Right now, I hate them, too.

W hat are you laughing at, you little scumbag?"
Karim is sitting handcuffed on a chair in a narrow,
closed office in the police station. He's been held
for questioning for fifteen hours now. This isn't his first arrest.
He's used to these little games. He isn't afraid anymore—not
really.

The cop opposite him has a head like a bull and a khaki
jacket. He's aggressive, provocative, he keeps pushing the
boundaries. It's always the same conversation. The same one-
way dialogue. The same protocol.

"Your ugly mug, asshole," Karim replies.

The slap makes his head swivel. It isn't the first and it certainly won't be the last. ·

They were picked up at dawn, just as they were getting
ready to go home after another night spent spray-painting public places. Saïd's face in close-up on all the government buildings, that really sticks out. Zahidi is a forbidden name here, an
unhealed wound, both in Les Verrières and at the police station. Several patrols just to arrest two young guys painting
graffiti. That's really what makes him laugh. Not them.

The Bull leans over him until their noses touch. Karim
doesn't bat an eyelid.

"What's your pal's name?"

They went their separate ways when the cops chased after
them. It was Karim they chose to follow. He was carrying the
bag with the spray cans.

"Sébastien Meunier," Karim says.

"Your pal's name!"

"Sébastien Meunier! Why should I lie to you? Oh, I see. You assume he's an Arab. Think again. I have French friends."

"We saw his face and he didn't look like a Sébastien."

"Are you putting that in the statement? The Human Rights League will love it."

"Shut up!"

"Okay."

Karim isn't too worried. It's just graffiti, they won't take it very far. Community service at the very most. He doesn't have a criminal record. A few arrests, but always for trivial things.

Bull Head asks him the question again several times. Karim keeps to his vow of silence and the cop finally sends him back to his cell.

They drag him out again after a few hours. Instinctively, he glances at the clock in the corridor. He's been here for twenty hours. Only four to go. Or twenty-eight if the prosecutor decides to extend it. It's a long time, but it's bearable.

He remains standing in the office until the Bull tells him to sit down. The cop types on the keyboard of a computer, then prints out a sheet of paper, which he shows to Karim.

"Sign the statement and you can go."

Karim can't quite believe it. He stares at him. Then he reads the statement, which is in very small print. He smiles and sits back in his chair.

"I'm not signing that."

"I beg your pardon?" the cop says.

"I'm not signing it. I never said what's written here."

The Bull has recorded his words accurately, with one exception: he's said to have uttered death threats against the officer responsible for the death of Saïd. *"We're going to find that dickhead and cut his throat."*

"For a start, I never use the word 'dickhead.' And then I

don't cut people's throats. Only sheep. Preferably in the bath-tub, or the blood goes everywhere."

The Bull stares at him. For a long time. To force him to lower his eyes. Another game. Karim won't play ball.

"Are you going to sign?"

"No."

"Do you want to be here for another twenty-four hours?"

"I'll sign if you take away this crap I never said."

Another slap. Another eyeball-to-eyeball confrontation.

"So you're not going to sign it?"

"No."

Back to the cells.

Karim waits. They bring him pasta in tomato sauce. The pasta and the sauce are both cold. It's disgusting, but he eats it all the same. Any distraction is welcome. He's all alone in his cell.

After four hours, a uniformed cop takes him to the same office. The Bull is still alone. Karim sits down obediently. A paper is lying on the desk. He rereads the statement, then looks up.

"I'm still not signing it."

"It's up to you."

He takes back the paper. Karim waits without expressing any impatience. Double or quits. Either he goes or he stays one day more.

The cop gets up, comes around to the front of the desk, and sits on it, legs dangling in the air, very close to Karim. They look at each other for a moment, then the Bull grabs him by the neck of his T-shirt.

"I know what you're planning, you and your pals. Don't you think it's a little late to take your revenge? Listen carefully. You may not have signed, but I have three colleagues who can testify you threatened that cop. So if anything happens, any-thing at all, you're the one we'll come for."

"What kind of thing?" Karim protests. "It's just graffiti."

"That's what it is, is it? Just graffiti." He lets go of Karim. "You can leave, but this isn't the end of it. You'll receive a summons to court for damage to property and death threats. In the meantime we don't want to see any more graffiti mentioning Saïd Zahidi, because again you're the one we'll come looking for. Pass the message on to your pal."

"You think there are just two of us in this?" Karim retorts as the cop takes him back down to the cells to collect his things. "There are plenty of people who remember him and what you did to him. Even a judge will believe me. There's lots of different handwriting."

"Go ahead, then, test your luck," the cop says by way of farewell.

Karim blinks in the daylight as he comes out onto the forecourt of the police station. He hails a passing woman who's smoking and bums a cigarette from her. It's his first in twenty-four hours, so he really savors it. He's in a hurry to get away, but then slows down when he sees a car parked a few yards from the police station. He shakes his head at the driver, a woman, who responds with the same signal. They meet up in the next street.

"How are you?" Siham asks as he gets in next to her.

"I'm fine, but you wouldn't believe how seriously they're taking this."

"What did they pin on you?"

"Damage and death threats, and I'm going to be summoned to court, but I didn't sign anything."

He sighs and rubs his forehead. He needs a shower, a decent meal, and a good sleep.

"Did you see Ross?" Siham asks.

"No. Are you sure he's still in town?"

"No."

Karim heaves a deep sigh. He looks at Siham. The car has

stopped at a red light, and she's staring out at the street. She's inscrutable.

"Siham."

"Yes."

"I don't know how far this is going to go. The cops aren't messing around."

"Of course they aren't. They have every reason in the world not to fool around."

"So what do we do now?"

20

. . . Des empires détruits je méditai la cendre:
Dans ses sacrés tombeaux Rome m'a vu descendre;
Des mânes les plus saints troublant le froid repos,
J'ai pesé dans mes mains la cendre des héros."[5]

L'Homme, by Lamartine.

It's after midnight. Lying in my makeshift tent in the toy aisle, eyes wide open, I listen to Zé reciting poems that others have created. His voice soothes me. It's warm, calm, serene. It's reassuring, even if Lamartine won't solve our problems for us.

It's Friday evening. Gabrielle has been in Charcot for two days. She isn't allowed visitors yet. Zé calls every day to ask how she is, but they won't tell him anything because he isn't family. She isn't allowed to make phone calls either.

The weekend arrives as a liberation. I sink into a bottomless pit when I think about the years of school I still have to endure. I can't see any farther than sixteen, the legal age for stopping my studies. There's no way I could continue beyond that point. And if Zé tries to dissuade me—provided he's allowed to continue as my guardian—he won't be able to offer a convincing

---

[5] I pondered the ashes of ruined empires:/Rome saw me descend into her sacred tombs;/ Disturbing the repose of the holiest shades,/I weighed the ashes of heroes in my hands.

argument. Because he stopped. And if he'd stopped earlier, he wouldn't have ended up in Charcot.

And we would never have met.

"... *J'allais redemander à leur vaine poussière*
Cette immortalité que tout mortel espère!
Que dis-je? suspendu sur le lit des mourants,
Mes regards la cherchaient dans des yeux expirants . . ."[6]

His voice has come closer. He puts his head inside the tent and smiles at me.

"Can't you sleep?"

"No. Keep reciting, it's great."

But he bends almost to the ground to get into the tent, and sits down cross-legged on the blankets. He scratches his head several times, a sign that he's embarrassed. I raise myself onto my elbows, sensing that something is going to happen.

"I spoke to your brother this afternoon. I asked him what you were doing there."

Silence.

"He told me you asked him lots of questions about what happened at the time of Saïd Zahidi's death."

Silence.

"And that he told you the truth."

"Unlike you."

He looks at me with big innocent eyes. "I never lied to you."

"No. Grown-ups never lie to children, it's a well-known fact. When I asked you what they wanted, you swore to me you had no idea."

---

[6] I was about to ask their vain dust once again/For that immortality for which all mortals hope!/What am I saying? hovering over the beds of the dying,/My gaze was seeking it in eyes that expired.

"And it's true," he insists.

I look at him closely. There's a sincerity in his voice that I find hard to question. Because he's right. So far he's always told me the truth.

"I hid some things from you," he admits. "But I would have told you the truth if you'd asked me."

"Great. How would I have known it had happened?"

"It wouldn't have gotten you very far if you had known. So listen."

He lies down next to me, his chin in the palms of his hands.

"Your father told me about those cops following him when we were together in the hospital, but he had a tendency to babble away, and I thought it was paranoia. He may have confided some very important things in me and I didn't even realize. It was your mother, later, who told me the story. But I don't know any more about it than your brother does. The cops thought your father was in possession of items that contradicted their version of events. They were afraid these items would end up in the hands of Internal Affairs, that was the reason for the burglaries. And clearly something has happened that's revived that fear. They must think this evidence or whatever it is survived your father. That he passed it on to someone he knew. Your mother. Or me, since we shared the same room and I inherited custody of you."

He heaves a deep sigh. He sticks a cigarette in his mouth, looks at me, and changes his mind. In the tent, the smoke would suffocate us. He slips the cigarette behind his ear.

"And did he?" I ask, since he seems ready to tell the truth if I question him.

"No. I have no idea what it is. In my opinion, Amélia is the only person who knows."

"And she's disappeared."

"Yes."

Silence. I'm suddenly tired. I blink my eyes to stop myself

from falling asleep. It isn't every day he gets the itch to talk like this. He turns over onto his back, folds his arms behind his neck, almost lights his cigarette, and stops at the last moment, cursing under his breath.

"Do you think they've killed her?"

"What?"

"The cops. Do you think they've killed my mother?"

He immediately kneels to face me, looking incredibly serious.

"Mattia. Look me in the eyes."

I do as he says.

"Of course not. She's alive. I'm sure she decided to get away after the burglary. She must have felt threatened. The cops don't kill people just like that."

"They killed Saïd just like that."

"I mean they don't kill in cold blood, at least not for something as dumb as that. That kid's death happened a long time ago, and there was a trial. It's too late for an appeal, because of the statute of limitations. The cop can't be tried again, whatever happens. Even if there was evidence that it didn't happen the way he said."

"So why are they still searching for it?"

"Maybe they're afraid there'll be unrest if this evidence falls into the hands of the media."

Another long silence. I stare at the sheets that hide me from the security cameras. I wonder how he can stand being constantly filmed when he's at work. I guess after a while he doesn't even see the cameras anymore.

"Your mother will come back. Or else she'll find a way to let us know how she is. In the meantime, sleep. It's late."

I agree to this. He strokes my hair to bid me good night and resumes his round. I close my eyes, listening to him recite the next part of the poem.

"J'aimais à m'enfoncer dans ces sombres horreurs.
Mais en vain dans son calme, en vain dans ses fureurs,
Cherchant ce grand secret sans pouvoir le surprendre,
J'ai vu partout un Dieu sans pouvoir le comprendre!"[7]

He's sewed the ping-pong ball back on my pajamas to stop the thing from bothering me again. But I have the feeling that the suffocation in my chest is permanent now, even if I don't sleep and don't have hallucinations.

* * *

The family judge looks like Father Christmas. He's old and stunted, with a white beard and round red cheeks—he looks like a Coca-Cola ad. He seems a lot nicer than Zé's parents, a lot less austere.

He sees us one after the other in a ridiculously small office in the county court. Our lawyer has also come. He has two testimonies: my brother's and Nouria's. Against us, the police report and statements from the doctor and from my teacher, who's of the opinion that Zé is a bad influence on me. I wait patiently on a red bench in the vast lobby of the courthouse. There's a lot to see. It's fifteen feet from floor to ceiling, giving the building an effect of carefully calculated grandeur. There are lots of statuettes depicting justice, plinths with Mariannes, and grandiloquent quotations about duties and rights.

Imitation marble staircases lead up to the other floors. The banisters are translucent, as if to impart a notion of transparency to those who climb them. But if you do climb those

---

[7] I loved to sink into these somber horrors./But in vain in his calm, in vain in his rages,/Seeking this great secret but unable to find it,/I everywhere saw a God but was unable to understand him.

stairs, you're already in deep shit, and in my humble opinion the statues, the quotations, and the Mariannes won't do much for you.

For a while, I watch the comings and goings of the judges, the lawyers, the guilty, the victims, their nearest and dearest, the employees of the court, and all the others. This place is a world apart, a self-sufficient organism like a hospital, but I hope I never have occasion to penetrate its workings. I look at the doors leading to the courtrooms. Was it here that Saïd's murderer was acquitted?

"Mattia?"

I look up in surprise. The female voice is coming from the hot drinks dispenser next to the toilets, a few yards away. A woman of about twenty-five, in jeans and a black coat, cooling her heels while the paper cup fills. Her face is familiar but I don't recognize her. She smiles at me from a distance. She waits for the machine to give her back her change, then walks up to me.

"Siham," she says. "I'm a friend of your sister's. Do you remember me?"

Her brown eyes are surrounded by slightly smudged lines of black pencil, reinforcing that feeling of general exhaustion that strikes me as affecting the whole town these days.

We kiss each other on both cheeks. She sits down next to me on the bench, blowing on her coffee.

"What are you doing here?" she asks. "Are you on your own?"

I don't feel like telling her the whole story. I shrug, as if to say it doesn't matter, and she doesn't insist. I ask her the same question.

"I'm here with a friend. He has a trial coming up, he's with the court-appointed lawyer."

"What's he accused of?"

She smiles. "Spraying graffiti."

"Is that all?"

"I guess they don't have anything else to do."

But I don't listen to her. I remember Karim the other night, Karim and his friend pursued by the cops. I don't dare ask if it's him.

An embarrassed silence follows. We share part of our respective stories, but we have nothing else in common, and what connects us is death. I, too, would like to have been a teenager in Les Verrières before they demolished it, I'd like to have experienced that wind of insurrection that blew through the high-rises when Saïd was killed, I'd like to have known him, too, not just as a face sprayed in red on the walls.

Siham stirs the sugar in her coffee. She stares at the empty eyes of the bust of Justice hanging on the wall several yards above us.

"Have you seen Gina recently?" I ask.

She doesn't change her angle of vision. "Yes, I saw her a few weeks ago."

"Do you know where she's gone?"

She shrugs. "No."

"What about my mother?"

"Amélia? Haven't seen her in a while."

"Did Gina tell you she's disappeared?"

She nods after a tiny hesitation. And I have the increasingly weary feeling that she's hiding something from me, like everyone around me. I'd like to talk to her about my father. To ask if by any chance she knows what this famous evidence is that the cops are still searching for after his death. But I know she wouldn't answer me. There are some things that are just not meant for the ears of children.

The door of the judge's office opens, and Zé and his lawyer come out, deep in conversation. Siham stands up. She strokes my hair distractedly, which is what all grown-ups do when they don't know what to say to me.

"Ciao, Mattia."

"Ciao."

She greets Zé with a nod of the head, to which he responds in kind. He joins me.

"Your turn."

"Did it go well?"

"No idea."

The judge motions me to a comfortable padded armchair. He gives me a kindly smile that's intended to be more than just a routine greeting, but it's the forced smile of nurses and social workers and all those who are supposed to want what's best for you and who've rather forgotten what that is after years on the job.

On his desk there's a computer and some framed photographs. Behind him, hanging on the wall, children's drawings signed in clumsy lettering. Houses. Forests. Little families. A father, a mother, brothers and sisters, and the happy artist with a big smile.

"Hello, Matéo. My name's Frank Kowalski. Has your guardian explained to you why I've asked you to come?"

"Yes."

"I'm going to ask you a few questions and I'd like you to be as honest as you can. You know what 'honest' means, don't you?"

I raise my eyes to heaven.

"Yes."

"The purpose of these questions is to help me find the best solution for you."

I nod. I hide my hands under my thighs so as not to show how nervous I am. He drops me for a minute to type something on his keyboard, then folds his arms on the desk in a relaxed pose.

"Your guardian has been taking care of you for five years. What do you think of him?"

I think for a moment.

"I don't know. He's kind."

"Kind."

"Yes."

"Do you get on well?"

"Yes."

"Does he ever lose his temper?"

"Not often. I behave myself."

He smiles at me. "I'm sure you do. What happens when you don't? You must do stupid things from time to time, like all children."

"He punishes me."

"How does he do that?"

"He doesn't let me watch TV. Or he makes me stay in my room, things like that."

"He makes you."

"I mean I'm not allowed to come out."

"Does he ever yell at you?"

"No. He's very calm."

"Does he ever hit you on your backside, or slap you?"

"No, never."

"Not once?"

"Never."

He glances inquisitively at his computer. I suddenly remember the duty doctor when I was sick.

"Once," I quickly correct myself. "Not long ago. He slapped me."

"Did it hurt?"

"A little bit."

"Why did he hit you?"

"I called him a murderer."

He taps the frames of his glasses.

"Why was that?"

"I was angry because of school. I don't always get good grades even though I do what I can."

"Were you angry with him? Don't you think he helps you enough?"

"He does help me."

"So why did you insult him that time?"

"I didn't want to admit that it was my fault."

He looks at me. I put on a sheepish smile, the smile of a lost little boy. It works. He also smiles.

"Your guardian says that you know he's been through some, let's say, difficult times in his life."

"Yes."

"And you don't have any problem with that?"

"No."

"Do you ever feel threatened at home?"

"No. I feel fine. Zé protects me."

Next, he mentions the night the cops found me asleep outside in the cold in the middle of winter, drunk on energy drinks. I more or less tell him the truth, leaving out the fact that Zé had asked me to keep my eye open in case Gabrielle tried to kill herself again. He asks me a few questions about her. Zé and I have agreed on what to say—supposedly, I don't know that she's been trying to die, he's told me they were accidents—and the judge refrains from telling me the truth. I pretend I haven't been upset by her various stays in hospital.

In the end, he cracks his fingers.

"Very good. Thanks a lot, Matéo."

"It's Mattia, monsieur. You're welcome."

He walks me out into the lobby. Zé is waiting for me, but his overworked lawyer has already taken off. We walk together in silence to the car.

"I'm going to see Gabrielle in Charcot," he says after a few minutes. "Do you want to come?"

I think about the walls. About the room where my father hanged himself, which stank of sweat. About the white coats and the empty looks, the unsteady walks. I don't want to go. But I say yes.

* * *

There she is, Gabrielle, so frail in her blue pajamas. She's been in Charcot for a week, behind the high walls of Les Orchidées—4C, to those in the know. It was here that my father and Zé shared the same room, the same aimless strolls. I remember the corridors very well. The room where he killed himself is opposite hers.

Gabrielle is sitting cross-legged on her bed, looking through the window. Her eyes seem not to notice us. There's a TV set on the wall, but it's not connected. A night table. A telephone. A desk beneath the window looking out on the smokers' yard, in which one or two people dressed in the same pajamas are now pacing.

The section hasn't changed much, although now there are security cameras.

Zé is sitting on a chair to the right of the bed, his hand on Gabrielle's, his eyes blurry. Her eyes are tired and swollen, with red circles under them, it's as if she's aged ten years in a week. People age more quickly here, within a health regime that takes away a little more of your substance with every passing day, on the pretext that this substance can bring nothing but pain.

I'm standing with my back to the door, my hands in my jacket pockets, watching the world moving in slow motion beyond the window.

And between us, of course, the silence, which once again separates us more than it unites us.

We've been here for at least thirty minutes when she at last opens her mouth.

"You should have stopped them."

She isn't looking at him. And I can feel each of the syllables drive itself into Zé's heart. He tightens his grip on her hand.

"I tried."

"Yeah, right."

Her voice is thick, and she speaks slowly. It's the drugs. In five years of treatment, my father never got rid of that artificial slowness.

"If it had been you, I'd have fought them physically to stop them bringing you here. I thought you cared about me."

"I do!"

"Then get me out of here, for fuck's sake!"

A stunned silence. She doesn't often swear, let alone raise her voice, and this time she did both. Zé lowers his eyes, fighting back the tears. She pulls her hand away.

I leave the room. I'd like to get some air, but I can't go out without a nurse opening the door for me and there are none in sight. I fall back on the smokers' yard, which has a fence around it. A man in his twenties is busy tearing off the ivy that covers the fence. A woman squatting on the grass watches him from a distance. She smiles at me when she sees me. I force myself to return her smile. It's obvious she needs help, but I can't give her anything. I can't give anybody anything.

I stand in the middle of the yard and try to empty my head. That's hard to do with the guy nearby tearing away at the fence, emitting sharper and sharper squeals as he does so. I'm bound to end up here one day, on the wrong side of the fence. I might as well get used to it.

I try to imagine my daily life here, but quite simply, there's nothing to do. So people smoke. They go for walks. They get bored. The meds, the meals, the sound of footsteps, the silence.

I kneel in the grass. I feel like crying. I wipe my eyes angrily. The woman asks me if I'm all right, I say yes—I have no desire to talk—and she goes back inside. I don't know how much time has gone by when Zé crouches beside me.

"Let's go, Mattia," he says in a very gentle voice.

I grab hold of his sleeve. He helps me up, and I'm surprised by this sudden physical contact, we don't touch each other often. I cling to his arm, seized by the irrational fear that someone will stop us from leaving. That the nurses will bar our way and say: "You're going to stay here forever." Because if that happened, who would get us out?

But nobody intervenes.

21

S he's going to die in that place."

"You don't know that, Mattia."

"I tell you she's going to die. Only Zé can prevent it, and even he doesn't always succeed. The pills certainly aren't going to convince her that she's actually happy."

"That's not what it's about."

"What is it about, then?"

Nouria sighs. She gets up and looks out the window, as she always does when she's confronted with a difficult question. I follow her with my eyes, but don't get up. My fingers hurt from twisting them so much, and I scratch furiously at the insides of my wrists, where the scars, white and raised, still haven't disappeared.

"They won't just give her drugs. The treatment involves psychotherapy."

I give a nervous laugh.

"She doesn't even talk to us."

"Sometimes it's easier to talk to a therapist. Look at us. Do you tell Zé or Gabrielle what you tell me here?"

"No," I admit.

"You see. When it comes down to it, the hospital may do her good."

"The only thing she wants is to go. They're trying to force her to live."

"Who are they?"

"All of them. Zé, the doctors, her brother . . ."

"Her brother?"

I tell her about the night I caught him in our apartment. One thing leading to another, I end up blurting out everything I've gleaned in the past few days about my father and the madness they instilled in him—because, despite what they've always said, everything started with his being followed. That's the reason my father went from legitimate mistrust to "paranoid schizophrenia." Hallucinations and persecution mania don't burglarize you.

She moves back behind her desk and sits down.

"It's like a movie."

"Dad killed himself," I retort. "There's no doubt about that. But they did everything they could to push him to it."

"So you think it was their fault he went over the edge?"

"It was Saïd's death, it was the judges' verdict, it was all that shit around us."

"I didn't know you were a revolutionary."

"It's not that. I'm not talking about politics. I'm talking about what goes on here."

"That *is* politics."

"I don't care what people call it. I don't understand everything. I've always lived here, I haven't seen much. I haven't lived enough to know how the world is made. But the little bit I see . . . I understand Gabrielle and I understand my father. You have to be crazy to want to live here. We're the ones who should be in Charcot."

She looks at me for a long time.

"Do you want to die?"

I give a start. I wasn't expecting such a direct question. But I remember when it was that I started seeing Nouria, just after using that damned knife that lost me my mother's love, and I realize it's something she never stops thinking about.

"No," I say. "But I understand people who do."

"Anyone can understand them. That's not the question."

"Then what is the question?"

"Life . . ."

"I know. Life's a precious gift, I know."

She dismisses my remark with an irritable gesture. "If everyone who couldn't stand the world they lived in had killed themselves rather than fighting, nothing would ever have changed."

"And look where we are now."

I point to the world outside. I feel tired.

"Things never really change. It's just an illusion because life is movement, because the Earth turns. But what then? It's shit. It's always been shit. End of story. What do you want to change? And how?"

She smiles sadly.

"Some people spend their lives looking for the answer."

"For a very good reason: there isn't an answer. Things don't change. Ever. They jump about, that's all, but in the same place. That's the only thing I've realized."

A long silence. I scratch my wrists frantically. Nouria stares at me with her deep-set eyes. She sighs again.

"If that's what you really think, all you can do is try to slip through the net."

When things go beyond what you can stand, you have to change your angle of vision. Where are you, Gina? Come help me I need you . . .

* * *

Zé keeps his promise: he makes every effort to get Gabrielle out. He goes to Charcot every day. He contacts a lawyer who specializes in wrongful confinement, who explains to him that only two people can release Gabrielle: her psychiatrist or the third party who made the initial request for committal. Zé himself has no power, especially as he's crazy, or has been. It's the same old problem: zero credibility.

So he sets off in search of Gabrielle's brother, believing that he's the only way out. The problem is that Thomas is nowhere to be found. He isn't in the phone book. There are no records of his presence, either in the region or in the country. The hospital sends him packing when he asks them for a telephone number, arguing that the information is confidential.

"Why don't you inquire at the police station?" I ask him one evening when he's despaired of ever getting his hands on the man.

He doesn't seem to have heard me. A cigarette is burning down between his lips. In front of him, a plate of canned beans he hasn't touched. I was the one who cooked. I've learned a little more with each of Gabrielle's suicide attempts. Whenever she's sent to the hospital or is convalescing, he stops eating. It's as if even his vital functions are in sympathy with her distress.

Love is a beautiful thing. Beautiful and stupid.

As for me, I've finished eating. I wash the plate in the sink. With my back to him, I ask my question again more loudly this time.

"The cops all stick together," he replies. "His colleagues would think I want to kill him. It'll only make them suspicious."

"Do you think they were just looking for Gabrielle when they were following us?"

"Maybe. Her brother knows I live with her and I use my mother's maiden name for the lease, my real name only appears on the letterbox. It wasn't easy to find out where I lived."

"Why don't you use your real name?" I ask, sitting down again opposite him.

He heaves a deep sigh and looks away.

"I'm always scared that one day someone who was close to Émilie . . ."

The girl he killed. He doesn't bother to finish the sentence. I lower my eyes, embarrassed. He never talks about her. I wait a few seconds before changing the subject.

"Where does Gabrielle's brother work?"

"No idea. Not in this town."

"So how are we going to find him?"

He shrugs, then seems to remember his cigarette, which he stubs out in the ashtray.

"If there's no other solution, we're going to get her out of there without their consent."

"They've already tracked her down once."

"We'll move."

"He's a cop. He knows everyone's address."

"It took him a long time to find her."

"He knows which school I go to, and it wouldn't be difficult for him to find out the next one if you move me."

He sinks into a desperate silence and I leave him to his anguish, aware that this conversation has merely underlined how powerless he is. Later in the night, when I get up to drink some water, I find him still in the kitchen, scribbling on loose sheets of paper. He doesn't even notice I'm there. Out of the corner of my eye, I make out whole series of numbers and abstract signs, an infinity of equations.

He'd vowed to give up mathematics after Émilie died. Obviously, math had nothing to do with her death, but I suppose Zé needed to put the blame on something, anything, and since he couldn't find a person, he fell back on that poor subject that couldn't defend itself. Be that as it may, I tell myself it's a bad sign.

* * *

He goes to see her every day in the hospital. Two or three times, he asks me if I want to go with him, and I decline the invitation, claiming that I have homework. He pretends to believe me.

Everything is going badly. I've stopped making any effort to get good grades at school. Now that the custody hearing is over, I feel justified in going back to my usual mediocrity. My teacher threatens to summon Zé, I come clean about Gabrielle being in Charcot and take advantage of the opportunity to remind her that my father killed himself in that same hospital, and that it's Zé who found him hanged. She stammers something that sounds like an apology and stops talking about any possible educational meeting.

My mother is still missing. I start to seriously envisage the prospect of her death, just as I prepared myself in advance for my father's death in order not to be caught by surprise when the time came. Every morning, in the mirror, brushing my teeth, I whisper to myself, "She's dead, Mom is dead," and gradually grow accustomed to the idea. Her memory gradually fades. Like my father's face, which I can't even remember.

One night, since nobody is looking after me, I go back to the construction site that's replaced Les Verrières. The work is making progress. There's a huge crater where the high-rises once stood. They've erased the graffiti from the billboard.

I climb to the top of the crane and look down at the world, but even from up here I can't see any beauty in it.

I go back down without anybody having seen me. I cross a large part of the town on foot, taking side streets in order not to run into a police patrol. And it suddenly strikes me.

Saïd's face has been erased from all the buildings, as before. But this time nobody has tried to put it back. This small detail is like a cold shower to me. It's as if they've won.

I get back right at six, just before Zé. On the landing, I trip over a sleeping figure lying across the corridor and jump a mile. A female voice lets loose a volley of curses.

I know that voice. I lean over her, holding my breath.

"Gina?"

"Can't you look where you're walking, you little bastard?"

No doubt about it, it's my sister. I avoid apologizing or taking her in my arms. Without a word, once the surprise has passed, I clamber over her and insert the key in the lock. Behind me, she gets to her feet.

"I was waiting for Zé. What were you doing outside on your own?"

I don't reply. Acting as if she wasn't there, I go straight to my room. She tries to follow me. I put my back against the door to bar the way. She knocks very softly.

"Mattia . . ."

Silence.

"Mattia, don't sulk."

"Why don't you go—" I reply without finishing the sentence, remembering I'm talking to my sister and that it's not much of an insult.

She doesn't reply. Her footsteps move away. I make no attempt to find out if she's left. I go to bed, just to get an hour's sleep before school.

Zé wakes me a little later to drive me there. I register that Gina has fallen asleep on the couch. Zé doesn't say a word throughout the ride. I don't ask him if he's spoken to my sister.

I was kind of expecting it, but I'm surprised all the same to see her during the noon recess. She's signaling to me through the railings. I walk over to her, without hurrying. I climb on a bench to be the same height as her.

"Zé told me about Gabrielle."

I nod mournfully.

"I'd like to go see her," she continues. "Will you come with me after school?"

I make to leave. She calls me back.

"Or we could go right now and I'll write you a note for school."

I immediately return. She bursts out laughing and ruffles my hair.

"I know you so well."

* * *

She has her hand in mine as we approach the high walls. I'm wondering why she feels the need to visit a woman she barely knows. I guess Charcot hasn't marked her as much as it's marked me, unless this is a way of facing her own ghosts.

She's still wearing the same gray jogging pants and the sweatshirt with the white hood. Her hair has grown a little. Apart from that, she's the same. Why do I feel as if I haven't seen her in years?

"I'm sorry I left without warning," she says. "Things weren't working out with Zé. I preferred to leave before he threw me out."

And why do I know she's lying?

A nurse refuses us admission. Visitors aren't allowed until two in the afternoon. We sit down on a bench about thirty feet from Les Orchidées. Gina has bought sandwiches on the way. We indulge in a little picnic in the grounds, watched by a few patients who bum cigarettes from my sister. She hands out so many that the pack is soon almost empty.

Several times I think about bringing up the subject that's most on my mind, the question of that famous evidence. But my voice systematically sticks in my throat. Because against all expectation, I feel good. It's been quite a while since I was last with a grown-up who wasn't on the verge of despair. My sister's self-confidence is contagious, and I don't want to ruin this first moment of calm since they took Gabrielle away.

When she sees a family approaching Les Orchidées, she looks at her watch.

"It's two-thirty. Shall we go?"

I'm the first to stand up. She gets ready to follow me but suddenly freezes, as if struck by lightning. I look where she's looking. She's peering into the smokers' yard. It should be hidden from us because of the ivy, but the ivy was torn out by that guy the last time I was here. We can see two figures walking side by side, both with cigarettes in their mouths. One of them is Gabrielle. The other is her brother.

"That's Gabrielle," I say just in case.

"And the guy?"

"Her brother. Did Zé tell you the story? He's the one who had her sent here, he's been trying to contact her for two—"

"Her brother?" Her voice is as toneless as her face is white. She pulls down her hood over her forehead and gets to her feet, her legs unsteady. "Mattia, answer me seriously, I'm not joking. Is he really her brother?"

"Yes, he is. He's a cop. Do you know him?"

"I know he's a cop." She sticks a cigarette between her lips. "His name is Thomas Ross," she says, speaking very quickly, as if ridding herself of something that's become a burden to her. "He's the man who killed Saïd."

My mind is a complete fog. I turn to look into the yard. She's right. Thomas Ross, I know that I know the name and that it evokes something bad, but I've never heard Gabrielle's brother's first name and surname put together. I've never made the connection. I've tried to forget that name, just as I tried to forget my father's, and it seems I succeeded, because I never suspected the family ties between Zé's partner and the murderer who sent Saïd to his grave and my father to Charcot.

Nausea seizes hold of me. I stare at the man from a distance. Neither he nor Gabrielle has noticed us. I think of all the times I've mentioned Saïd in front of her or Zé, and I remember the strange looks they occasionally exchanged, looks whose meaning I didn't understand. I thought it was compassion, but it was the sign of yet another silent secret.

When exactly did they decide that I didn't need to know this?

For the first time in my life, I feel like hitting someone. I mean really hitting them. Even someone who hasn't done me any harm, just for the pleasure of hearing bones crack. I've never been in a fight. I've never felt the need. But I look at that cop, and my desire for violence turns into a desire for murder.

Gina takes me by the hand and yanks me away, bringing me back to reality.

"Come on, I don't want to see him."

Her voice is imbued with anger. She must be feeling the same thing I am, minus the sense of betrayal, but a thousand times stronger, since she experienced the events first hand.

We retrace our steps. She drags me along the paths of the grounds without looking back. I'm surprised she didn't want to confront him. Maybe she's afraid of losing her cool and making a mistake that can't be rectified. And anyway, she's always run away . . .

I'm out of breath by the time we reach the bus stop next to the hospital. Much to my dismay, Gina hands me a bus ticket.

"You'll have to get home by yourself. I need to go."

"What?"

"Don't tell me you've never taken the bus."

"But where are you going?"

She crouches in front of me and squeezes my hands in hers.

"I can't explain it all. There's someone I have to see urgently."

"Is it in connection with that cop?"

She hesitates imperceptibly.

"Yes."

"But wait! Things have happened . . . Mom was burglarized, and so were we, and Stefano told me the same thing happened after Saïd died, and that Dad had evidence . . ."

She straightens up, brushing the dust off her jogging pants. She looks away. The bus arrives. She hails it.

"We'll talk about all that later, I promise. I'm staying in town anyway. We'll meet again soon. Get home safely, and hang in there."

I don't know if she's talking about the depressing atmosphere in the apartment, the memories stirred by Gabrielle being in the hospital, or life in general. But I give up. Nobody has ever managed to keep Gina anywhere. She walks off in the direction of the town center while I get on the bus with a heavy heart and the rusty taste of anger in my mouth.

22
GINA

G ina is walking, her hands deep in her pockets, trying to forget the bitter, accusing look she sees every time she thinks about her little brother. How long is it since he stopped hoping for anything? How long has he been forcing himself to go through life without rubbing up against it, as if he had the power to keep the surrounding unhappiness away from him?

She'll tackle that problem when all this is over. For now, she has more important things to deal with.

Gina is walking, her hands deep in her pockets, in her head the distant figures of a man and a woman in the smokers' yard. She's angry with Zé. With Gabrielle. With the law, and pretty much with everybody.

The supermarket puts an end to her jumbled thoughts. She makes out Siham through the window. She goes in, rummages on the shelves for a while, decides on a pack of potato chips, and goes to Saïd's sister's checkout to pay for it. Siham greets her with a warm smile.

"The cop is still in town," Gina says. "I saw him less than an hour ago."

"Where?" Siham asks as she registers the item.

"Charcot. His sister's a patient there. I'll tell you all about it."

"I finish at eight. Let's meet at my place. Will you let Karim know?"

"Not Nadir?"

Siham shakes her head.

"His probation officer never leaves him alone. He'd rather we didn't get in touch with him."

The customers are getting impatient. Gina leaves the store with her pack of potato chips. A few streets away, she rings at an entryphone, but gets no reply. Karim isn't home. She wanders around town for a while, then shuts herself in a phone booth, inserts a card in the appropriate slot, and dials a number. There are a good few rings before someone picks up.

"Latifa? Hi, this is Gina. Is my mother there?"

A minute later, Amélia's voice echoes in the receiver.

"Hello, Gina."

"I just saw Mattia. He really isn't too good. Don't you want to get in touch with him? Just to let him know you're okay?"

A pause. Gina waits for the silence to end.

"I wouldn't know what to say to him," Amélia admits. "Why don't you tell him I'm fine?"

"He wouldn't believe me. He's found out that we've been hiding things from him. He doesn't trust me anymore."

"Tell him I'm fine," Amélia repeats, and hangs up.

Gina stares at the telephone for a moment or two, holding in check the bitterness that twists her stomach. She could hear the guilt in her mother's voice. Not that it makes any difference. She didn't ask after anybody.

"Selfish bitch," she mutters, hanging up in her turn.

She wanders about the streets for a few more hours before trying her luck again. This time, Karim opens the door, and Siham soon joins them.

"What's all this about Nadir?" Gina asks immediately.

"His probation officer is putting pressure on him to find a job. He can't afford to get into any trouble while he's on parole. We'll have to do without him."

"We don't need him," Siham says decisively. She turns to Gina. "Tell us about the cop."

I go to Charcot with Zé just a few hours after I left it. He bawls me out for skipping school, I tell him it's Gina's fault and he doesn't pursue it. Now that the hearing's all in the past, he doesn't give any more of a damn than I do.

The nurse who lets us in raises her eyebrows when she sees me for the second time in a day, but makes no comment. I grab hold of Zé's sleeve before we enter the room.

"Could you give me some time alone with her?"

He consents, too preoccupied to ask any questions. For a fraction of a second, I expect to find Thomas Ross by Gabrielle's bedside, but she's alone, sitting at her desk, gazing at the world through the window, or at least the meager portion of the world she's allowed. She turns when she hears us coming, her face swollen with weariness.

"Hi," Zé says with a smile.

She doesn't reply. Her silence is the worst of punishments as far as Zé is concerned. Like the first time, I leave them alone together and wander in the corridor, trying not to go too close to the room opposite. In the end, I sit down on a chair near the treatment room and watch the nurses coming and going. I'd like to empty my head but I can't. There are too many things swirling around in it, too many questions without answers.

The medical staff look at me in surprise when they see me. Children aren't often brought to visit the lost souls in Charcot. It's actually supposed to be forbidden, although in practice they tolerate it. I've spent so much time here that this section is an integral part of my childhood, but I still don't feel at home.

Unconsciously, I look out for the white coats, searching for that male nurse who instilled the ultimate fear in me and transformed my future into a dead end, but I don't see him. Maybe he doesn't work here anymore. I don't even know his name.

After what seems like forever, Zé sits down next to me.

"I'll wait for you here," he says.

Gabrielle hasn't moved from her desk. With her finger, she's drawing invisible patterns on the plastic table whose rounded corners are intended to reduce the possibility of violence. She isn't allowed a razor. She can't even wear a bra in case she tries to hang herself with it. It's all crap. From experience, I know that the desire to die stimulates the imagination, and even in a room padded from floor to ceiling you can always find a way to take your own life.

I close the door gently, taking care not to make too much noise. My father, walled up in his silent universe, could never bear it.

I clear my throat behind her.

"Zé told me you wanted to talk to me, just the two of us?" she asks without turning.

Her voice sounds more or less normal. Her treatment hasn't knocked her out too much.

"Yes."

I hesitate. I remember Gina. *Do you know how to talk to people?* No, and I don't know how best to express what I want to say. I decide to cut to the chase.

"I tried to see you earlier, but you already had a visitor."

Still with her back to me, she tenses.

"I was with Gina. She saw him, too. She told me who he was."

Silence.

"Gabrielle?"

Silence.

"Gabrielle!"

I go closer to her. She turns before I get to her. Maybe she heard the violence throbbing in my voice.

"Your brother is the cop who killed Saïd."

She gives a strange laugh and shakes her head vigorously.

"Why do you think I cut off all ties with him?"

"I thought it was because he wanted to send you here."

"No, I was better at that time. I was able to work, leave the house without panicking. I stopped seeing him because of that business. So drop the accusing look, Mattia, he's the one who killed him, not me."

And she tells me the story. Because I don't leave her any choice, because she at least owes me that.

L es Verrières is one huge graveyard.
Thomas Ross hasn't been back here since the police
reconstruction years ago. He's been told it's changed,
but he never thought he'd find nothing but a construction site.

"They'd have had to take them down eventually," Rassiat
remarks at the wheel.

His ex-partner is driving the unmarked car. He hasn't
changed much since the days when they worked together. A
massive body thrust into an everlasting khaki jacket, a neck as
thick as a tree trunk. The kids in Les Verrières didn't try to act
smart when he was around.

Thomas is one of those types that easily flies under the
radar. The local hooligans often didn't even peg him for a cop,
even though they could spot an unmarked police car from
miles away.

The vehicle slows down outside the last remaining building.
Younès's building, Thomas realizes.

"She still lives here," Rassiat says.

"Who?"

"Amélia Lorozzi. The teacher's partner. She's never left the
neighborhood. She's refused all offers to rehouse her. Strange,
don't you think? The Zahidis left quickly. If I was her, I'd have
gotten out as fast as possible. Too many bad memories.
Anyway, she may have gone in the end, because she's missing."

"Did you find anything in her apartment?"

"Nada. Maybe she wasn't in on it."

"Then why has she gone missing without leaving a forwarding address?"

Rassiat is silent for a moment. Like any self-respecting cop, he knows that innocent people rarely run away. The car does a U-turn and heads out of Les Verrières.

"She went off the rails after Younès died. She even handed over custody of her third child to the Palaisot boy. I don't think she's any kind of threat to us."

"I know she isn't behind it, but I think she's an accomplice," Thomas Ross replies distractedly. His thoughts are elsewhere, somewhere in the heart of Charcot, in Les Orchidées. He sees Gabrielle, hears her harsh words, her hatred—God knows he's had to absorb plenty of hatred in his life, but he didn't think he'd ever see that feeling in his own sister's eyes.

"I wonder if I should allow her to be released," he says as Rassiat drives in the direction of the town center.

"Your sister, you mean? Didn't you say there was a risk she might—"

"Oh, yes. I'm starting to think it won't make any difference. If she really wants to kill herself, she'll do it, even in Charcot." He closes his eyes and presses his palms to his temples. He needs to get some air. "I'd just like to understand why she . . ."

He can't finish the sentence. Rassiat finishes it for him, in a low voice:

"Why she wants to die."

"It's been going on for so long and she's never been able to explain why. I mean . . . our parents . . . She was loved, she never suffered particularly, there's nothing . . . There's no reason for her to be like that."

Embarrassed, his colleague concentrates on the road. He doesn't know what to say, because once again there is no answer. Thomas wasn't expecting one. For twenty years he's been sifting through the void that surrounds Gabrielle, and for twenty years he's come up with nothing but a multitude of question marks.

They stop at a red light. A lump in his throat, he puts a hand on Rassiat's shoulder.

"I'm getting out here."

"What? Are you crazy? With what's happening, I don't think it's a good idea for you to show your face around town."

"I need air, and I can take care of myself."

He opens the door, ignoring his ex-partner's curses. The sun is going down behind the buildings. Thomas Ross ought perhaps to fear for his life, but they've left Verrières behind, and he doubts that many people remember his face. For security reasons, his photograph never appeared in the media. There's still a possibility he might meet someone who was close to Saïd Zahidi, or someone who knew him when he spent most of his time doing identity checks. But what the hell? Right now, he doesn't even have enough energy left to worry about his own life.

He walks, his hands in the pockets of his suede jacket—a gift from his sister in the days when she was still talking to him—searching for some fucking reason to keep fighting. Fighting whom, fighting what? He's never really known.

His steps should take him to the hospital but without understanding how, he finds himself outside the cemetery. Half-heartedly, he looks up at the huge gate. With a slightly trembling hand, he grabs hold of the handle, but the cemetery is already closed. So without even making sure that nobody's watching, he grips the bars. Climbing the gate is child's play. He picks himself up on the other side, wipes the dust from the sleeves of his jacket, and sets off along the paths that wind between the graves.

He soon finds the Muslim section with its dozens of crescent moons. He wanders for a while before stopping by the grave that interests him. It's better maintained than its neighbors, even though it's fifteen years old.

The name Saïd Zahidi is there, above two dates and some words in Arabic that he can't read. Thomas Ross kneels to get a better look at the inscriptions carved on some marble stones placed by the headstone. There are also flowers and a little porcelain sculpture depicting the Qur'an open at a particular page.

He closes his eyes, remembering that night. Even after fifteen years, he still finds it hard to understand what happened—why, at that particular moment, he lost his cool and kept hitting until it was too late.

In his family, they've been cops from father to son since the Revolution, according to legend. Thomas didn't have much choice in his future. His father urged him to put on the uniform as soon as he was old enough to think about "what he might do with his life."

With hindsight, it was probably a mistake to follow his family's advice.

Graduating from the Police Academy with excellent grades, Thomas Ross benefited from the immense privilege of being able to choose where he wanted to be posted. Against all expectations, he buried himself here, in this "godforsaken hole"—as his father, an inveterate Parisian, had called it—in order to be close to his sister.

Gabrielle was a community organizer at the time. She was doing the job more to earn a living than because she was passionate about it. In fact, she'd chosen it mainly because it only required a few weeks' training and allowed her to work in lots of different places. She often worked with the community center in Les Verrières, where she'd met—and gotten to like—that teacher who was known to the local police for his annoying habit of showing up at the station, teary-eyed, every time a kid was arrested.

Brother and sister weren't on the same wavelength politically, but they managed to get along in spite of everything.

Maintaining his relationship with Gabrielle was one of Thomas's priorities at the time. It was for her that he had left everything behind.

Except the police.

"You're going to become as stupid as Dad," she predicted. They would laugh about it when they met up in a café once or twice a week at the end of their respective days. It was a nice time—and it wasn't to last.

Thomas came up against hate as soon as he put on his uniform. A visceral hatred overflowing from the eyes of those kids who hadn't had time to grow up, who'd been flung into an adult world by necessity, bad influences, boredom, or simply because the future looked bleak.

He thought he'd be able to take it. He'd overestimated himself.

After a few months of this, he, too, was gripped by hate. He saw the process get under way. He clearly saw contempt grow inside him and spread to his whole way of thinking. He saw it, because his colleagues were a mirror image of what he himself would be like in a few years' time, when he'd forgotten everything except the bitterness. He tried not to let himself be swept along by it. It was hard. He'd been unable to build up a new circle of friends since he left Paris, so very soon, the only people he saw were his partners—and Gabrielle. It was a very limited vision of the world that could only lead to the worst.

The worst happened one December evening. Its name was Saïd Zahidi. The curses the blows and the blood, the blood, the blood.

The patrol he'd been with when the events happened took things in hand while he, once he'd gotten over the shock, sank into a kind of stupor. They put together the least damning version and made him repeat it endlessly until he had it at his fingertips. This was the version they told their superiors. And

Internal Affairs. And the media, the lawyer, and the examining magistrate.

And everyone believed them.

Suspended for an indefinite period while awaiting trial, Thomas suddenly discovered in himself a keen interest in whiskey, an interest he indulged until Rassiat, his closest colleague, paid him a visit at home. Throwing the bottles away, Rassiat told him it wasn't over. That there were things to be settled. That he couldn't afford to let go.

Evidence. There was evidence that Saïd hadn't struck the first blow. This evidence was held by the teacher from the community center in Les Verrières, and it had to be found before the prosecution got hold of it.

At first, Thomas thought he would just let things play themselves out. He didn't feel as if he had the energy to stand it anymore, to keep lying in response to the constant questioning to which he was subjected. What's more humiliating for a cop than to have to undergo interrogation?

But his colleagues rallied around him. Especially Rassiat. "We won't let you go to prison just because you lost your cool with that little scumbag." Thomas let himself be persuaded. He couldn't do anything himself. He was being watched, and it was in his best interests to make them forget about him. But he gave the green light. Rassiat and a few others set about getting rid of that famous evidence and intimidating the teacher to make sure that he kept quiet until the trial was over.

* * *

"You shouldn't be here," a voice said behind him, cutting the thread of his thoughts.

Thomas gives a start and instinctively moves his hand to his belt. He turns. A woman of twenty-five or thirty stands looking at him. Her face is familiar—and what's even more familiar is the hate in her dark eyes.

She looks down at the gun he's ready to draw.

"Go on, kill me, you have impunity!"

She opens her arms, challenging him. Thomas moves his hand away from his gun. He's racking his brains, trying to remember her name, the name of that girl who almost got herself arrested as she tried to push through the cordon of CRS protecting him, crying, "He was my brother!"

Siham. Siham Zahidi.

"I'm sorry," he says. "I didn't expect to see you here."

"Why not? It's my brother's grave."

"You recognized me."

"But you didn't recognize me. Get out of here, lieutenant. You may be a cop, you may have the authority, but even you should know there are times when it's best to shut up, bow your head, and go."

He opens his mouth to respond to the affront. A second later, he gives up on the idea. What could he possibly say?

Carefully avoiding the woman, Thomas walks back to the gate. Without appearing to, he watches the shadows on the ground to make sure she isn't following him. This encounter has reminded him that he's unwanted here. As long as he walks the streets of this city, he'll be in danger.

The gate is still locked. She hasn't respected the opening times either. He climbs back over to the other side and strides away, although turning frequently to look back. She hasn't followed him. That's reassuring. Maybe, like Rassiat, he's overestimated the importance of the graffiti and what preceded it.

Maybe everyone really has forgotten about that business. But something tells him they haven't.

25
SIHAM

She watches him walk away, trying to contain her anger. It's as if her chest is in a vise. She's familiar with that feeling of suffocation. She felt it so often, every morning for weeks, after her brother died.

She's very tempted to run after him, but what would she do then? She left home earlier, wanting to pay Saïd a visit—not to take revenge. She has no weapon except her hands, and they won't be enough. He's armed. Armed and on his guard.

Siham takes several deep breaths. The cop disappears down the street. She gets a grip on herself and turns to the grave, her eyes moist.

"If I could have, I swear I'd have done it."

What on earth possessed that son of a bitch to come to the cemetery? Was he savoring his victory? Or does he have regrets? Siham smiles. Even if he can't sleep at night, it wouldn't make any difference. Saïd is dead, that's all there is to it, and nobody has ever bothered to punish his murderer. If it had been the other way around, the guilty party would have spent twenty years rotting in prison.

As for any apologies, they would be fifteen years too late.

Siham stands gazing down at the grave for a moment or two, drawing from it the strength to keep standing. Then she nimbly climbs over the cemetery railings. She looks up and down the street. No sign of any cops.

She was planning to go back home and join Gina, who's waiting for her there, but now she changes route and heads for her parents' place. She hasn't seen them in weeks even though they're almost neighbors.

Latifa and Tayeb Zahidi live in a housing project in the town center, in a modern building that's a lot more comfortable than the apartment they had in Les Verrières. Not that they're any happier.

Siham's father's hair turned white overnight—no need to specify which night. Her mother's face is prematurely lined. It barely lights up with a smile when she discovers Siham on the landing.

The three of them sit and have coffee in silence, a silence punctuated by the TV news.

"Isn't Amélia here?" Siham asks, glancing absently at the TV screen.

"She's asleep," Latifa replies, then lowers her voice. "I'm really worried about her. Couldn't you ask Gina to drop by and see her?"

Siham shakes her head. She knows her friend well. There's too much resentment between mother and daughter, too many things unsaid for Gina to make an effort to pay her a visit. She's like a gust of wind, Gina.

"She's increasingly paranoid," Madame Zahidi continues. "All she talks about is the police and what happened fifteen years ago. Since that burglary . . ."

"I know, she refuses to go home."

"We'll let her stay here as long as she likes, but I'm afraid she'll end up in Charcot, too."

Siham smiles sadly.

"She isn't crazy, Mom. It wasn't a burglary. It really was the police."

"What are you talking about?"

Siham takes the plunge. Her father lowers the volume of the TV and turns slowly to her as she recounts the latest events. How she ran into Lieutenant Ross in the store, then at the cemetery. How his sister is back in the hospital. How Mattia's guardian was also burglarized.

Her parents turn pale as she tells her story.

"Why didn't you tell us any of this before?"

"You've already suffered enough because of this business."

Latifa gives a dry laugh.

"You don't have to protect us, Siham."

But she does. They went to pieces after Saïd died. Not her. She's still standing, still able to face up to things—able to rebel perhaps, when they no longer have the strength.

"And what are you planning to do?" Tayeb asks suddenly.

Siham sustains his anxious gaze. She's getting ready to reply when Latifa grabs the remote control and turns up the volume. The voice of the newsreader bounces off the walls and echoes in their heads.

"... *verdict has just been delivered. Here is a brief recap of the case: four years ago, Baptiste Dioury, 23, died of asphyxiation in the van taking him to the 20th arrondissement police station in Paris. The three police officers present at the time of death, charged with bodily harm leading to unintended death, have just been acquitted. We join our reporter outside the Palace of Justice.*"

Siham leaps to her feet.

"Shit! How many deaths is it going to take before someone does something?"

She has screamed the words. Someone bangs on the ceiling with a broomstick. Siham stares at her parents, first one, then the other, she doesn't know what she's looking for in their eyes but doesn't find anything except exhaustion. They gave up a long time ago, one December night, and at this moment she realizes that nothing more can be expected of them.

They're angry, of course. But what then?

What can we do, Siham? Her mother would repeat those words every evening during the year the legal proceedings dragged on, in the vain hope of lessening her daughter's rage. *What can we do?*

Siham puts on her coat and slams the door behind her. She runs down the stairs, out onto the street, and all the way to her own building. Gina and Karim haven't moved. Standing by the radio, they turn when she comes in.

"Did you hear?" she asks, out of breath.

Yes, they heard.

"It can't go on," Gina says.

They look at each other, conscious that they've reached the point of no return. Karim turns away. Where they want to go he can't follow.

26

S o, basically . . .

One of the people following them is Gabrielle's brother. Not the worst cop possible. Or the best. A normal guy. Except that he killed someone. For a while, there were proceedings against him. But when he was reinstated, he was welcomed so warmly at the station that he ended up telling himself it wasn't so serious. And the law merely confirmed that feeling.

After all, he simply made an error. And to err is human, they say. The only problem is that errors are tolerated in some people and not in others, and it's always the same ones.

"I supported him at first, when I saw that he was going under and sincerely regretted what he'd done. But then his colleagues got involved. He ended up convincing himself that it really was self-defense, that he'd had no choice. And who was going to worry about a young delinquent, a persistent offender, who would probably have attacked someone eventually? Saïd Zahidi didn't deserve to have my brother ruin his life because of him."

Gabrielle is speaking, one bitter word after the other, I've never heard her talk so much, it's as if I was discovering her real voice. I listen to her without interrupting her even though her story revives my desire to burn everything—how right you were, Gina, I've grown up and now I understand.

"I broke off all ties with him. When he was reinstated, they transferred him to another town. He tried to get in touch with me, but I never responded. Until the other day, when he showed up at our place."

She looks at me. There's hatred in her eyes.

"So don't go thinking I'm on his side just because he's my brother. And don't make me pay for his sins. It's because of him that I'm here. If you were expecting me to defend him—"

"I don't blame you because he's your brother," I retort. "I blame you because you never told me."

"What difference would it have made?"

"I'd have known the truth!"

"I didn't want you to hate me. You didn't like me much at first, do you remember? You were afraid I'd steal Zé from you."

Which is exactly what she did, but I don't say anything.

It's thanks to my father that they met. Gabrielle would visit him from time to time in Charcot. She would sometimes talk with Zé, because my father rarely spoke, and they met again by chance years later in a store. They recalled their respective stays in the hospital. They talked about my father, and their loneliness did the rest.

"If I'd told you the truth, you would never have trusted me," she continues, a hint of supplication in her voice.

"And didn't you ever think that if you wanted people to trust you, you shouldn't lie to them?"

She doesn't reply. She turns to the window. She hasn't moved since she started telling her story.

I wait for a moment, looking for something to say, but all I find inside me is silence. I soften my voice to say goodbye and good luck, because however angry I am, now's not the time to heap blame on her. I hold my tongue and swallow my venom, as usual. I know that one day it'll poison me, but in the meantime, knock on wood!

I walk back along the corridor. I hear continuous moaning coming from the room where my father hanged himself. I walk faster. I calm down. If there's one thing I'm sure of, it's that I'm

not the unhappiest person in this hospital, an impression confirmed by Zé's face. He hasn't moved from his chair, and he's
staring into space, into the deepest of chasms, rings six miles
long under his eyes. When was the last time he slept? I have to
snap my fingers half an inch from his face for him to notice that
I'm there. He seems to realize all at once where he is.

"Her brother came to see her earlier," he says in the car.

I say yes as if I'm hearing this for the first time.

"I plugged in the phone in her room. She'll let me know if
he comes back, and I'll try to catch him and get him to sign her
release." A pause. "It's too much power for one person," he
adds, choking on his own cigarette smoke.

I don't have the courage to accuse him of being on the side
of the liars.

This time, when we get back to the apartment, I don't take
the trouble to cook for two. I make myself a bowl of cereal and
immediately rush to my cartoons. He lets me watch TV until
it's time for him to leave for the store. I end up falling asleep
on the couch. It's still warm from Gabrielle's body.

* * *

Both Zé and I have forgotten one little detail, and we're
both equally surprised by the phone call from our prestigious
lawyer: the family judge has decided to leave me in the custody
of my guardian. What with the testimony from my brother the
surgeon, the pressure from Zé's parents, and the lawyer's gab-
bing, it was a foregone conclusion. Zé isn't in the mood to celebrate the news. Neither am I, to be honest.

The days pass. Despite her promise, Gina doesn't appear,
and my mother's telephone rings forlornly without anybody
picking up. I don't even care about her anymore. I'm sure she's
dead somewhere. I try to convince myself that it doesn't matter. That she's been dead for me ever since she handed me over

to a stranger, a man she knew nothing about except that he'd been dangerously close to going crazy and may even have committed a murder.

I've stopped dreaming about her death, evidence that my self-conditioning is bearing fruit.

Gabrielle's brother comes back to see her a week after his last visit. Zé jumps in his car as soon as she hangs up, but by the time he gets to the hospital there's no trace of the cop.

One evening, as we're vegetating in front of the TV just before he leaves for work, the telephone rings. Zé stretches his long legs and gets laboriously to his feet to answer. I listen for the voice at the other end without seeming to. Zé frowns.

"There now? How many of them are there? Can you describe them to me?"

A pause. He nods and takes a gulp of his coffee. He's been in a kind of hibernation since Gabrielle went into hospital, but now he seems to be coming back to life.

"Right. Thanks for calling. No, no idea. Let me know if they ask you any questions. Yes, have a good evening. Thanks again."

He hangs up and turns to me.

"That was your mother's neighbor."

That's it, she's dead. I nod without betraying the slightest interest.

"The cops are at Amélia's. There are four or five of them, in uniform or with police armbands. They've come officially this time."

"What do they want?"

"I don't know. She'll call me back if they come and ask her questions." He glances at his watch. "I have to go to work. Will you be all right?"

"Of course."

He looks at me with unprecedented anxiety.

"Don't move from here, okay? Whatever happens, it's

bound to go against you if you show up there on your own. They'll let us know if anything has happened to your mother."

I nod absently. He goes to his room to get dressed before leaving for the store. I stay where I am on the couch, watching a documentary about the first Gulf War, in unconscious tribute to Gabrielle, who was always excessively affected by all the shit in the world.

The telephone rings twenty minutes after Zé left. I pick up without saying a word.

"Monsieur Palaisot?" a female voice asks, probably the neighbor.

"No," I say. "This is Mattia. Amélia's son."

"Could I speak to your guardian?"

"He's at work. Have the cops been to see you?"

A long hesitation. She doesn't know if I'm ready to hear what she has to tell me. Mom's dead, that's for sure.

"Nothing's happened to your mother," she says at last. "They aren't looking for her. They're looking for your sister."

Just then, there's a loud knock at the door. I hang up without bothering to say goodbye. I put my bowl of cereal down on the coffee table and walk casually to the door, cold sweat running down my shoulder blades. I get up on tiptoe to look through the peephole. It's the police. There are five of them. I recognize the guy in the khaki jacket who was following us with Thomas Ross. He must have been the one who urged him to give the green light to harass my father. He's the only one of them in plainclothes, but his orange armband is clearly visible. He really does have a head like a bull.

"Open up, police!"

I open the door. They calm down when they lower their eyes to me instead of the tall figure of Zé they were expecting to see. Two of the uniformed cops exchange annoyed looks.

The Bull himself hesitates for a few seconds before giving me a reassuring smile.

"Are you on your own?"

"Yes," I say.

"Where is Monsieur Palaisot?"

"He's at work."

"We'd like to see your sister, Gina Lorozzi."

As if I'd forgotten her name. Mind you, given how little I see of her, it doesn't seem so ridiculous.

"She isn't here. She hasn't been here in a long time."

"I'm sorry, but we're going to have to check."

"Do you have a warrant?"

He smiles. One of the other cops gives a nervous laugh.

"You watch too many movies. They only have warrants in the States. We have letters rogatory."

He shows me an official paper signed by a judge. I don't know how legal it is to conduct a search in the absence of the tenant or any responsible adult, but I'm not knowledgeable enough to play the smart aleck. I move aside, for fear of arousing their suspicions. They come in and divide into two teams of two while the Bull motions me to follow him into the kitchen. He doesn't seem particularly aggressive for somebody who's done unauthorized searches and burglaries, and who drove my father into a state of hard-core paranoia.

He assumes his friendliest air. That's not so easy when you're as big as he is.

"Lieutenant Rassiat," he says, holding out his hand, which I don't shake. "Mattia, is that your name?"

"As if you didn't know."

"Do you have any idea where your sister might be?"

"No."

"I can't tell you the whole story, but she's in danger. We're looking for her so that we can warn her and get her to a safe place."

You can't fool me, you son of a bitch. I may be eleven, but I'm not completely stupid.

"Is that also why you were waiting for me outside my school?"

He nods, but doesn't take it any farther. What a bastard! I take advantage of his avoiding my gaze to get a good look at his face and I see that, behind the facade he's put on, he's really agitated. Something important must have happened.

He tries again to get information from me, asking me who she sees in this town, to which I don't reply—especially as I have no idea—then lets me go back to the living room. It's been a quick search and they haven't found anything.

Lieutenant Rassiat scribbles something on a piece of paper and hands it to me.

"Give this to your guardian when he comes back."

It's a summons to the station. I say I will. The cops leave the apartment. I rush to the window and see them getting back into their police cars.

It's impossible to sleep tonight. I stay up, watching TV in order not to be trapped by my own thoughts. Morning comes after what seems like forever. Zé arrives at seven. The rings under his eyes have gotten bigger. I hand him the summons.

"They came after you left. They're looking for Gina."

"Why?"

"I don't know."

I get to school late. The teacher has given up telling me off about anything. She doesn't ask me any questions, and the others watch me curiously as I take my place. It's impossible to figure out what they're in the middle of studying.

At recess, while I'm walking up and down in the yard, Youcef strides up to me. He's taller than I am. I look up at him, a tad apprehensively. I'm not used to anyone approaching me.

"My brother's being held for questioning," he says.

"Really? Why?"

He keeps looking around, afraid our conversation will be overheard.

"I'm not sure. The cops came to our place last night. They searched everywhere and took him away."

"Who is your brother? Do I know him?"

"Karim. He used to go out with your sister. They're looking for her, too. They asked my parents if they'd seen her. They said no. It's the truth."

Karim. I remember the night when I caught him hiding from the police, him and another guy I didn't recognize. There's no doubt about it anymore: all this is definitely connected to the death of Saïd Zahidi. But why are they looking for my sister? Is it just about the graffiti?

"I ran into Siham on my way to school this morning," Youcef continues.

"Saïd's sister?"

"Yes. She gave me a message for you."

We go into the covered playground, which is almost empty on this sunny morning. It's March 15. Winter is finally fading. When nobody can see us, he stuffs a sealed envelope into my pocket.

"She told me not to worry about Karim, she said he'd be out soon. I asked her what was going on but she wouldn't tell me. She just rushed off." He gives me an intense look. "Aren't you going to read the message?"

"Yes, of course," I stammer.

I shut myself away in the toilets to open the envelope. It doesn't have any name or address on it. Inside is a sheet of paper folded in four. I recognize Gina's handwriting.

> Mattia,
> I assume the cops went to your place. I'm sorry I kept you out of all this, but it wouldn't have made any difference if you'd known about it.
> Zé and you may be being watched, or even followed. I'm going abroad soon. For much longer this time. I don't have any choice. But I want to see you first to explain why I'm

leaving you again. I swear I never imagined things would go this far.

I can't tell you all of it in writing, it would take much too long and I can't take the risk that someone else might read this letter.

I'll wait for you tomorrow evening (Saturday) where dad's ashes were scattered, from eight o'clock. Make very sure you're not followed.

I hope we'll be able to see each other tomorrow. If not, take care of yourself.

I love you.

Gina.

P.S. You can bring your guardian if you want. Mom trusts him, so I do, too. Mom's fine, by the way. She's hiding for the same reasons I am.

"Well?" Youcef asks when I emerge from the toilets.

He looks at my hands, but I threw the paper down the toilet and flushed several times. I feel as if I'm in a fucking spy movie. I look at him, feeling a bit lost. He's looking for some explanation about what happened to his brother, but I don't know any more about that than he does.

"It was a message from my sister."

"I thought it was from Siham."

"I guess they're in touch."

He gives me a solemn look. Outside, in the yard, the other kids in our class are playing tag, taking advantage of these last few months when they can still allow themselves to behave like children. Come September, in middle school, it'll be too late to play.

"So it has some connection with Saïd," Youcef says.

"Yes."

The bell ringing shrilly for the end of recess echoes in the covered playground, cutting short our conversation.

27

LIEUTENANT RASSIAT

Lieutenant Rassiat is smoking a cigarette at the window of his office. He isn't allowed to, and he quit smoking six years ago, but desperate times call for desperate measures.

He watches Karim Benafa's reflection in the window. The young man's head has fallen to his shoulder. He's constantly dozing off. Rassiat hasn't been able to get anything from him. He watches him, thoughtfully, while a thick drizzle spreads over the town. The suspect has been answering his questions. He's cooperating this time, aware that he risks a lot more than just community service over this stupid graffiti business. He's cooperating, but not telling him anything useful. Hard to figure out if he's lying.

Rassiat heaves a deep sigh and throws his cigarette butt out the window. He sits back down opposite Benafa. He feels a sharp pain in his knee, what remains of a badly mended fracture that sometimes keeps him from running. It's started hurting again quite recently.

"Do you want a cigarette?" he asks.

"I don't smoke," the young man replies weakly.

"A coffee?"

"A coffee, sure . . ."

Rassiat handcuffs him to the radiator and goes out into the corridor. For a moment, he leans back against the door of his office, his eyes closed. He's overcome with a terrible sense of despondency, even though he's done everything he can not to get to this point. He pulls himself together, sluggishly walks over to the coffee machine, inserts the coins, and presses the button for two espressos. Karim Benafa hasn't moved. Rassiat puts the cups down on the desk and sits down again. With one finger, he wipes away the nervous sweat running down his temples. He feels tired.

For a while, the only two sounds are swallowing and the pressing of computer keys as Rassiat rereads the statement.

"Tell me again where you were between ten and midnight on Tuesday, March 8."

Karim laboriously raises his head. He repeats word for word what he's already declared a good dozen times since he was first brought in for questioning. Rassiat listens without taking notes.

"It's incredible," he says.

"What is?"

"You say exactly the same thing every time. Almost word for word."

"That's because it's the truth. You just have to check."

"We are. But I swear you rehearsed your story."

"All I'm doing is telling the truth," Karim says. He blinks vigorously to wake himself up. There's a knock at the door. A woman looks in. Rassiat joins her in the corridor.

"Monsieur Palaisot is here. Do you want to question him or shall I?"

"I'll deal with him. Will you take over with Benafa?"

"Okay. Is he still sticking to his story?"

"Yes. He prepared for this interrogation, that's for sure. I don't think we'll get anything else from him."

"Do we have enough to hand him over to an examining magistrate?"

"His alibi holds up."

"Do you think it's him?"

"He's a bit too obvious as a suspect after that graffiti business.

I'm starting to figure out how his mind works. He's no fool. I don't think he'd have taken a risk like that."

He nods goodbye to his colleague and heads for the lobby of the station. Young Palaisot is waiting there, standing by the water cooler, a paper cup in his hand. Rassiat immediately notices the purplish rings under his half-closed eyes and the weariness that weighs down his every gesture. The cop is unmoved. He doesn't sleep well at night either.

"Monsieur Palaisot?" he asks, pretending he hasn't seen him before.

"Yes."

He hasn't brought the child. The lieutenant leads him to another deserted office.

"Sit down," he says, taking off his jacket. "Thank you for answering the summons."

"If I hadn't, you'd have come to get me anyway."

Rassiat forces himself to smile. The young man sits down opposite him, bending his long, tall figure with some difficulty.

"Are you anti-cop, too?"

"Anti-cop?"

"You don't like the police?"

Palaisot seems to be seriously thinking about a question that was only intended to throw him.

"Neither more nor less than anyone else," he says at last.

"An excellent answer."

Rassiat opens a new page in his computer program. Zé obediently states his particulars and tenses when the officer mentions his previous experience in the legal system.

". . . acquitted in court."

"Is that why you called me here?"

"Your parents are judges, aren't they?"

"Yes, they are."

"With parents like that, I guess you can do pretty much

what you like, or am I wrong? Having that kind of impunity must go to your head."

Zé shakes his head vigorously.

"What are you getting at?"

"What were you doing on Tuesday, March 8 between ten and midnight?"

"Working."

"Don't you need to think about it? It was a week ago."

"I work every weekday from 8:30 in the evening to 6:45 in the morning. I don't need to think. Call my employer. Better still, ask to see the store's security footage."

Rassiat notes down the name of the manager and his telephone number. He'll check, just to be conscientious, but he already knows that what Palaisot has said will be confirmed. He wipes his eyes and looks the young man up and down.

"Your adopted son must have told you—"

"He's not my adopted son, he's my ward."

"All right. He must have told you that we went to your apartment last night."

"Yes."

"We're looking for Gina Lorozzi. We need to question her. When did you see her last?"

"Just after the Christmas holidays, around January 4, I think. She spent Christmas and New Year's Day with us and then left."

"Where did she go?"

"No idea. She always does that, she passes through and then leaves again, she never gets in touch. I never know where she is when she's not at my place, and she's not often there. She comes to see the boy from time to time. Apart from that, she lives her own life."

"Does she ever call?"

"No. She travels a lot."

"Where?"

"I'll say it again: I have no idea."

Rassiat massages his temples. He can feel a migraine coming on. He quickly rereads the statement. Palaisot is perfectly motionless.

"Where is your partner Gabrielle Ross right now?"

The young man gives a painful smile.

"You should know that. You're close to her brother, aren't you?"

"What makes you say that?"

"I can't prove it and I don't intend to, but I know that you two followed me several times."

"Where is she?" he asks again, clearly articulating each syllable.

"In Charcot, thanks to her brother. By the way, I've been trying to get in touch with him for a month. I don't suppose there's any point in asking you for his number, but could you ask him to contact me urgently?"

"Why?"

"His sister won't be able to leave the hospital until he speaks to the psychiatrists."

Rassiat looks at him for a good long while before transcribing these last words. He tries to read Palaisot's expression, but all he can see is an immense weariness.

"Do you think your partner is in a fit state to be questioned?"

"No," he says immediately.

"I'm going to pay her a little visit all the same. You can come with me if you like. She may be more forthcoming if you're there."

The young man clenches his fists on his thighs.

"Why? Don't you think she has enough problems already?"

"Because her brother, Thomas Ross, was killed last week. He was shot eight times. And it's considered normal to question the family in a case like that, although I very much doubt his sister had anything to do with it."

He studies Palaisot's features as he imparts this information. Zé's eyes open wide. He's stood up in order to leave, and now his whole body sways.

"Are you serious?" he says in a low voice.

"Yes. Do you want to come or not? It's best if you're present when she learns about her brother's death."

"Of course."

"Where is your ward?"

"At home. Do you want to question him, too?"

"I already did that last night. Follow me."

The two men get into an unmarked car. Charcot is only fifteen minutes' drive away. They are silent at first, but after a while Rassiat turns to his companion.

"Don't look so grief-stricken, it makes you seem ridiculous. I know you hated Lieutenant Ross, and now that he's dead your partner will be able to leave the hospital. You're allowed to smile. We won't put you on our list of suspects for that."

"Death is never a laughing matter."

Palaisot allows himself to abandon his expression of false compassion.

Gabrielle Ross hears Lieutenant Rassiat through to the end without batting an eyelid. Sitting cross-legged on the desk, her hands hidden in the folds of her huge pajamas, she doesn't take her eyes off him, and it's the lieutenant who has to turn his gaze away. From time to time, she turns to Zé, as if asking for confirmation, and Zé nods in silence, standing with his back to the door, his face as inscrutable as hers.

She nods to indicate she has understood. Rassiat looks her up and down, in surprise.

"Is that your only reaction?"

"I'm sorry. I'm on mood stabilizers."

She unfolds her legs and slides them gently to the floor,

then walks toward the lieutenant. Her bare feet make no sound on the tiles. She is as tall as her brother. She has his eyes, too, and his hair, but not the same expression. She must be thirty-five. A little younger than Thomas, Rassiat tells himself. What a waste.

"What do you want from me?" she asks in a thick voice.

"Nothing. I just wanted to inform you of your brother's death." He hesitates for a moment. "I was quite close to him."

If he was hoping for compassion, he doesn't find any in this woman's attitude. That was to be expected. Thomas did tell him their relationship was extremely complicated.

"Do you think I had something to do with it?"

"I don't know. Did you?"

"If I could get out of this fucking hospital, believe me, I'd have much more important things to do than kill someone."

She bends her elbows to bring her hands up to the level of the officer's face. Rassiat squints at her fingers, which are shaking noticeably.

"It's impossible to do anyone any harm in this condition."

She lies down on her bed, on top of the blankets.

"I'd like to get a little sleep now, if you don't mind."

Rassiat is about to say something, then changes his mind. He won't tell her that Thomas was killed just after paying a last visit to his sister, or that he took a big risk in insisting on coming to see her in this town that was forbidden to him.

He'd be too afraid she just wouldn't care.

28

Zé forgets to pick me up from school. I walk home, too preoccupied by Gina's letter to think about cursing him. I remember her warnings, and peer into every store window, looking for a familiar face. I don't see either of the two cops who followed me those other times.

The apartment is empty. I get through my homework in a few minutes, just to have my mind free for the weekend. I watch TV, waiting for it to be tomorrow evening, torn between fear and the anticipation of finally getting some answers.

Zé gets back just after eight, slamming the door behind him. He comes into the living room, still fully dressed, takes off his coat, and switches off the TV without warning. I glare at him.

"I know," he says before I can get a word in. "I let you walk home, I'm sorry. I was at Charcot."

As usual.

"Mattia, can you listen to me? Gabrielle's brother is dead. He was murdered."

I turn to him slowly. His expression is solemn, as if to underline how serious this is.

"And I think they suspect your sister."

I close my eyes.

You'll understand one day. The only solution is to burn it all down.

Gina, dammit, Gina . . .

"We have to help her," Zé adds, but I hear him through a thick fog of noise, my ears ringing. "Mattia?"

He kneels by me and squeezes my hands in his.

"If they catch her and she doesn't have an alibi . . . you know what'll happen. Do you know where she is? Tell me. She needs us."

He's wrong. She's always coped perfectly well by herself. But she's never been in this kind of trouble before. I imagine her, wandering alone in her everlasting hooded sweatshirt, jumping whenever she hears a police siren.

"Do you know where she is?" Zé repeats, and his voice echoes dully in my head.

* * *

When my father died, Mom and Gina argued over what to do with his ashes. He'd wanted them to be scattered over the park in Les Verrières, not far from the community center. Mom was okay with that, but not Gina. She said it was his job that had driven him over the edge and she refused to reduce him to being just a special needs teacher. He was more than that.

My mother won that battle in the end.

Today, the park is gone, there's just the construction site. The bulldozers have gained ground. In a month, the last people living in the last high-rise will have been relocated and the final traces of this uncomfortable affair will be wiped out.

A new apartment building is under construction where the park used to be. There's a security camera trained on the main entrance, but it's easy to get around it. I know, because a number of my classmates meet here to get away from their parents.

I haven't been able to stop Zé from coming with me. He's too afraid that something will happen to me and I couldn't leave the apartment without his noticing. We leave at about seven in case someone tries to follow us. Gina's instinct was right: we soon notice a car dogging our heels after a few blocks.

Zé drives into the underground parking garage of the shopping mall half a mile from Les Verrières, and lets me out at a point where our pursuers can't see us.

"I'll meet you there when I've lost them."

I take the elevator while he parks the car. The stores are packed. I mingle with a small family in order to pass unnoticed in case they try to spot Zé and me on camera. The parents look at me in surprise but don't say anything, and thanks to this technique I'm able to cross the entire shopping mall. Once outside, I continue walking for a while without turning around. Then, at an intersection, I stop and pretend to tie my shoelaces. The street is deserted. I start walking again, a tad paranoid, turning around every five seconds, but I'm not being followed.

It's about five after eight when I climb over the fence around the construction site, carefully avoiding the one security camera. And there she is, Gina, sitting on a concrete step, not far from Siham, who's keeping lookout.

They smile when they see me arrive without incident. The sad, weary smile of those who've had enough of fighting every day.

I look at them, Saïd's sister and the girl who loved him in secret, in the way children can love. It isn't my story, but all the same it's part of me, and I've earned the right to hear it.

"Are you sure you haven't been followed?" Gina asks, getting to her feet.

"I'm sure."

I go to her. She takes me in her arms. I don't dodge the embrace, but I don't return it either. When I close my eyes I see two corpses, a teenager with his skull smashed in and a cop, his body riddled with bullets. I'm not here as a judge, or a juror, or a lawyer. I'm only a listener. A belated witness.

Standing on tiptoe, Siham keeps watch. Steam emerges from her mouth as she breathes out. The weather has turned cold again after a brief improvement.

"Can you hurry it up a little?" she says.

Gina sticks a cigarette in her mouth. She motions me to sit down next to her on the steps of the staircase that will soon lead to a beautiful apartment building for families, an ideal place to bring up children, provided the police don't kill them before they're fully grown.

My sister holds out a bottle of wine and looks at me questioningly.

"For the cold."

I refuse the gift with a shake of the head. She understands that I don't want anything from her, except the truth.

So she tells me the story.

* * *

Before Saïd died, the window of the community center in Les Verrières was smashed several times, so the director decided to have a security camera fitted. It was trained on the main entrance to the center and the path winding for about thirty yards between two apartment buildings. The center was at the end of this path. The culprits would have had to use it to cause their damage.

Dad was against the idea. He suspected it was local people, and he didn't even want to know who they were.

On the evening of the murder he was indeed present at the center, and it was along that path that Saïd had come to escape the cops who were running after him, hoping to find help in the form of my father.

Dad didn't lie. He didn't see or hear anything. But the camera did. After a while, he was alerted by a sudden commotion coming from the path. He went out and saw them, all these cops bustling around Saïd's lifeless body. Thomas Ross and the others had already alerted their colleagues and put together their version of events.

My father broke down when he saw Saïd, blood on his face, an expression of extreme pain still frozen on his lips. The cops tried to question him, he said he hadn't seen anything, he waited just outside the security cordon for the family to arrive, then, gradually, all the neighbors, and soon Les Verrières was echoing with cries of anger at the death of a fifteen-year-old kid, a glass bottle was thrown at the cops, followed by many others, and everything exploded.

It wasn't until the next day, after a sleepless night spent trying to calm the rioters and overcome his own grief, that he remembered the camera. The cops, too, had forgotten about it in all the excitement. When he got back to the community center, he hastened to view the footage. What he saw chilled him. He made a copy of the cassette and came home with the only two recordings in existence. The only evidence that Saïd had been killed for nothing, because a lousy cop had lost his cool, because he'd been in the wrong place at the wrong time, getting in the way of a patrol that had had a bad day.

The only evidence that Thomas Ross hadn't acted in self-defense.

Back home, he confided in my mother and my sister, who were also in a state of shock from Saïd's death. They all came to the same conclusion: the video shouldn't be given to Internal Affairs. They were cops, too, and nobody here trusted them.

So they hid the cassettes and waited.

The riots soon died down by themselves. The reporters who'd been covering the story announced a triumphant return to order thanks to the work of social mediators and the tactics of the riot police. The real reason they stopped was because everyone was in prison, or at least the most hardened of them, and there was nobody left to keep any kind of movement going.

One evening, coming back from the university, Stefano

found the door broken open and the apartment turned upside down. The cops had requested the security footage from the director, who had looked for it in vain. The cassette wasn't anywhere in the center. It was easy to guess who had taken it.

In our apartment, they found the original cassette but not the copy. At the same time, thanks to an appeal for donations, the Zahidis were able to hire a lawyer to help them bring a civil case against Thomas Ross. My father decided to get the copy to this lawyer. He was already being followed, and so was Mom. By a strange coincidence, they had to undergo an extensive identity check every time they got in touch with the Zahidis. They were afraid the police would seize the cassette during one of these checks if they tried to hand it over to Saïd's parents or their lawyer, so Gina volunteered. She was the same age I am now.

The lawyer's office was in the town center, not far from the courthouse. She took several buses to make sure she wasn't being followed. The cops weren't behind her.

* * *

Gina breaks off to stub out her cigarette and light another one. I'm brought abruptly back to reality. Siham is still pacing back and forth, as nervous as it's possible to be. My sister has vanished into her memories. She's looking straight in front of her, but just like Gabrielle, she doesn't see anything.

"So, this evidence . . ." I say in a low voice. "Did the lawyer get to see the video?"

She doesn't reply.

"Did they search his office and get rid of the copy?"

"No," she whispers.

She buries her face in her hands. Her voice comes from a long way away. From the time when she was ten, perhaps, as powerless as I am now.

"The cassette was in a backpack I'd put down between my legs, on the bus. I was too busy checking that nobody was following me to keep an eye on it."

"So . . ."

"When I got to my stop I realized the bag was gone. Someone had stolen it, and the video with it." She stifles a despairing laugh. "What an idiot, honestly, what an idiot . . ."

"Was it the police?" I ask softly.

"Or somebody else. Whoever it was never got in touch with the authorities. And I lost the only evidence that could have sent Thomas Ross to prison."

"But hadn't you made any other copies?"

I almost yell the words. Siham signals to me to shut up. I obey.

"We were relying on the lawyer to do that. It was all so urgent, we were afraid they would come back, we didn't have time, it all happened very quickly."

"That was stupid."

"I know, Mattia! Why do you think Dad went off the rails? The guilt was slowly eating him up. And the cops harassing him every day . . . They suspected him of having another copy of the video. Even now, that's the reason for those burglaries at your place and Mom's."

"But why almost fifteen years later?"

* * *

Because you did something very stupid, Gina, that's why.

It was one night a few months ago. Passing through town, you met up with your old friends, the only ones you hadn't lost touch with after you left, Karim, Siham and Nadir. The three of you had grown up together, and you hadn't forgotten. You drank to the memory of Saïd. You drank a lot, especially you,

Gina, and you cried, overcome with guilt, even though Siham kept telling you it wasn't your fault, you'd done everything you could, it was too late now, but you couldn't stand it anymore, Gina, knowing that he was free, that he was still a cop and free to do the same thing again.

No, it went farther than that. Thomas Ross was just a cop and Saïd just another symptom. There was something else at stake, something bigger than the four of you, because every time a cop presses the trigger and someone falls to the ground, the same scenario is played out in court.

And you remembered all those names. You didn't know even a tenth of them, because everyone had forgotten them, just as everyone has forgotten Saïd, and so on until the next police killing.

You'd had enough, that was all.

So you wrote to that cop. A threatening letter in which you said that you had evidence he'd committed a cold-blooded murder, evidence that would soon be sent to the media.

You were bluffing. It was just to scare him. You couldn't do anything to him. There's a statute of limitations. He couldn't be tried again, but he could be scared. And his superiors, too, while you were at it. And the whole of the police force if you produced evidence that they were killing people and getting away with it.

You just wanted him to have sleepless nights. You sent the letter to his parents in Paris—even though he was nowhere to be found, their address was in the phone book—you mailed it at four o'clock in the morning, still under the effects of alcohol, and that was your undoing, Gina, because of course you didn't think of wearing gloves.

And your threats worked. Gabrielle's brother got scared. So scared that he had the letter analyzed by his pals in forensics and they found your prints.

But he couldn't make a formal complaint about being

threatened. He believed in your famous evidence because you were that teacher's daughter. He didn't want that video to be found. He turned to his colleagues for help. His colleagues from here, who had already helped him the first time. The Bull being the first among them.

They went looking for you at Mom's. They didn't find you, you'd already left, you barely remembered that threatening letter. They turned the apartment upside down. Coming home, Mom realized it was starting all over again and ran away. She wouldn't have had the strength to stand it all again, the questioning, the tailing, the searches. She wasn't as strong as before.

When you came to us at Christmas, I told you about it and you immediately realized what was happening. Later, you saw Siham again and she told you she knew where your mother was: with her own parents, the Zahidis, who'd been rehoused in an anonymous apartment building somewhere, like all the inhabitants of Les Verrières. My mother and the Zahidis were great friends. The deaths of my father and Saïd had brought them closer together.

Mom didn't want to go back home. She was scared of the cops. She was scared of everything. She, too, was going under, and that really riled you, Gina.

You talked a lot, you and Siham, then Karim and Nadir. You all agreed it was time to do something. You weren't sure what. Just something. Anything.

And suddenly that cop was back in town. It was like an omen. None of you could stand the fact that he'd dared show his face here again, out in the open, head held high, completely shameless. He shouldn't have been allowed to set foot on our streets again—but they aren't ours, Gina, we've never owned anything, everything belongs to them, you know that perfectly well.

The hatred was there, as vivid as on the first day, it was in you and it was in Siham, and the two of you decided to put an end to all of it.

* * *

"So the two of you killed him?"

Gina slowly nods. Siham has come closer to listen. I feel cold. Huddled over, my knees against my chest, in a fetal position as if that could protect me even from what has already happened, I'm waiting for morning to come at last. I know it's still early, and this endless night scares me. It was on a night like this that Saïd lost his life.

The moon shines over Les Verrières.

"It was never meant to go that far," my sister murmurs. "We only wanted . . . to confront him."

"Confront him?"

"Make him face up to his own actions. Tell him that we'd seen the video, that we knew . . . We wanted to see if he was sorry for what he'd done."

"But why?"

"We knew how it was going to end," Siham cuts in.

Her voice is steadier than Gina's. She takes a cigarette from my sister's pack, which is lying on one of the concrete steps.

"We knew it was going to end that way. We just didn't want to admit it to ourselves."

"I never wanted that," Gina says.

But her voice lacks conviction. It isn't Siham she's trying to convince, it's me. Siham realizes that and falls silent. I smile.

"You're still lying."

The only solution is to burn it all down.

I'm not your judge, Gina. It's not up to me to determine what's right and what's wrong, who deserves to live and who deserves to die. All I know is that I have no desire to live here.

"Which of you killed him?" I ask.

"What difference does it make?" they reply in unison.

I assume they did it together. Eight shots, that proves it. That's how to measure accurately the extent of someone's anger, counting the number of times the index finger has pressed the trigger, or the number of blows it took to smash Saïd's skull and leave him like a dislocated doll at the foot of the high-rises.

"What about Nadir and Karim?"

"They weren't there. They wouldn't have wanted to go that far. We just advised them to find themselves good alibis. Karim was a ready-made suspect because he'd been caught red-handed spraying *Justice for Saïd* on walls. Nadir had already been in prison."

"And what about you two? Do you have alibis?"

They exchange inscrutable looks.

"Nothing that would hold up for very long under questioning," Siham says.

"So what are you going to do?"

"Get out of here," Gina says.

"And go where?" I ask, in a panic now.

But I'll never find out where they were planning to go to escape pursuit. Because just then my eyes catch the reflection of the moonlight on a metal object behind one of the pillars of the building.

They're there. Who? The cops. They're like ants. First you see one, then two, then the whole colony. About ten of them have slipped through the fencing around the construction site. They have guns pointing straight at us. They're close enough to shoot, but not close enough to have heard what we've been saying.

Siham gets abruptly to her feet. Gina does the same, taking up position in front of me to protect me from any possible gun-fire. Next to one of the pillars, I recognize the huge bulk of the bull-like cop, Lieutenant Rassiat. My sister is the first to put her hands up, cautiously, followed by Siham, who simply heaves a sigh to acknowledge defeat.

I'm about to piss myself.

"Move away from the child!" the Bull calls out.

Siham obeys. Gina hesitates. I cling to her jacket.

"Move away, Mademoiselle Lorozzi!"

"Let go of me," she whispers.

"Don't leave me!"

"Let go of me! They're not after you!"

"Don't leave me!" I cry. I don't want them to take her away. They've already taken my father. They've taken Gabrielle. They've taken my mother in a way. They won't take Gina.

What happens next is a blur.

The cops move closer, the barrels of their guns held out in front of them. Siham is pushed up against a wall and searched from head to foot. The Bull and others I don't know grab me by the waist and force me to let go. As I do so, the sleeve of Gina's sweatshirt gets torn. They take me off to one side and the two women to the other. They force them into the police cars and try to calm me down, I struggle with all my might to join Gina, but I can't, I can't, I'm not strong enough and there's this rage inside me that I'm powerless to do a fucking thing . . .

The cars drive off, blue lights flashing, goodbye Gina goodbye Siham, the next time we see each other there'll be bars between us, all because a fucking cop lost his cool one day, all because justice only applies to one side, all because they have their own criteria for determining who's a monster and who isn't, who's a murderer and who's made a forgivable error, *to err is human, isn't it, it is if you're a cop, it isn't if you're a delinquent, so knowing all the facts, choose sides, my friend . . .*

I burst into tears, unable to stop myself.

By the time I recover, I'm sitting in the back seat of a police car, a paper cup of hot chocolate in my hands. I'm shaking all

over, but I don't feel the cold anymore. It's as if I've been anes-
thetized from inside.

"There he is, monsieur. See if you can calm him down."

Zé's warm hands close over mine. He's kneeling in front of
me, looking at me with a mixture of relief and sadness. He has
a black eye, his right one.

"Are you all right, Mattia?"

No, I'm not all right, I'll never be all right, I wish I could
just go to sleep and when I wake up everything will be different. I don't answer. I have nothing to say.

They force us to go with them to the police station. From
what I hear, I gather that Zé arrived after they'd surrounded
the construction site and already formed a security cordon,
and that he tried to force his way through in order to find me
until a cop stopped him in his tracks with a punch to the eye.
He gets away with a warning.

Nobody asks me any questions. When I ask to see Gina, I'm
kindly sent packing.

We get home around midnight. I fall asleep on the couch,
watched over by Zé, and I wake up in the early hours of the
morning, bathed in sweat, unable to breathe, opening my eyes
to see a shadowy figure perched on my chest. The hallucination fades after a minute. There's only me. Me and Zé. I almost
miss that shadowy figure.

29
LIEUTENANT ROSS

One week earlier

Without thinking, he reaches out his hand and takes hers; Gabrielle pulls violently away.

"Don't touch me!"

A flock of crows is flying over the grounds of Charcot. Thomas Ross turns away in order not to see the anger inflaming his sister's face, but it's almost palpable. He can feel it digging into his flesh like a thousand talons.

"Gabrielle, please—"

"Get out."

"At least let me say one thing!"

"Get me released and I'll listen to you. In the meantime, just fuck off."

He goes on speaking anyway. First she insults him, then puts her hands over her ears. He goes on in the mad hope that she'll hear him at least unconsciously. He tells her how sorry he is that things have come to this. How much it pains him to see her in this state, but how necessary it is, too, because what matters is staying alive, just *surviving*, Gabrielle, anything is better than death, and anyway what the fuck gives you the right to turn your nose up at Life, do you care so little about the people who love you?

As he speaks and she refuses to hear him, he gradually loses his cool. He gets to his feet, red in the face. He raises his voice.

"Do you think you're the only person who wants to die? Don't you know it happens to everyone at least once? But what do you think other people do? They face up to things! Life is shit, nobody denies that, life grinds your face in the dust every day, so what? You endure, that's how it is. You don't throw yourself out the window every time things don't work out, or there'd be nobody left on earth. You've always been so selfish—"

Gabrielle abruptly takes her hands from her ears, a sign that she's been listening all the time.

"Selfish? Are you fucking kidding me?"

He doesn't answer her. She moves toward him, step by step, at last breaking the distance between them that she's insisted on for nearly fifteen years.

"What do you call having me confined and keeping me here by force? I don't owe you anything and I've never asked you for anything. Who are you doing it for? You or me? For *you*, Thomas, of course, for you! You're not a believer. Just like me, you don't think there's anything after death. I won't be unhappy there, at least no more than I am here. The only reason you want to stop me ending it all is to preserve your own peace of mind. You're afraid you won't get over it, afraid you'll suffer. Asking me to stay just because you don't think you could bear my death—what is that? Altruism?"

She's spat out the last word. He's looking at her, unflinching.

"So I should just ignore what I see, should I, ignore what I experience every day, things that push me past my breaking point, forget the nausea that grabs hold of me as soon as I open my eyes, live with all that, make do, because my brother asks me to? What do you call that, Thomas?"

She stops, disheartened, out of breath, and collapses onto the mattress, which sinks beneath her weight. She looks at her hands, at the level of her face. They're shaking. She has tears in her eyes. Thomas bites his lips when he sees that and lowers his head.

A long silence settles over them. Gabrielle breathes deeply, trying to calm down.

Her brother gets to his feet.

"Forgive me," he says quietly.

She doesn't reply. He can't see her face, which is hidden by her hair. He nods by way of farewell and leaves the room.

He walks back through the section, hails a male nurse to open the door for him, and finds himself out in the grounds, feeling as if he's regained his freedom. He doesn't notice the two figures watching him from the cafeteria.

A bus takes him to the town center. He was planning to go to his ex-partner's place—Rassiat always puts him up when he passes through town—but he can't stand the thought of company. He goes into a grocery store and buys a bottle of whiskey, the way he used to, after that boy died, when alcohol was the only thing he could find to help him bear the endless days and nights.

He sits down in a little park, not far from Les Verrières and the scene of his final defeat. Lovers have carved their initials on the bench: J + A = 4 EVER. He lets out a hopeless laugh. Night falls. Gabrielle's words go around and around in his head on a loop. *What is that, altruism?*

No, she's right, he isn't doing it for her, he's doing it for himself, and what gives him the right to assume such power, to keep her alive at all costs? It's some kind of therapeutic harrassment . . .

Getting drunk has always cleared his head.

And here they come.

Two shadowy figures, one quite tall, the other shorter, walking side by side, making no attempt to hide. He doesn't feel any kind of suspicion when they step over the low fence around the park, he's too preoccupied by Gabrielle and the high walls to remember that he isn't wanted here.

But they come toward him, and he frowns and lowers the bottle. The light of the street lamps is reflected in a metal object aimed at him.

Being a good cop, he can recognize a firearm when he sees one.

"Move and you're dead," a female voice says.

He recognizes it as Siham Zahidi's—and part of him knows that the die is already cast.

She's dressed in black jeans and a hooded jacket. The person with her looks up slightly. Thomas easily identifies Gina Lorozzi from all the times he studied her face in photographs.

He's been looking for her for months, and she's the one who's found him.

He slowly puts the bottle down on the ground.

"Don't do it," he says.

"I can't think of a good reason why I shouldn't."

"It won't bring your brother back. Siham . . ."

Hearing her name, the young woman raises her eyebrows.

"I'm sorry."

The hands gripping the gun don't shake.

"What were you thinking?" she says, taking a step closer, followed by Younès's daughter. "When you killed him, what were you thinking? And when they acquitted you? Were you relieved? Did you ever tell yourself that one day someone might decide to take the law into their own hands? Your impunity . . . the fucking law, always on your side . . ."

Your side. The way she says it, he can tell she isn't addressing just him. She's addressing the whole of the police force. He's thinking fast, but his blood hasn't yet flushed away the alcohol and his mind is hazy.

The two women are getting dangerously close, step by step. When he makes a move toward his belt, the barrel of the gun is pressed between his eyes.

Gina Lorozzi grabs the semiautomatic he was getting ready to take out. Her eyes gleam, even in the darkness. After fifteen years, Thomas Ross realizes that nobody has forgotten.

"Please. I beg you. I never wanted it to happen."

"When you hit someone on the head with a baton, you have a pretty good idea what's going to happen!"

He swallows with difficulty.

"I was . . . I beg you. I lost control. I didn't mean to. I swear. It was pure chance. The wrong day. The wrong place. Les Verrières . . . I couldn't stand it anymore. The contempt, the hatred every day . . . I'd asked for a transfer, I knew I had to get out before . . . I was waiting to hear. I didn't want to be out on those fucking streets anymore, I—"

Gina interrupts him with a burst of icy, stunned laughter.

"Contempt and hatred? Poor you, it must have been hard, but nobody asked you to do that job, Saïd didn't ask you to do it, you can survive hate but you can't survive having your skull smashed in, no, that you can't survive, Saïd didn't survive, and you did."

"Not a night goes by without my praying to turn the clock back. But it's . . . it's done, it can't be wiped out, I'm sorry, if you kill me it won't make any difference, they'll put you in prison, your lives will be ruined, is it worth it?"

He's almost screamed these last words. It doesn't even occur to him to cry for help. Siham Zahidi has his life at the end of her index finger, and they're a long way from anywhere except Les Verrières, whose inhabitants Lieutenant Ross doesn't hold in very high esteem.

"You don't understand a thing," Gina says in a weak voice. "It isn't you we're going to shoot. It's everything you represent."

"But I'm the one who's going to die!"

"You or another cop, it doesn't matter. I've lost count of the number of your colleagues who've walked free from court thanks to the false testimonies of their cop friends, it's great the way you stick up for each other, it really is, I wish we were the same, I also wish we were equal when we appear before the judges, I wish they questioned what you say the way they never believe what we say, unfortunately they never dare find you guilty, and that's why you're going to die."

"It has to stop," Siham says. "Someone has to make up their mind to do something. Anything. Even if it's pointless."

They're making him bear, alone, the shortcomings of a whole system. Thomas Ross looks at them in turn, out of ideas. He can defend himself but he can't take responsibility for so many errors. He's only one man. A cog in the machine. It doesn't matter. They don't want anything from him. No excuses. No justifications.

"Gina, can you pass me his gun?"

Gina hesitates for a few seconds before she obeys. Siham throws away the gun she's been pointing at his face, much to his surprise. Then he understands. It was only a very good imitation. A toy for holdup men with consciences. They weren't armed. He shouldn't have let himself be taken in. It was the whiskey. The fear.

The resignation?

Siham Zahidi presses the trigger and Lieutenant Ross thinks about Gabrielle before a bullet digs a rough black tunnel in his skull.

30

It's impossible to see Gina and Siham. They're being held for questioning. The day after they were arrested, Zé tells me they'll probably be kept for forty-eight hours before being handed over to an examining magistrate, who'll decide whether or not to charge them with the murder of Thomas Ross. Then they'll either be released, put on probation, or more likely sent to prison while awaiting a trial, which won't take place for another two years.

I listen without saying a word. I've been in a state of shock since yesterday. He's put a bowl of cereal with warm milk down in front of me, but I haven't touched it.

"I'll put in a request for you to visit her," he says. "It takes so long, it's best to do it now. They won't be able to refuse you. You're eleven years old."

I don't reply. He sits down opposite me. He's worried.

"Have something to eat, Mattia. You haven't had anything in your stomach since yesterday." Then, when I still say nothing: "What would you like? Pancakes? A chocolate pancake, how about that?"

He opens the fridge, but of course it's empty. He's hardly done any shopping since Gabrielle went into hospital, and for the past month we've been eating expired food from cans and pasta without sauce. It's about time he came to. Too bad that it's just when I've decided to let go.

He makes up his mind. "I'm going shopping. The grocery store should be open, even on Sunday."

He starts to put on his coat, but then changes his mind and sits down again opposite me. I guess he doesn't want to leave me on my own.

"Say something. It'll be fine."

I look him straight in the eyes.

"I dare you to tell me to my face that everything's going to work out for my sister."

Silence.

"Go on, say it if you're so sure of yourself. Say she's going to get out. Say they won't send her to prison. Say they'll understand. Say it. I dare you."

He turns his head away. Thank you, Zé. I couldn't have stood yet another lie.

* * *

Tired of going around in circles and short of arguments to persuade me to eat, he takes me to see Gabrielle early in the afternoon. He doesn't ask me if I want to come, but I do nothing to stop him from putting a coat and cap on me and securing my seat belt.

Nothing new inside those high walls. The same deathly pale faces. The same white coats. The same corridors. I stop before I get to Gabrielle's room. Zé turns and throws me a questioning look, I don't move, standing in the doorway of the TV room, looking at images of rioting on the screen.

"... the confrontation continued until dawn. The cause of the unrest is the death of a twenty-two-year-old man, Selim Sandjak, of Turkish origin. The circumstances remain unclear."

"Mattia? Are you coming?"

I'm listening.

"Selim Sandjak, who was known to the police, was at the wheel of a car in the company of a young man of nineteen when he was flagged down for a roadside check. The two men

refused to stop, and a chase ensued, at the end of which a mem-
ber of the Anti-Crime Squad fired several shots at the vehicle.
Selim Sandjak died a few hours after being taken to hospital;
his accomplice, whose name has not been divulged, was
unhurt."

The footage shows a car that has smashed into a lamp post, with forensics officers bustling around it. The bullet holes are clearly visible on the windshield. I suppose they aimed at the tires . . .

And again there are flames reflected in the opaque visors of the CRS.

I already know what'll happen. Everyone knows, unless they live in an alternate universe. A few years from now, some prosecutor or other will timidly ask for a suspended sentence of two or three years. The cops will claim self-defense (Selim would surely have killed them by the sheer force of his will if they hadn't fired first), they'll be acquitted with the blessing of public opinion, everyone will shake their hands, and they'll be sent back out into the field.

Maybe the culprits will regret what they did. But a fat lot of good that'll do for Selim up there.

I'm understanding more and more, Gina.

"Come on," Zé says—I hadn't realized he was standing next to me. "Watching that won't help."

He takes my hand and drags me to Gabrielle's room. My head is empty, I don't even have the strength to be angry anymore, there's nothing but this dull resignation.

But Zé gives a start when he opens the door. His face lights up. He takes me by the arm and forces me into the room, just when I was hoping to keep in the background. I open my eyes wide on seeing the woman who's sitting at the foot of the bed. She has very dark eyes with no make-up, she's quite short, and she's dressed in faded jeans and a gray woolen jacket that seems to have survived the centuries. Her brown hair is tied in a simple ponytail from which a few tow-colored locks escape, falling over her eyes.

It's my mom, Amélia. And I swear I'd like to scream at her, to let out all my resentment at her abandoning me, but I can't help myself, I swallow and rush into her arms when she opens them to me. I hug her with all my might, for fear she's just an illusion, but no, it's really her.

She strokes my hair with one hand, the other hand flat on my shoulder. She nods a greeting to Zé over my head, then bends and whispers in my ear, "I'm here now."

And where were you before? I feel like yelling at her. I can't. Not now. I've already lost everyone. She's all I have left. I can't lose her, too. Not again.

"Do you know what happened?" I ask in a low voice.

"Yes," she says solemnly. "Gabrielle and I were just talking about it."

Gabrielle now opens her mouth. From her voice, I'd guess she's in her usual place, sitting on the chair by the window. I can't see a thing, with my head buried in the hollow of my mother's neck.

"Because I'm in this fucking hospital, I have a cast-iron alibi," Gabrielle says, oddly angry. "Even if I handed myself in, it wouldn't hold up for a minute. I couldn't have left the hospital and come back without someone noticing I was gone."

"What are you talking about?" Zé says.

I've already understood. I free myself from my mother's arms, though I stay next to her, her hand in mine. I turn to Gabrielle. She and Zé are looking at each other so intensely that the air between them seems to vibrate.

"You know perfectly well," she says, "that if we don't do anything, those two women won't get out of prison until their lives have been ruined."

"And you wanted to give yourself up in their place, is that it?"

She turns away.

"I'd have been the ideal prisoner."

He looks at her, trying to make her regret these words, but she doesn't refute them. She isn't planning to stay alive much longer. So, here or behind bars . . . If you're going to die anyway, you might as well save someone who wants to live.

"Don't look at me like that," she says. "Nobody would have believed me anyway."

She stands up, unfolding her long legs. Her hands are shaking. She takes Zé by the wrist.

"Come on, I need a smoke."

They disappear into the corridor, leaving me alone with Mom. We instinctively let go of each other's hands. She smiles at me. I don't smile back. She reaches out her hand to me, but I dodge it. Her eyes cloud over.

"Mattia, please."

Silence.

"I've made a lot of mistakes, I know. But that's going to change."

I can't hold back a sneer.

"Are you going to take me back?"

"No."

I wasn't expecting her to be so honest. I feel like crying, but I choke back my tears. I make to go and she grabs hold of my arm.

"I've talked a lot with Gabrielle. She's really determined to go."

"What about Zé? Does she really care so little about him?"

Mom heaves a sigh as distressed as the world.

"You can't stay alive just for the love of someone. That didn't stop your father from killing himself either. It's best if you stay with Zé. He's going to need you in the next few years."

"Shit, I'm eleven years old! I'm the one who should rely on him!"

"Theoretically, yes. But there's the way things should be, and the way they really are. Saïd shouldn't have died, Thomas Ross shouldn't have been acquitted, your father shouldn't have killed himself, and I shouldn't have abandoned you. Nobody ever said it was fair."

"So you're going to tell me you handed me over to Zé because he needed me, and that's why you lost interest in me?"

"No. I didn't have the strength, and now it's too late. It can't be mended." She lifts a hand to her temple. "I'm tired."

"So am I," I retort in a somber voice. "Everyone's tired. Being tired is no excuse, or everyone would be throwing themselves off bridges."

"*You* tried to die. Not me. I've always held out, although I admit the idea did cross my mind more than once after your father died. But you didn't wait very long."

She takes my arm and touches the fine scars on my wrist. I shiver at the touch of her cold fingers and the sternness of her judgement, and I realize that she still hasn't forgiven me. That she'll never forgive me, just as she'll never forgive herself for abandoning me. That there's too much unsaid, too much guilt between us, for all those years when we didn't speak to be wiped away with a gesture of the hand.

"You were seven when you tried to die," she continues, relentlessly. "Forgive me for not being strong enough to bear that."

I tear myself from her embrace. I want to run away from her, far away. To go back and wipe it all out so that I can start all over again but differently. It's impossible. And it's so unfair.

Mom gets to her feet, pushing back behind her ear the locks of hair that are impeding her view.

"Your sister won't go to prison."

I subject her to the same test as Zé.

"Swear it."

Without the slightest hesitation, she looks me straight in the eyes.

"I swear. They destroyed your father, and Saïd's family, and they destroyed me, too. That's quite enough."

"What are you going to do? Burst into the police station with a Kalashnikov?"

"Not exactly."

* * *

The cops think they're dreaming when she demands to make a statement about the murder of Thomas Ross. Lieutenant Rassiat takes it down on his computer without saying a word, too stunned to speak.

She asked me to go with her for moral support. I agreed, as surprised as the cops. We left without saying anything to Zé and Gabrielle, knowing they'd be against the idea. I'm sitting beside her while she talks to the Bull, who's listening to her religiously.

"It's a nice story, madame," he says when she's finished, "but nobody will believe it."

"Why not?" Amélia says.

"It's obvious you're protecting your daughter."

"Has she confessed to the murder?"

Silence.

"What about Siham?"

Silence.

"Have you recovered the weapon, lieutenant?"

"No, madame."

"Do you want to know where it is?"

He listens.

"In Les Verrières, in the last remaining high-rise, 16b Allée des Pissenlits, fifth floor, door on the right, the kitchen. It's soaked in dishwashing liquid, but you might be able to find a few traces of DNA belonging to Monsieur Ross. The barrel of the gun was covered in blood."

He stops taking this down.

"So you took the murder weapon away with you?"

"I was in a state of shock after what I'd done. It wasn't

premeditated. In movies, that's often how the murderer gets caught: he throws away the murder weapon and the cops find it with his fingerprints. I was trying to wipe out mine."

"I don't believe you for a second."

"Maybe not. But you have to pass it on to the prosecutor. My children's father killed himself because of the death of Saïd Zahidi and I'm very friendly with Saïd's parents, that'll be easy to prove. He'll have to take it into account." She counts on her fingers. "I don't have an alibi for the night of March 8. I have a motive. I have the weapon. All you have is two suspects who haven't confessed, and nothing against them apart from my daughter's fingerprints on a threatening letter, but making a threat doesn't mean you're going to carry it out."

"How do you know that? The evidence we have is confidential."

"I don't know. I assume."

Silence.

"I wasn't sure about giving myself up," Mom goes on. "But when I heard you'd arrested Gina and her friend Siham, I couldn't just sit back and wait for you to send two innocent girls to prison."

Lieutenant Rassiat still hasn't started typing again. Amélia leans toward him with a sigh.

"A man is dead, lieutenant. Someone has to pay. You have your guilty party and you're still hesitating. What more do you need?"

"The truth," he says.

My mother bursts into a magnificent laugh.

"The *truth*," she echoes contemptuously. "We both know it has no place here. You saw the video of Saïd's murder. So did I. Talk about truth to the media, or to your superiors if you want. But don't give me any of that bullshit. Not me."

They stare at each other for a very long time. I look around the room. Two desks. The other occupant isn't here. A cabinet filled with files. The Civil Code. The walls are plastered with posters warning against drunk driving, rape, domestic violence, and so on. Last year's calendar, forever stuck at December.

There's a single window looking out on the street. Two sparrows are pecking at something on the ledge.

"What about your son?" Rassiat asks. "Have you thought about your son?"

"He needs his sister more than he needs me. She's strong. She'll take care of him. I can't do anything for him."

"Is that why you're taking her place? You're going to pay for a crime you didn't commit."

"I'm going to pay for a crime I should have committed a long time ago. When you murder our children with impunity you can't expect there to be no repercussions."

For a moment, weary, she falls silent. Rassiat waits for her to continue, one eye on her, the other on the screen.

"You know," she resumes in a low voice, "the reason it's come to this isn't because a teenager was killed, or even because his murderer wasn't punished. It's because nobody spoke up. When a police officer is killed by a delinquent, he's mourned, salutes are fired in his memory, he's decorated, and even ministers file past his grave with tears in their eyes. When a delinquent is killed by a police officer, the silence is deafening. Ditto when the police officer in question goes unpunished. I'm surprised they don't award the killer the Legion of Honor."

Nobody said it was fair.

"Given that," my mother concludes, sinking deeper into her chair, "how can we talk seriously about social harmony? Achieving harmony requires sacrifices. By killing your colleague, I've tried to restore the balance a little, but I know we'll never be even."

She stops there as if everything has been said. The silence takes over, devours us, and purrs with satisfaction.

It's interrupted by the clicking of the keyboard.

EPILOGUE

S o they've let Siham and Gina go?" Nouria asks, unable
to conceal the fact that she's hanging on my every word.
I smile, taking advantage of this interest I'm not often
accorded, and pause for a moment to increase the suspense.
Not that there's anything to smile about. There's nothing funny
in this story. But I made the decision a long time ago to concentrate on nice things and neglect the bad ones, even if that
requires constant vigilance that I don't always have the
strength for.

"Yes. They're on probation, they're not allowed to leave the
region, and they have to show up at the police station once a
week, but their lawyer says they'll soon be completely free."

"What about your mother?"

I look down at the dusty linoleum. Nouria has never taken
much interest in keeping her office clean. She says getting the
cobwebs out of people's heads is already a big enough chore.

"She's in prison. She'll appear before the parole judge in six
months. Her lawyer says there's a good chance they'll release
her until the trial, even though she's sure to be given a prison
sentence. Maybe it won't be too heavy. There are extenuating
circumstances."

"Not too heavy. What does that mean?"

I grimace.

"He was a cop, so ten years minimum."

Nouria remains silent. I shift on my seat.

"That means five years with good behavior, and Mom isn't

the kind of person to cause a riot. She may be out by my six-teenth birthday."

Nouria smiles weakly, which is good because it means I'm the one who has to reassure her, and that forces me to look on the bright side—not easy in this situation.

"The court has just accepted my request to see her. I can visit her if Zé goes with me, and he will."

"What about your sister? How's she holding up?"

I shrug.

"She's Gina. She's invincible. A brick wall."

"Like you, you mean?"

"When I'm grown up, I want to be like her."

We look at the world through the window. Unlike the rest of the room, the window panes are always meticulously pol-ished.

"What about the gun? How did it end up at your mother's?"

I lower my voice just in case. She leans in toward me to hear my whispering.

"Gina didn't know what to do after . . . after what hap-pened, she was in a panic. She told my mother everything. Mom went and recovered the gun when she heard they'd been arrested."

Nouria gives an admiring whistle.

"Your mother is very brave."

"In some cases, yes."

"And what about Gabrielle?"

"She left the hospital with a ton of meds she won't take."

"And Zé?"

"I saw him crying in Gabrielle's arms the other day. He kept saying the name of that girl. Émilie."

She smiles.

"You should stop spying on people."

"But it's useful. People only show their best sides—or their worst—when they think they're alone. I've felt closer to him since I've realized how sad he is over her. I understand him better."

"You're amazingly advanced for your age."

"That's not an advantage."

"How do you feel generally? You seem in much better shape than the last time."

I smile.

"So-so."

"How's school?"

"Not good, but I don't care."

I burst out laughing for no apparent reason. She looks at me questioningly.

"I have lots of friends suddenly."

"Why?"

"I'm the son of the woman who killed Saïd Zahidi's murderer. Half the kids come from Les Verrières. At school, my mother's a heroine."

I'm exaggerating a little. There are also lots of my classmates who call me the son of a murderer, and some of them grew up in Les Verrières. I don't give a damn. I know what's just and what isn't. Siham, my mother, and my sister are the only people who've done something to right those wrongs. Gina may be a murderer. But the fact is, I've been sleeping better since Dad and Saïd were avenged. The thing has gone for good. I don't need a ping-pong ball sewed to my pajamas anymore.

"And your brother?"

"We haven't told him the truth, although he probably suspects it. He sends money to my mother every week in prison."

Nouria walks me out into the lobby.

"By the way, Mattia . . . you've never told me your father's name."

I smile.

"Ryad. His name was Ryad."

* * *

Zé and Gabrielle are waiting for me in a nearby bar, drinking to Amélia's health. We're invited to dinner this evening at Siham's parents' place. They feel indebted to me for what my mother did. I don't know if their daughter has told them the truth, if they've guessed it themselves, or if they still don't know all the ins and outs of the story, but sometimes I see Monsieur Zahidi's eyes come to rest on Siham and Gina with a silent question and a great deal of anxiety in them.

Mom made Gina promise to keep an eye on me before she went into prison. And Gina's taking her task very seriously. Being obliged to stay in the region, she's sharing an apartment with Siham. One evening I heard her talking with Zé, telling him that she could take me to live with her if he wanted and I agreed. He replied, "No way," with a kind of panic in his voice that made me smile. That's fine by me. She isn't working and has plenty of time to hang out with me.

Karim was released as soon as he was able to prove his alibi. I see him and Nadir from time to time, when I'm invited over to Gina's.

Gabrielle hasn't given up on her desire to go. I think she's only staying long enough to get Zé gradually used to the idea. I don't like thinking about it, but I think I'm prepared. It remains to be seen how Zé will get over it. Little by little, he's learning to accept how powerless he is. As my mother said, you can't stay for the love of just one person.

I'll be there for him when she goes.

* * *

I look up at the grim building that houses the women's

prison. Barbed wire everywhere, watchtowers, armed guards. You have to go through a metal detector while the guards watch you suspiciously, then down a narrow corridor until you get to the visiting room.

There's Mom, a little thinner than she was but still cheerful. A miracle occurs: no silence during the thirty minutes allowed, or very little. She says she's fine. That at last she's able to rest. That it isn't so bad here. That she isn't unhappy.

Meeting Zé's eyes in the rearview mirror as he drives us back to town, I know he isn't taken in, and that he's wondering if I've figured out she was lying. Hey, I may be only eleven, but I'm not completely stupid. I pretend to believe her, though. I'm a child. I'm entitled to be carefree for a few more years.

I'm fine, I swear. None of the world's shit can reach me. I have my brick wall.

ABOUT THE AUTHOR

Cloé Mehdi was born in 1992. Her novel *Monstres en cavale* received the 2014 Beaune Prize. *Nothing Is Lost* is the winner of the 2016 Polar Student Prize, the 2017 Dora Suarez Prize, the 2017 Mystère de la critique Prize, the Blues & Polar Prize, and the Thousand and One Black Leaves Prize, among others.